# WANDERINGS

# WANDERINGS

Dana T. Moore, II

# CONTENTS

# HEY, SANTA! PLEASE WAIT FOR ME!

## BY: DANA T. MOORE, II

"I don't know, Maw," Santa said, his tone of voice heavy with sadness. "I think," he continued, wearily pulling on his heavy, winter clothing. "This will be the worst Christmas of my life. I hate to even think of the mothers and children in the New York area. Over 6,000 souls lost in the World Trade Center in that terrorist attack. Think of the number of people who lost parents, husbands and wives when those two buildings collapsed! In the past, in declared wars, people have been emotionally prepared, as much as they could be, for the possibility of losing loved ones. This was different. Think of the terror those airline passengers must have felt as they closed in on the Twin Towers. Even the firemen and police who were trying to help evacuate those poor souls from the buildings were, in a manner, too occupied to suffer fear. Their death was sudden, and overwhelming in its horrible brevity." Santa paused, his face a study in dejection.

"Santa, don't let it get you down," Mrs. Claus answered. "Think of all the little ones who desperately look forward to your visit each year. You know this will be even more important to many in the New York area. In a way, millions are dependent upon you for a small portion of happiness. I know you won't disappoint them."

"Maw, if it weren't for you, I don't think I could face the terrible sadness and loneliness I run into on my trip each year. Millions of people have you to thank for my annual delivery of Christmas cheer. You're the one who keeps my spirits up."

Mrs. Claus leaned over, and gave Santa a kiss on the cheek. "You're good, Santa. I know you will make this a happy trip as you always do. I'm looking forward to the stories you will have for me when you get back. Now, dress warmly, and drive carefully."

Santa resumed his preparations for the cold night ahead. Already his mind was on the many details of his round-the-world Christmas trip. "Were the deer well fed? Was the sleigh loaded? Were the heavy winter blankets in the sleigh?" He knew the brownies took care of these important details just as he knew they had carefully checked the many letters from children all over the world, and compared them to the list of toys and gifts loaded into the sleigh. The very last thing Santa wanted was to leave a disappointed child with no gift to open on Christmas morning. He knew that sometimes some were overlooked, but he did his very best to prevent it if he could. He never forgot the central theme of Christmas; love for the little ones.

Finishing his dress preparations, Santa walked toward the door into the barn where the deer impatiently awaited his arrival. "Bye, Maw!" he shouted as he pulled the door open.

"Have a good trip, Santa," Mrs. Claus replied.

Striding into the barn, and toward the sleigh facing the open barn door, Santa spoke to the deer. "Ready, Fellows?" The reindeer pawed the barn floor, anxious to be on their way. They looked forward to this trip nearly as much as did Santa. After all, it wasn't every night they had a chance to go around the whole world, and in doing so, bring untold amounts of love and cheer to many young children. Christmas was truly the highlight of the year for Santa, the deer, and the children fitfully sleeping, anxiously awaiting the arrival of the jolly old elf and his sleigh full of Christmas gifts.

After mounting the sleigh, and tightening the safety belt, Santa pulled the heavy fleece blanket up around his waist, and shouted, "On Donder! On Blitzen!" With that, the deer leapt joyously into the night, pulling the heavily loaded sleigh on their annual Christmas joy trek.

Halfway through the round-the-world trip, Santa arrived over the New York City area. The loom of light surrounding the huge city, normally giving off the happy and gay appearance of a brightly lit Christmas tree, now exuded an air of sadness. The gaping opening in the familiar skyline showing clearly where the Twin Towers of the World Trade Center had once stood proudly tall. Now, Santa saw the still simmering, smoking stone and metal mass, a repugnant symbol of hatred imposed by the terrorists who had committed this atrocity against humanity.

"Can't let this get me down," Santa thought. "There are many children and families down there in desperate need of the reassurance Christmas brings." With that, he swooped down for a landing in a residential neighborhood not too far from the once mighty World Trade Center. Pulling to a stop before a small, but brightly decorated home, Santa noted the heavy snow cover on the ground and houses, and observed also falling fresh snow. "A white Christmas!" he thought to himself, carefully dismounting the sleigh.

Very quickly, Santa became engrossed in his Christmas cheer delivery. He hefted his heavily loaded gift bag over his shoulder, and entered the house. Contrary to popular concept, he did not use the chimney. The house didn't have a fireplace, so no chimney. Santa was used to this. Many homes he visited on Christmas did not have fireplaces, so he used the front door. There was no such thing as a locked door for Santa. Quietly entering the house, he noted the absolute quiet within. "Good!" he thought. He loved children, but tonight was not the night to visit with them. Very quickly Santa placed gifts under the tree, and into the socks hanging over the backs of chairs. He had already compared the gift list with the requests of the children living here, and knew he was delivering what had been fervently prayed for.

Completing his delivery, Santa paused momentarily, and ate several cookies left out for him. Scooping the rest of the cookies in one hand, Santa quickly departed the home. Placing the now empty gift bag in the sleigh, Santa walked to the reindeer, and gave each of them a cookie. They happily munched, clouds of steam rising from their nostrils. Turning to reenter his sleigh, Santa caught sight of a figure standing in the snow a few yards from the sleigh.

The figure was the personification of a Charles Dickens street urchin. He appeared to be about 12 or 13 years old. His clothing was in complete disarray. He wore a baseball cap turned backwards. His hair was unkempt; hanging in greasy tendrils from beneath the cap. His trousers were several sizes too large, rolled up at the ankles, and had holes in the knees, showing pink skin beneath. His shoes were also too large, turning up at the toes like slippers from an Arabian Night's tale. The coat he wore appeared to be that of a woman; a too large woman, but nevertheless, providing warmth on this cold, snowy night. His face gave evidence of a long lapse since it last experienced soap and water. "A pitiful sight," Santa thought; looking intently at the youngster.

"May I help you, Young Man?" Santa asked, tone of voice friendly, but not overly so. "Do I have Christmas gifts for you?" Santa asked further.

"You don't have anything for me, Old Man!" the boy replied, tone of voice exuding contempt.

"What do you mean?" Santa asked, taken aback by the vitriolic tone in the young man's voice.

"You're not Santa!" the boy replied. "You're a fake! Santa is a fake! There never has been a Santa Claus!"

Santa was now truly nonplussed. He stared intently at the urchin, wondering what had brought on this release of verbal venom. He wondered what terrible catastrophe had befallen this youngster. "If I'm not Santa, what about the sleigh and reindeer? Where did they come from? How did they fly me in here?"

"A trick!" the boy replied, although his facial expression showed less determined, bitter assurance than it had moments ago.

"A trick, huh?" Santa replied. "What about the toys, and other gifts in the sleigh? If you're so sure it's a trick, go look at the toys. Look at the sleigh. Pet the reindeer."

The boy walked hesitantly over to the reindeer. Stopping beside Blitzen, he gently stroked the deer's shoulder. Blitzen, as if sensing the enormity of the moment, turned, and affectionately nuzzled the boy under the chin.

"He sure seems real," the youngster said. Turning to Santa, he said "It's gotta be a trick!"

Perceiving an opportunity, Santa broke in. "On Christmas Eve, a most important night, which you can't deny, how come you aren't home with your mother and dad?"

"Don't have any mother and dad," the boy replied.

"No mother and dad?" Santa asked with disbelief in his voice.

"That's right," the youngster replied. "My dad was a fireman with the New York City Fire Department. My mother worked in the World Trade Center. They were both killed in the terrorist attack on September 11." As he said this, two large tears dripped from his eyes, and oozing down his cheeks, left a rivulet in the dirt and grime on his face.

"Now I understand!" Santa thought, his old heart swelling near to bursting with pity. "Do you have any other family?" Santa asked.

"No. Even our home is gone," the boy replied. His home had burned to the ground, ignited by the falling debris from the collapsing Twin Towers. The boy's face now showed a steady flow of tears.

"This boy is really suffering!" Santa thought. Then, Santa had an idea.

"Son, would you like to come with me?" Santa asked.

"Come with you?" the youngster asked, tone of voice reflecting incredulous disbelief. "What would you do with me?" he asked.

"Oh, I need many young people to replace my aging brownies. We have lots of work that has to be done; work enough to take all year just to get ready for Christmas."

"I always wanted to be a fireman," the boy answered.

"Believe it or not," Santa replied, "but we need a few firemen around our place at the North Pole. We can't afford to let our place burn down, and up there, we need a lot of heat all year long. The risk of fire is pretty high."

"You mean you would take me to the North Pole and let me be a fireman?"

"There would be some things to do first," Santa replied. You would still have to get your school work done. You would have to learn the trade of a fireman. All during this, you would work as a brownie."

"Me? A fireman for Santa at the North Pole? I can't believe it," the boy replied. Then, as if in attempt to throw off what he couldn't accept, his face hardened, and he said, "Not on your life, Santa. I still think you're a fake!"

Santa noted the title of address the boy used. "Well, if that's the way you feel, I'll thank you to stand clear of my reindeer, and the sleigh. I have many places to go before the night is through." Santa then climbed back into the sleigh.

Gently slapping the deer with the reins, Santa slowly turned them to face a clear takeoff spot. Looking over his shoulder at the boy, Santa saw a face of abject sorrow.

Turning to the deer, Santa said, "Let's go boys!" The deer pranced in preparation for their takeoff lunge. The sleigh began to move.

"Santa! Please wait for me!" Santa looked around, and saw the youngster running as hard as he could through the deep snow, not quite able to keep up with the sleigh.

"Whoa!" Santa yelled, pulling back on the reins. The sleigh came to a halt.

The young boy stopped beside the sleigh, gasping great gulps of air. Looking through a sheen of tears at Santa, the boy said, "I want to go with you, Santa. Please!"

Throwing open the heavy blanket, Santa smiled, and said, "Climb in. Beginning to think you weren't going to change your mind."

The boy, shivering now, climbed in next to Santa. Santa wrapped him in the heavy fleece blanket. "On Donder and Blitzen! The sleigh leaped into the air, almost with a happy bound.

MERRY CHRISTMAS!

# THE HATE TREE

## BY: DANA T. MOORE, II

Immediately following the recent terrorist attack on the World Trade Center, and the Pentagon, in the midst of the evolving variety of emotions throughout America was the question, "Why?" I think the following true story illustrates the answer.

I grew up in the coal mining area of the mountains of southern West Virginia. This was during the midst of the great depression of the 1930's. My father was the company doctor. As such, he occupied an elevated position, both socially and economically. The miners looked up to my father and our family with a mixture of awe, respect and intense dislike.

During the early history of the coal mining industry, obtaining labor was a serious problem for the production of coal. Many immigrants were brought in to work in the coal mines. Some prisons in the southern states, with appropriate persuasion, released many of their inmates to move to the coal fields. These released convicts were relocated by the trainload. A condition of the convict's freedom was his continued servitude in the coal mines. This forced labor environment produced a social strata of uneducated, illiterate, hate filled men of all races, creeds, and ethnic backgrounds. Violent life was common. Refined social graces were near non-existent. People with an education were objects of distrust, fear, and very often, contempt. Illiteracy is fearful of knowledge. This social condition spawned the intense dislike for my father and our family.

My family subscribed to culture, education, and a loving environment. An enduring example of this was our celebration of Christmas. We always had a plentiful and joyous Christmas. My brother and I were too young and innocent to realize that this privilege could, and did generate considerable hostility in the local people who frequently ignored Christmas entirely. These people were too poor to afford a nice Christmas. Why?

The coal company economically controlled their workers by paying them in scrip. The scrip was accepted in the company owned stores. If the miner attempted to use scrip in a non-company store, the scrip was devalued 25 to 50%. Because of this, the miners, and their families, spent their wages at the company store. The company store encouraged the miners and their families to run a charge account. The charges were then deducted from the miner's wages. In addition, the miners and their families lived in company-owned houses, little more than hovels. Rent was also deducted from their wages. This economic system ensured servitude of the miners. As the country singer, Tennessee Earnie Ford, would later sing, "I owe my soul to the company store."

The aforementioned conditions produced a laboring element of a near disenfranchised mass of people. Many of them lived an existence of seething, hate filled frustration. The immigrant employees had come to America to escape exactly what they became ensnarled in. Additionally, many of these laborers came out of prisons with their mental philosophies permanently hardened to distrust all forms of authority.

One year, as the Christmas season approached, my father decided he would plant, and decorate a living tree in the front yard. He purchased, and planted a six foot tall, shapely pine tree. We then decorated the tree with strings of beautiful, multi-colored outdoor lights. I was probably seven or eight years old, but still remember that tree as a perfect reflection of Christmas. My father truly meant for others to take pleasure at the sight of the tree; a tree meant to display the loving theme of Christmas.

After decorating the tree, and following the evening meal, my parents took my brother and me to the movie theater in a nearby town. After the movie, we returned home around 10:00 PM.

Pulling up in front of the house, we noted the Christmas tree lights were not illuminated. They were on when we left for the movie. Closer examination showed the tree was nearly completely destroyed. All the lights were broken, and even the strings torn apart. Many of the limbs on the tree were missing. The vandals had used lumps of coal to throw at the tree to make sure the lights were not only extinguished, but totally destroyed. The tree was dead!

When I asked my father why people would do this, his answer was simple, "They have nothing so don't want anyone else to have anything." It was a long time before I was able to understand the venom of the have-nots for the haves. It might be called jealousy, but I don't think so. Some people who have nothing don't really want anything. They just don't want anyone else to have anything. It is a form of anarchy.

People who are permanently infected with this vitriolic hatred for those more fortunate cannot be changed. The more they are given, the more they hate the giver. Nothing will satisfy them, not even the total destruction of everything they hate.

The people who destroyed our Christmas tree were motivated by exactly the same hatred as were the terrorists who destroyed the World Trade Center, and attacked the Pentagon. I don't believe their hatred can be erased by anything. To them, the World Trade Center and the Pentagon represented the same image as our Christmas tree did for the disaffected vandals. The terrorists hated those symbols.

OUR CHRISTMAS TREE WAS A HATE TREE!

# ALTER EGO

BY: DANA T. MOORE, II

The pain was bothersome, but tolerable. It was widespread throughout her body, but after years of experience, she had grown to accept it. The worst part was her certain knowledge that it was incurable. The only medication offering even the smallest relief was a strong pain killer, and when she took this, she was, as she called it, "Zonked." She couldn't even wake up for meals.

She was a ninety-four-year-old woman residing in a nursing home. When she entered the home a year previously, following a bad fall resulting in a fractured hip with subsequent surgery, and a therapeutic recuperation in a hospital, she was able to walk, using a walker. Then, after a few months, the walker was no longer sufficient, and she had to resort to a wheel chair. Gradually, over the succeeding months, her mobility decreased to the point where she now required assistance just to go to the bathroom. Her meals were served on a hospital table. "Oh! The indignity of it!" Most likely, the worst part of all was her mental alertness, aware of her worsening condition, and being unable to do anything about it.

This woman, at one time, was an active, amateur athlete. Her husband's income as a successful physician allowed her access to the country club with all the golfing privileges. She was a competitive golfer, winning many trophies around the state. Additionally, she was an avid water skier, never missing an opportunity to spend time on the water at their summer lake home. Now, her only access to golfing events was by way of the television in her room. Often, when viewing golf on her TV, and simultaneously suffering the arthritic pain, she would cry silently, evidenced by tears slowly coursing her wrinkled, weathered old face.

Aggravating an already acute emotional environment was her total aloneness. Her husband had died 25 years previously. Her daughter, the older of her two children, was killed in a tragic automobile accident, along with her husband and two children. Then, a few years later, her son, a much decorated, career naval aviator, was killed while attempting a night recovery aboard an aircraft carrier in the Atlantic. Her son was married but had no children. In the years following his death, his widow gradually terminated all their former contact with one another. This loss of contact with her daughter-in-law contributed to her loneliness.

This old woman was the sole surviving member of a family of nine children. She was without close relatives, and her few cousins had long ago died. As for close friends, she had none, having outlived almost all her contemporaries. She was alone. Like all fiercely competitive people, she had subconsciously avoided any close relationships, not having one friend caring enough to visit her in the nursing home. There was no one to talk to, other than the professionals in the home, and to them, she was an enigmatic, close-mouthed old woman.

Fortunately, her husband had possessed a keen ability to look ahead to her future financial requirements, and had established a trust fund for her. This trust was established in such a way that it was administered for her, providing for all her financial requirements. Her fees at the home were handled through the trust administrator. All her personal money needs were likewise handled. In essence, other than from her physical distress, she had not a worry in the world. True, she would have much preferred to be in her own home, provided for by her household staff, and enjoying the love of her dog and cat. However, along with her home, the staff and the pets were now part of her history. This left her much like a dead space satellite hurtling through the dark and impersonal void of emotional isolation. Even the monthly visit by her physician was an event she looked forward to, although knowing he could offer no solution to her never ending pain.

When her arthritis began many years before, her husband had tried to ease her discomfort. It was during this time she revealed to him that she had fallen from a horse several years previously, and neglected to tell him about the fall. Upon hearing this, her husband had ordered a full orthopedic workup. During this examination, he discovered she had suffered a broken neck incurred in the fall from the horse, and was extremely lucky she had not been paralyzed from the neck down. He felt this had a lot to do with the onset of her arthritic pain.

And now, adding to her emotional distress was the approaching Christmas holiday season. In the past, Christmas was always a time of brimming happiness for her. With her husband and children gone, she turned her boundless energy outward to try and bring Christmas cheer to those less fortunate, and more likely to suffer true depression during the season of love and giving. Her entry into the nursing home effectively halted her Christmas activities. This led to an intense, emotional turn inward, with a loss of the old feeling of sharing at Christmas.

She lay back in her recliner chair, watching a televised golf tournament on the golf channel. The tournament tended to get her mind off the pain in her back and legs. Resulting from the pain killer she took following lunch, she was in a floating mode between interest in the golf and her arthritic pain. Intruding through her medicated mental fog, she heard a soft knock on her door.

"Come in!" she called out, perhaps a little too harshly, at the same time muting the tournament TV announcer.

Looking toward the door, she saw one of the staff members entering. "Would you be interested in some Christmas music?" The lady asked. Behind her were several young faces peering curiously into the room.

"Christmas music would be nice," the old woman answered.

With that, ten young ladies of high school age crowded into the room. They were accompanied by a choral director. As soon as the group was in place, the director held her hands up, and signaled for the singing to begin. The young women sang a medley of Christmas carols. Inasmuch as they were singing without musical accompaniment, they did quite well. As the holiday sounds filled the room, the old lady began to softly sob. The singers apparently didn't notice her distress, continuing through their complete repertoire without pause. When the singers finished, the old lady thanked them, and wished them a Merry Christmas.

She sadly watched them file out of her room. The singing reminded her, if it were necessary, of how lonely she was. "Yes, this is going to be a rough holiday season for me," she thought. Her acknowledgement of the unhappiness accompanying the Christmas season was one more indicator of just how far inward she had turned. Unmuting the golf announcer, she drifted drowsily down into her state of semi-sleep and attention to the golf.

And now, it was Christmas eve. Outside, snow was falling in thick, blinding white clouds. "Well," she thought bitterly. "With this snow, Santa will have no trouble getting in here tonight."

She had stumbled upon an old TV rerun of Lawrence Welk Christmas music and was listening to it. As the hour progressed toward midnight, she gradually dropped off into fitful slumber, the pain killer having its way with her.

Some time later, she only surmised it was very late, she was wakened by a muted sound of Christmas music. She thought the young singers had returned, but then, the hour was late, and the tone of the Christmas music was a little different. It was more like the voices of mature women. She looked around her room, but could see no one. "Must be coming from next door," she thought. She had turned off her television before going to sleep, so, as the dark screen confirmed, the singing was not coming from her TV. Struggling to wakefulness, she allowed her eyes to again wander around the room, dimly lit by her night light. "What in the world!" she thought.

Standing at the foot of her bed was a familiar figure; Santa Claus. "Oh, no," she thought. "Not a visiting Santa at this time of the night!" Then she thought of Ebeneezer Scrooge in *The Christmas Carol*. "Bah! Humbug!" she thought somewhat naughtily. "There really is no Santa Claus," she reassured herself.

"But, there is!" Santa answered, even though not a word had been spoken.

"Did I speak to you?" she asked, puzzled at his response to her thought.

"No, but I heard you just the same," Santa replied. "And let me once again reassure you, there is a Santa Claus."

"Why are you here?" She asked.

"It's Christmas Eve. Christmas is a day all Christians celebrate."

"What do I have to celebrate?" she asked bitterly.

"The birth of our Lord and Savior," Santa replied.

The old woman was quiet for an extended moment. She then asked, "If I am to celebrate the birthday of our Lord and Savior, why doesn't He do something for me? Why does He leave me here alone, and in pain?" Her tone of voice was sarcastically contemptuous, reflecting a feeling of, "There! I stopped you."

"Maybe He will eliminate all your pain," Santa answered.

The old woman stared morosely at Santa, listening to the heavenly singing coming from somewhere in the background. She noted now the conversation between Santa and herself was entirely without vocalizing, the transmission of thoughts to one another seeming to occur instantaneously.

She took her eyes away from Santa for a moment to try and see if she could determine where the singing came from. When she looked back, Santa was gone, but in his place was a young, bearded man with long, brown hair. He was dressed in a white, flowing robe with a heavy cowl collar. He looked intently at the old woman, His blue eyes seeming to penetrate right through her.

"Who are you?" she asked, an uneasy disturbance beginning to penetrate her thoughts. She was very uncomfortable.

By way of an answer, He said, "I've come for you."

"Come for me?" she replied like a mindless parrot.

"Yes, and I'm sure you want to go," he continued, all the while His piercing blue eyes maintaining an unwavering gaze upon her.

"Where are we going?" she thought, a little fearfully. Again, the dialogue taking place without benefit of verbal sound, and as before, the speed of exchange was virtually without hesitation.

Then, she followed up with, what to her was a certain end to the conversation. "I can't even walk."

"Ah, but you can," he replied, with even more certainty in His tone of voice. He continued, "Go ahead. Stand up!" This last was almost in a tone of command.

"I'll show Him!" she thought, and threw back the bed covers. She then rolled to her side, and threw her feet and legs out of the bed. To her complete surprise, she stood very steadily, erect as an unwavering oak tree.

"I knew you could," he said quietly, with no surprise in His tone of voice.

The old lady was now very apprehensive. "You asked me to come with you. Where are we going?"

"Look behind me," the white-robed figure answered.

She looked, and was amazed at what she saw. Standing in the near distance was a small group of people. They looked vaguely familiar. Concentrating, she focused her eyes on one figure, a middle aged male. "My husband!" she thought unbelievingly. "How?" she further thought. Her husband stood, grasping her old golf cart. He beckoned to her with one hand, a motion indicating for her to join him.

The other members of the group waved to her. She then heard voices, noting that the people were talking happily. Staring intently, she recognized her daughter, and her family; the two children, and her husband. Standing by the old woman's husband was her son, resplendent in his medal bedecked naval officer's uniform. As if this wasn't enough to completely throw her into a state of deep shock, she saw her two pets. Mike, her old black and tan Airdale, and Marvin, her Maine Coon, gray striped cat. Mike and Marvin were somehow different. "Of course!" she thought. Mike was hopping with the youthful exuberance of a young dog, and Marvin was twisting around her husband's feet in an obvious display of excited happiness. The pets looked, and behaved as they had in years past. Her family looked just as she remembered them from the time when her life was all happiness.

"Well, are you coming with me?" a somewhat peremptory question came from the white robed figure.

Without a moment's hesitation, she thought, "Of course, I will go with you." Then, another shocking question popped unbidden into her mind, followed by another. "The pain! What happened to it?" Then, almost immediately, "Will I be coming back?"

"I took your pain, as I have for all mankind. And no, you will not be coming back anytime soon."

Noting her look of hesitation, he continued, "You need nothing more. You have Me, and you have your family, and it will be so for all time. Now, let us be on our way."

Taking a step away from the security of her bed, the old woman was very pleasantly surprised to note she now walked with the pain free, bouncy gait of a youthful woman. With another thought, she abruptly stopped. "Santa! What happened to Santa?" She looked to where Santa stood a few moments previously and saw Santa again. As she stared at the white bearded, jolly old figure in the red suit, the image changed again. Now she was staring at the white robed figure. While she looked, the image changed again, back to Santa.

"But Santa? Who is Santa?" she asked.

The Santa image again changed back to the white robed figure.

"Santa is My Alter Ego," He replied.

MERRY CHRISTMAS!

# BEAVER PATROL

BY: DANA T. MOORE, II

"I'll fix that New Testament, Mackerel Snapping, Irish Goy!" Major Abe Lipshitz said explosively, his eyes gleaming with anticipation.

"Shultz, get your butt in here!" Abe yelled at his personnel Sergeant.

Shultz appeared like Mephistopheles materializing. "Sir?" Shultz inquired respectfully, standing before Abe's desk.

Rolling an unlit cigar from side to side in his mouth, Abe stared at a letter clutched in his hand. Finally, "Shultz, this Pentagon letter is a directive telling us we gotta cut some orders sending the enlisted personnel to Fort Carson to serve in Major Liam Shaunessy's USAF detachment assigned to the 5th Infantry Division.

"Yes, Sir," Shultz acknowledged in a neutral tone of voice, glancing at the letter he had read, and placed on Major Lipshitz's desk earlier that morning. Shultz was also aware of the vitriolic feud between Major Lipshitz, Personnel Officer at the 6550th Tactical Air Control Wing, and Major Shaunessy, USAF fighter pilot, Air Force Liaison Officer to the 5th Infantry Division. This intense hatred evolved from Major Shaunessy's assignment to the U. S. Army. He took this assignment as a direct attack from Major Lipshitz, and at the pre-assignment briefing, unloaded his stored up invective upon the personnel officer, overlooking completely the fact that Major Lipshitz was merely carrying out orders directed to him by higher headquarters. Regardless, Major Shaunessy now had a permanent and vindictive enemy in a position to unleash a lot of problems upon him.

"Shultz, lemme see the records of Sergeant Lane, and Airmen Loose, Ruffle, and Ginn," Abe said, handing the directive letter to his personnel Sergeant.

Shultz's eyes opened wide in disbelief, mouth agape in surprise. "Sir, you wouldn't," he started to reply.

"The hell I wouldn't!" Abe answered, grinning wickedly. "Gimme those records!"

"Yes, Sir," Shultz acknowledged, resignation in his voice.

Two weeks later, entering his office at Fort Carson, Liam heard his name called. "Major Shaunessy, Col. Patterson wants to see you in his office right away," the administrative clerk said.

"On the way," Liam replied, turning to walk down the hall to the Colonel's office.

Knocking on the partially open door bearing a sign "G-3," Liam responded to the staccato "Come in!" by stepping smartly through the doorway. Saluting, Liam had a momentary, mental flash recall telling him that Col. Patterson, U. S. Army; West Point graduate, and the 5th Infantry Division Operations Officer, held little affection for the "USAF College Flyboys," as he often referred to Liam and his two Captains.

You wanted to see me, Sir?" Liam asked, noting the unreturned salute, military rudeness of the first order.

"How is the manning of your detachment coming along?" Col. Patterson asked, malevolence unmistakable in his voice.

"I have two Captains as Forward Air Controlers, one maintenance Staff Sergeant, three USAF jeeps, and one maintenance van, all equipped with the latest communications gear, and three Airmen First Class radio operators due in any day now," Liam answered, face showing quizzical reaction to the query. Liam knew that Col. Patterson was kept currently aware of special staff manning such as the USAF detachment.

"Well, Major, lemme ask you this," Patterson went on, an evil lear on his face. "Where is your Sergeant? When did you last see him? Where are the rest of the people for your detachment?"

"Sergeant Lane is in the barracks assigned exclusively to my detachment. I saw him three days ago. He's been working on the radio equipment. The three airmen are due in momentarily."

"Have you seen any orders on these enlisted people, other than your Sergeant?" Col. Patterson asked, voice dripping with sarcasm.

Liam paused, growing increasingly uncomfortable under the interrogation of this hostile, senior Army officer. Liam had wondered about the lack of info copies of the orders for his enlisted people, but had discounted it as a typical screwup by the personnel system for which he had nothing but contempt anyway.

"No, Colonel. Apparently the orders have been somehow misrouted. I'll check into it. Is this why you wanted to see me?" Liam was genuinely concerned now.

In reply, Col. Patterson shot back, vitriol in his voice, "You better check on your people, Major! One of my officers handle things this way, and I'd have him up on charges! Best you get busy!"

"Yes, Sir!" Liam acknowledged. Saluting, he turned, and left the G-3 office.

"What the hell's going on?" Liam thought, as he hurried to the barracks assigned to his detachment.

Taking the stairs two at a time to the second floor where Sergeant Shady Lane had established himself, Liam paused at the top. Looking down the long, open bay World War Two barracks, Liam spotted Shady asleep in bed, and noted three adjacent bunks in disarray, obviously having been used. He also noted baggage and personal belongings strewn about, evidence of the recent arrival of new personnel.

"Better have these people clean up the area," Liam thought, approaching the sleeping Sergeant.

Nudging the foot of Shady's bunk, Liam spoke. "Wake up, Shady. It's Major Shaunessy. I need to talk to you."

Shady rolled over, and groaned. As he did, an empty bourbon bottle bounced from beneath the bed covers, clattering loudly on the wooden floor.

"Damn it! Wake up, Shady!" Liam spoke again, forcefully now.

Shady sat up, hair tousled, eyes bloodshot, and deep, dark debauchery circles etched under his eyes. Liam was shocked at his intensely dissipated appearance.

"What the hell have you guys been doing?" Liam fired at the unsteadily upright Shady.

"Guys?" Shady echoed, apparently still drugged with alcoholic slumber.

"Yeah. What the hell you been up to? Where are the other three?" Liam was growing provoked with his muddleheaded Sergeant. Perhaps he could get some sense from the airmen.

Nodding his head weakly toward the end of the open bay, Shady muttered, "Latrine, Sir."

Walking into the old fashioned Army barracks latrine, with its rows of sinks, mirrors, and toilets, and large, open communal shower, Liam was totally unprepared for what awaited him. His jaw jolted open, and his facial expression ran the gamut from shock, to disbelief, and then finally, to total incredulity. Rinsing in the shower were three of the most beautiful women Liam had ever seen. Three Nude Nymphs! Voluptious Valkyries! Sensuous Sirens! The variety couldn't have been better arranged; one blue eyed blond; one amber eyed brunette; and one green eyed redhead; hair color confirmed by consistency; all statuesque, lean, lithe and lanky. True American beauties!

Catching sight of Liam rooted in the doorway, apparently in shock, the blond spoke. "Good morning, Major. Care to join us?" The other two continued their sensual rinsing, watching Liam intently.

"Who in the hell are you?" Liam exploded in response.

The blond spoke again. "I'm Airman First Class Wanda Loose. The redhead is Airman First Class Lacey Ruffle, and the brunette is Airman First Class Sloe Ginn. Sure you wouldn't like to join us? The water's great."

"How long have you been here?" Liam asked, ignoring the invitation, but showing less hostility now.

"We checked in three days ago, Sir," Lacey answered.

"You've been here in the barracks for three days?" Liam responded, voice rising in disbelief.

"Yes, Sir," Sloe answered, then went on, "Sure you won't join us? Ole Shady's shot. We could sure use a replacement."

"Good Lord! Shady! No wonder he looked as if he'd been drawn through a fine grade filter. The man's been worked nearly to death!" Liam's mind continued, "Oh, My Gawd! These three are my detachment! Communicating Concubines! Now I know what was on Col. Patterson's mind. That son-of-a-bitch! He knew all along, and let me hang before telling me." Liam's mind then jumped to Major Lipshitz at the 6550th. "That Hebrew Horses Ass! He really put it to me!"

Liam stared at his military maidens. The three women continued to rinse and enjoy themselves without the slightest trace of concern that they were under close scrutiny by their new boss.

Shaking himself free from the grip of this answer to a Satyr's fantasy, Liam spoke, this time with authority in his voice. You girls get some clothes on, and come back to the sleeping area! We've gotta talk."

"Yes, Sir," Wanda acknowledged, nodding knowingly to the other two.

With a twinge of regret, Liam turned, and walked from the latrine back to where Shady was again snoring loudly.

"Wake up, Shady!" Liam demanded imperiously.

Shady still snored. Were it not for the snoring, he might have been taken for dead.

Giving Shady's bunk a resounding kick, Liam shouted, "Damn it, Shady! Get the hell up!"

Shady rolled to a sitting position, looking not one whit better than when awakened before.

"Yes, Sir?"

"What the hell you been doing with these women in the barracks? No, don't answer that! I don't want to hear! Why didn't you get in touch with me? These women are assigned to me, or uh, rather, uh, these Airmen are assigned to my detachment," Liam lamely finished.

"Sir, I was going to get in touch with you. They had to be processed in, so I went ahead and finished that first. They're all signed in, and ready for duty."

"Duty, hell!" Liam exploded. "These girls are going back to the 6550th."

"I don't know, Major," Shady disagreed respectfully. "They got orders, and it all appears legal and official." With that, Shady climbed from his bed, and, clad in undershorts only, walked to his wall locker. Opening the door, he extracted a thick sheaf of papers and handed it to Liam.

Liam examined the papers; official transfer orders; one set for each of the airmen. "Official, all right," he thought. "Official but not irreversible."

Shaking his head, Liam sat on the edge of Shady's bunk. As he did, he turned, and saw the three girls; all sitting cross-legged like Buddhas on a bunk opposite him, clad in sheer brassieres and the briefest of nearly invisible bikini panties. They reminded Liam of the three monkeys who heard no evil, saw no evil, nor spoke no evil; in this instance, certainly a totally inaccurate analogy. Liam blinked, and tried to keep his mind on military business, rather than monkey business.

"Please get some clothes on," Liam blurted out plaintively. The girls got up to obey. Walking to their wall lockers, they pulled out a set each of kaki coveralls. Donning these, they returned to their stoic stations on the bunk opposite Liam and awaited further developments.

Looking first at the three girls, then at Shady, Liam spoke. "It's obvious, Ladies, that you can't stay here. I'm going to try and get your orders cancelled, and send you back to the 6550th."

"Major," Wanda Loose, the blond beauty, interrupted. "Are you aware of women's liberation? Do you have any idea of the sort of adverse reaction and bad vibes the press would give a situation like this if it became known you had us sent back to the 6550th? I'm not making a threat, but I really think you might be setting yourself up for a lot of headache."

"And, Major," Sloe Ginn, the brunette, chimed in. "The Army has women assigned here. Why can't the USAF? You're in the USAF, and so are we. We're well trained, and know our business." Sloe frowned at the lewd winks of the other two girls, then continued. "We're well trained in the communications career field, and know the USAF and Army Air Ground close air support system. You need us."

"You oughta give us a chance, Major," redheaded Lacey Ruffle admonished.

"What about field duty?" Liam enjoined. "You'll be exposed to a hell of a lot of field duty wherein you'll have to sleep in the bush. You'll not have the comfortable, convenient hygienic facilities of a dormitory. You'll be forced to share the hardships and privations of living in primitive field conditions, just as the doughfoot soldiers do, with bugs, spiders, snakes, and all kinds of hairy, creepy crawlers." With that, Liam stared at each of the girls, his jaw jutting in stubborn, male supremacy.

"Major," Sloe Ginn answered, "I grew up in a migrant farm environment, sleeping in a bed with five other kids of both sexes, until I was seventeen. I was twelve years old before I ever saw an indoor bathroom. Just having my own sleeping bag is a luxury. Field duty doesn't scare me."

"Me, neither," echoed Lacey Ruffle.

"Nor me," corroborated Wanda Loose.

Glancing first at Shady, then at the girls, Liam appeared to become lost in thought.

"All right! Enough talk," Liam said. "The four of you get into clean, starched fatigues, with shined combat boots. I don't want to see those coveralls again. The Army would laugh us off post. Get yourselves looking sharp, and report to my office in one hour. I want each of you girls to bring one of our new jeeps." With that, Liam stood, and strode from the barracks.

Stomping into his office, Liam nodded to Gil Kellerman, and Web Arthur, his USAF forward air controllers. Sitting at his desk, Liam muttered, "That Kooky Kike, Abe Lipshitz, really put it to me! Sending three women for duty in my Tactical Air Control Party! The Army will never let us hear the end of this!"

Gil and Web looked at one another, grinning widely. "Hell, Major," Gil opened, "I don't see why you're so upset. If these girls know their jobs, let's keep 'em." Web nodded his head in eager concurrence.

Looking at his two fighter jockeys, robust young lions, Liam shook his head and asked, "What about your wives? How do you think they'll take it when we go to the field with these girls?"

Grin gone now, Web asked, "Do they have to know?"

"Come on, Web," Liam replied sarcastically. "The Army wives will drop this artillery round on our wives before the flag goes down tonight. I suggest you tell your wives at lunch today. I'm telling mine."

Before either Web or Gil could reply, Liam picked up the phone, and placed an official call to Major Abe Lipshitz.

Momentarily, "Abe! You circumcised, fugitive money changer! You bastard! You've set USAF and Army relations back 50 years. How'm I going to operate with women assigned to my detachment? I'd like to make a personal gift of you to Yasser Arafat, and the PLO. They'd know how to deal with you!" Liam stopped for breath.

"Well, well, well," Abe replied in mock sympathy. "So the Papal Pimp is unhappy with his flock. Tsk! Tsk! Tsk! How about Sergeant Shady Lane? How's he doing? He should be a real asset to you with his specialized background."

"Huh?" Liam mouthed without comprehension.

"Yeah, Mackerel Snapper! I sent you a real winner for your enlisted honcho. Ole Shady's had a history of drinking, fighting, carousing, womanizing, and work release with the local civil authorities here. He's been reduced from Technical Sergeant to Staff Sergeant for fighting in a brothel. The only reason he wasn't busted all the way down is because he's an electronics genius. Listen, Ole Bead Clicker! Shady's guaranteed to keep things interesting for you. He really has a finely honed sense of appreciation for the three 'B's.'"

"Three 'B's?" Liam echoed, beginning to sound like a record player.

"Yeah, you Genuflecting Gentile! Shady really knows and loves Booze, Broads, and Brothels. And I'll tell you something else, you Confessing Creep! No absolution for the likes of you! You better make do with what you have, because you're really under the gun to do good with the Army. I tried to tell you this when you were here for briefing, but you weren't having any of it. You're supposed to placate the Army, and get them off the backs of our Pentagon people. Screw up the works, and you'll be the gift to Yasser and his cut throats, if you aren't nailed to a cross first!" With that, Abe Lipshitz hung up on Liam.

"He hung up on me," Liam said in disbelief, replacing the phone.

Almost instantly the phone rang. Liam nearly jumped out of his boots. Picking up the phone again, he answered, "Major Shaunessy."

"Yes. Yep. Understand. 0800 day after tomorrow, huh? Okay. We're ready." Liam replaced the phone again, staring at it in wide eyed shock, as if seeing a live viper in his hand.

"We're going out with the Division for extended field duty day after tomorrow. We're ordered to have the radio equipment manned and operational. There'll be simulated close air strikes from Tactical Air. Gil and Web, you'll be handling the strikes. This means the girls have to go to work and operate the equipment," Liam finished, sounding as if his death sentence had just been pronounced.

Gil and Web grinned. "Wives or no, orders are orders. Looks like some fun," Web observed.

"Hope you still think so when we return to garrison," Liam said, voice sounding apprehensive, thinking of the reaction from his wife upon receipt of this news.

Liam's worrying was interrupted by Shady reporting in with the three girls. "Sergeant Lane and Detachment reporting for duty, Sir," Shady stated sharply, saluting smartly.

Returning the salute, Liam replied, "We're going out for field duty day after tomorrow. We'll need all the equipment. Each jeep will have an operator and all the radio gear in working order. You checked out the communications this morning, Shady?"

"Yes, Sir. Everything working fine."

"Good," Liam acknowledged. "Girls, I've talked with people at the

6550th, and it appears you're staying. Needless to say, we gotta mind our manners, and don't give the Army any call to fault us. Now, girls, Captains Kellerman and Arthur will give you an orientation tour of the area, seeing as how your local exposure has been limited to Sergeant Lane. Shady, you stay here. I want to talk to you."

Gil and Web led the girls from Liam's office.

"Shady, Major Lipshitz told me about your fondness for booze and women. He also told me about your excursions with the civil authorities. Lemme say this. You keep outta trouble with the Army and the local law, and we'll get along fine. I don't care about your after duty shenanigans, as long as you don't get into trouble. Get hung up with the locals, or the Military Police, and you're on your own. Do we understand each other?"

"Yes, Sir," Shady replied, smiling innocently at his new boss.

"And one other thing, Shady. I'm moving the girls into the Division WAC barracks. I think they'll be better off with the Army women than with you. Don't want the Army to think we're trying to breed our own recruits."

Shady nodded glum concurrence, saying nothing.

Two days later, following a pre-dawn departure in convoy, the Division Headquarters pulled from the dirt road into a heavily wooded area. A sentry waved the line of vehicles through the opening in the concertina barbed wire enclosure to a place designated as the Division Tactical Operations Center.

Liam was less than pleased with the sign marking the location of his detachment; "Beaver Patrol, USAF." The girls grinned, pleased with the recognition.

"Beaver Patrol! The Army must think we're a bunch of Cub Scouts," Liam said, a querulous tone in his voice.

"I doubt it, Major," Wanda replied. "I think whoever printed that sign had a little more grown up idea in mind."

"How so?" Liam inquired.

"I'll explain it to you one of these dark nights, Sir," Wanda offered, shaking her head in disbelief at her naive boss. Lacey and Sloe grinned.

Shady smirked.

After four days of intensive operational field training, Liam was confident his detachment could do the job assigned to it. The Army staff officers had begun to accept Liam and his USAF people as functional and contributing members of the 5th Infantry Division combat team. Sergeant Shady Lane repeatedly demonstrated his electronics genius by keeping the USAF communications equipment working flawlessly.

The two Captains were professional in controlling air strikes, and in fire support planning for the Brigades. The girls, while drawing the expected cat calls from Army personnel, showed themselves to be well qualified in performing as radio operators and drivers. They surprised Liam with their ground navigation skills, finding their way around in the woods with far less trouble than their Army counterparts. Liam was pleasantly surprised with his detachment; however, there was one fly in the ointment.

Col. Patterson was relentless in his degrading, derogatory verbal attacks upon the USAF and its "Blue Beavers," as he now called Liam's detachment. He took particular delight in airing his dislike before the General Staff at the evening briefings where all the key personnel were present to enjoy the daily dose of caustic comments aimed at Liam. Being the outsider, Liam was hard pressed just to survive the verbal onslaught.

Observing this cruel campaign was the Division Commanding General, and the two Brigadier General Vice Commanders. Liam had the uneasy feeling the Commanding General was quietly waiting to see how he would cope with this vicious and often personal attack.

Late on the evening of the fifth night in the field, and a night when Liam had been the butt of some particularly demeaning jibes from Col. Patterson, Liam stopped by his maintenance van to see if Shady had everything in shape for tomorrow's operations. Climbing through the blackout curtains on the rear of the large van, and blinking in the bright flourescent lights shining on all the expensive test equipment, Liam walked to an empty work stool, and sat facing Shady and the three girls.

"You've all done good work, and I'm proud of you," Liam said.

"You don't look too happy about it," Shady replied.

Liam then told Shady and the girls about the ongoing attacks from Col. Patterson, and of his apparently intractable hostility to the USAF, and to this detachment in particular. In summary, Liam said, "Col. Patterson is a real bastard. He's worse, if possible, than that no good Personnel Officer, Major Abe Lipshitz!" Shady looked at the girls, but saying nothing, raised his eyebrows knowingly.

Moments later, Liam got up to leave. "Thanks for listening to my problems, Troops. See you tomorrow." Parting the curtains to leave the van, Liam failed to note the exchange of meaningful glances between Shady and the three radio operators.

Two days later, returning from the midday meal in the officer's mess tent, Liam didn't observe Col. Patterson drop into step beside him. Several paces passed before the Colonel intruded upon Liam's preoccupied mental isolation.

"Your guys are doing good work, Liam," Col. Patterson began, making unusual use of Liam's first name.

"Huh?" Liam said, equally as surprised at the compliment as he was at the out-of-character friendliness.

"Yeah, your detachment is doing a bangup job, Liam, no pun intended," Patterson said, a weak smile on his face. He was obviously uneasy with this camaraderie charade.

"Well, thanks, Colonel," Liam acknowledged, a trifle uneasy himself.

"And those girls really know their job," the Colonel continued.

Liam made no reply.

"Well, thanks again, Liam," Col. Patterson said, a somewhat strange, and overly solicitous tone in his voice. "See you back at the Command Post later," he said, turning to continue on his way.

"Yes, Sir," Liam replied, his own voice reflecting uncertainty at this new, and uncharacteristic display of appreciation.

That evening, following a very routine, uneventful general staff briefing, during which not a single sarcastic, stinging remark was winged at the USAF by Col. Patterson, and with a head more full of questions than after the curious conversation following lunch today, Liam was stopped as he departed the briefing tent.

"Major Shaunessy," Liam heard.

Turning, Liam recognized the Commanding General's Aide de Camp.

"Yes?" Liam replied.

"The General would like to see you in his field van, Major."

"Now?" Liam inquired.

"Yes, Major. If you will, please, come with me now," the Captain requested, turning to leave the tent.

"Major Liam Shaunessy, USAF Air Liaison Officer, Sir," the Aide said, formally introducing Liam to the General, standing inside his van.

"I know the Major, thanks. You may take the rest of the evening off now, Captain," the General said, dismissing his Aide.

"Yes, Sir. Goodnight, General. Goodnight, Major."

"Drink, Major?" the General asked politely, nodding toward a small table upon which sat a bottle of good bourbon, several clean glasses, and a large ice bucket. "Pour me a couple fingers neat, please."

Liam poured two glasses with an equal amount, and extended one to the General. "Thank you, Sir."

Taking a swallow of bourbon, the General spoke. "Have a seat, Major."

The two sat, facing one another, the table of refreshments beside them.

"Major, I've been waiting to see how you would handle Col. Patterson. I could have intervened, but I think this was a test of wills best left to the outcome of the smarter of you two."

Liam said nothing, waiting for the General to continue.

"I admire a shrewd survivor, Major. I also admire a clever tactician. I normally don't hold with blackmail, but under extraordinary circumstances, extraordinary maneuvers are called for. Knowing the maneuvering stops here, I approve."

Not having any idea what the General was talking about, Liam took refuge in the safest reply. "Thank you, Sir," he said uneasily.

"What I don't understand, Major, is how you got it all wrapped up so quickly. I only wish my intelligence people could get me the results of their photo recon as fast."

Still following the noncommital vein, Liam replied, "Necessity is the mother of invention, Sir."

The General chuckled. She sure came through this time." Reaching down to a briefcase beside his chair, the General extracted a manila envelope, and handed it to Liam. "Thought you might want this back. I have no further use for it."

Taking the envelope, Liam finished his bourbon in one long gulp. "Thank you, Sir," he said weakly, hoping the bourbon would be blamed for his whispery tone of voice.

The General stood. "Enjoyed the photo work. Enjoyed seeing you come out on top. You really fixed Col. Patterson's wagon. Don't think he'll bother you any more. I enjoy a combat gamble. Welcome to my team. Again, good show." The General extended his hand in welcome.

Taking the proffered hand, Liam encountered a warm, sincere grasp.

"Thank you, General. Thanks for the bourbon, too. Good night, Sir."

Saluting, Liam left the field van, still wondering what had taken place.

Stopping by Shady's maintenance van, Liam climbed inside, and in the bright light, with Shady and the girls watching quietly, examined the contents of the manila envelope. His eyes opened wide in disbelief. Shady and the girls fidgeted and squirmed nervously. Finally, Liam broke out in a peal of gut laughter. Placing the stack of glossy photos on the metal work bench behind him, Liam turned, and examined them more closely. They had been taken in Col. Patterson's private, three man, field duty squad tent, his living quarters in the field.

Col. Patterson was clearly identifiable in all the photos. He was also obviously very drunk, with booze bottles evident. With the Colonel, in various compromising conditions in the different photos, were three nude women.

Liam chose not to make an issue of the identification of the women in the photos. He looked at the four members of his Air Control Team, and commented, "Looks as if Col. Patterson has placed himself in a rather compromising condition. Wonder how the General got these photos?"

With tongue in cheek, Shady said he would never presume to explain the actions of senior officers, particularly those of a senior officer from a sister service.

The three girls nodded in agreement.

"Well, whatever, can't bite the hand that feeds," Liam said. Continuing, "It would appear that a bridge of cooperation has been crossed. I'm very thankful."

Pausing, and looking directly into the eyes of each of the girls in turn, Liam went on, "I'm certainly grateful for the outcome of this field duty. Think I'll keep these 'After Action Reports,'" Liam said, returning the photos to the envelope, and standing to leave the maintenance van.

Still grasping the envelope, Liam said, in a sincere tone of voice. "I'm very grateful. And one other thing. I have no doubts as to the efficiency, and capability of this control team. Good night."

# THE CHRISTMAS PRESENT

## BY: DANA T. MOORE, II

"Now be sure, Son, to give me a call when she starts into labor. We want to be there with you during the delivery."

"Dad, you can't. I'll be in the delivery room during delivery. The best you can do is wait in the waiting room."

"Okay, Son. The waiting room will be good enough. Just give us a call when the countdown starts."

"I will, Dad." With that, the phone connection was broken, and the anticipated long wait begun. His son, the last of his three children to marry, and thus the last to begin his family, had gotten into the game. His wife of two years was about to birth their first child, a son, if the sonograms could be trusted. And so, it looked to the old man and his wife, like the circle was just about complete. Their other two children, both daughters, had married, and brought forth two children each. The daughters were securely entrenched in their life pursuits, and his son, was also firmly on track in his professional life. And now, on the eve of another grandchild, and at the beginning of the Christmas season, the old man allowed himself the luxury of a brief review of his family begetting.

He and his wife were very fortunate. Their three children were all born in good health, and had remained that way throughout their lives. Each of the daughters had in turn born two children, and they were in excellent health. Now, the son and his wife were about to tie another knot in the genetic string. The old man had no doubts the birth would be as normal as sun up and sun down. With this reassuring thought, he turned out the bedside lamp, and joined his wife in peaceful slumber.

Some time later, the old man wasn't sure just when, the sound of bells awoke him. "The phone!" he thought, reaching for the receiver, his hand shaking with excitement. A loud dial tone was the rude response to his grasp of the phone. The bells continued.

He looked over at his wife, and saw that she was awake, but not moving. "Do you hear them?" he asked. She nodded an affirmative reply.

"What are they?" he wondered aloud.

"They sound like Christmas bells," she answered.

"They sure do," he acknowledged, climbing from beneath the bed covers. They both could still hear the bells. They weren't loud, but nevertheless, very clear. The bells pealed softly in a rolling tone as if there were banks of them, with the nearest being the first bank, the farther ones being behind the first, diminishing in volume, but still clear, crisp, and beautiful.

The old man walked slowly before the foot of the bed, gazing intently around the now dimly lit room. He noted that all the lights in the bedroom were off, but still there was a dim glow of light from the east wall of the room; dim but sufficiently bright enough to illuminate the whole room. The bells continued pealing, but now there was another, beautiful sound in the background.

"Women's voices!" he exclaimed.

"No! Those are angels," his wife said, her voice reverently soft, but firm.

Before the old man could absorb the impact of his wife's statement, he felt something in his arms. An incredulous expression on his face, he looked down to see what was moving in his arms.

A babe wrapped in swaddling clothes! The old man looked into a pair of clear, blue eyes gazing steadily up at him. The bells and the angelic voices grew louder, rising to a crescendo of beautiful sound. And then, the bells and voices dropped off to a low background level.

The old man then heard, in a deep masculine voice, "BEHOLD! UNTO ME THIS DAY A SON IS BORN!"

Gradually, the sounds, and light faded away, as if they had never been there. The small figure in the old man's arms was the last to disappear.

And then, the old man found himself sitting up in bed, his wife sitting beside him. Rubbing his eyes, the old man muttered, "Must have had a dream."

"If you did, so did I," his wife responded.

Then, before any serious discussion could develop, the phone on the bedside table jangled loudly.

Hands shaking, the old man picked up the receiver. "Hello."

"Dad! We've got a boy!" his son spoke excitedly.

"I know. How's your wife?" the old man asked.

"She's fine, and the baby is fine also," his son replied. Continuing, "When are you and mom coming up to see what we've done?" his son asked.

"Would it be all right if we come on up now?" the old man asked by way of an answer.

"Know what time it is, Dad?" his son asked.

Glancing at the clock by the phone, the old man noted it was a half hour past midnight.

"If we came on now, we'd not stay long, and then the three of you could get some uninterrupted rest," the old man said.

"Dad, you two come on. We'll be looking for you."

In the car, driving the 20 miles to the hospital, the old man and his wife were at first hesitant to mention the dream they had had. They preferred to call it a dream rather than a vision. People today had some very harsh ideas about those who had visions, or claimed some sort of a religious happening in their lives.

"Well, what do think we saw, or what happened to us?" he asked his wife, keeping his eyes on the road.

"I certainly don't think our grandson is the Messiah," she answered. She continued, "I think what happened to us was a very unusual message, with perhaps an even more unusual delivery."

The old man then took up the dialogue. "The message wasn't so unusual, but the delivery certainly was. I think we were told, in a heavenly fashion, that every childbirth is a link in the divine chain back to the Babe born on Christmas day. Parents need to be aware of the Hand of God at work when they are allowed to bring a healthy new baby into the world." With that, the old man paused, and gave his wife her turn.

"I agree with you," she said. "Also," she went on, "I don't think we need tell anyone about what happened to us."

"You're right," he said. "Everyone will think we're senile."

"Maybe we are," the old woman answered, a twinkle in her eye.

After 44 years of marriage, the old man knew when he was being joshed. It was good for him. Kept him from taking himself too seriously.

Arriving at the maternity ward reception desk, they told the duty nurse who they were, and who they wanted to see.

"Room 116. Down the hall on the right," the nurse answered, not bothering to take her eyes off the paperwork she was bringing up to date.

Gently pushing the door open, the old man leaned in and asked, "Is it all right for these old grandparents to come in?"

"Come on in," his son answered.

Stepping cautiously in, the old couple saw their son standing by the side of the bed. Their daughter-in-law was propped up on the adjustable bed, holding their new son in her left arm, a look of radiant pride on her face. The baby was wrapped in hospital baby garments, with a little pointed, knit cap on his head. He appeared to be soundly sleeping.

"How are you doing?" the old man asked, looking intently at the new mother. "And how's he doing?" he continued, looking at the new baby boy.

"We're both doing fine," she answered, although I think I'm running on adrenalin right now."

"How about you, Son?" the old man asked.

"The same, Dad," his son answered.

The old man's wife produced a small camera, and receiving no objection, proceeded to take a few pictures, with the three adults shifting around to be next to the baby, and the new mother.

Following a few minutes of small talk, and assurances the new baby, mother, and father were all doing well, the old man suggested it was time for them to go. He could tell that his son and wife were tired, and needed rest.

"Before we go, can I have a picture of the grandfather and grandson together?" the old woman asked.

"Sure," the new mother responded.

The old man leaned over, and gently took the baby in his arms. Turning, he faced his wife while she took two snap shots. He then looked down at the baby nestled in his arms. Again, he was aware that he was looking into a pair of clear, blue eyes gazing intently up at him.

"Thank you, Lord," he thought to himself. Then, he heard the bells, and angels' voices in the background. "Hear that, Son?" he asked.

"What's that, Dad?" his son asked.

"Oh, nothing. Guess I'm hearing things," the old man answered, glancing quickly at his wife, who nodded almost imperceptibly. "Probably because we're all tired," the old man went on, handing the child back to his mother.

Then, making their farewells, the old couple started to leave. Pausing in the doorway, the old man turned and said, "You know, Christmas is only a little over a month away. I think we have just received an early Christmas present.

MERRY CHRISTMAS!

# CHRISTMAS BUGLES

## BY: DANA T. MOORE, II

W alking through his beloved mountain woods, the old man was keenly aware of the imminent onset of the first winter snows. It was past mid-November, and the crisp, woodsy air was full of the sharp tang of wintry promise. The leaves were dry and crunchy under foot; the limbs of the hardwood trees were bare and glistening in their seasonal sleep. The tall pines pointed majestically toward the blue, mountain sky, almost as if to urge and hasten the arrival of the first mantle of dry, white snow to complete their dignified beauty. The snow would dress them as a group of tall, proud ladies, adorned in ermine wraps of white, with brightly flashing diamonds scattered throughout their attire, adding a touch of heavenly angel's eyes to their radiant appearance. It was no wonder to him that the snow covered pine tree had been selected centuries before as the fitting symbol to celebrate the birth of Jesus. The pine tree, with its permanent green of youth, mingled with its wintry angel hair of white, was truly symbolic of life. And to him, life and the birth of the Christ Child were inextricably entwined as the true ingredients of eternity.

He paused from his walking, and lit his pipe. As he drew the flames of the match into the bowl, he allowed his mind to wander back over the past few years. As much as he loved his mountain forests, the past two and a half years had been very lonesome for him. His wife had died then, and from that point on, his life had been empty. What little solace there was for him was drawn from his mountains, and his frequent walks through the woods. This was where he and his wife had spent their twilight years together. It was she who had likened the snow covered pines to stately ladies dressed in ermine. It was she who had seen the reflected sunlight as flashing diamonds in the snow, and had compared them to angel's eyes. They had frequently bundled up, and walked hand in hand through the snow covered woods, usually in the sunlight of early morning following a fresh snowfall, and in particular, they loved to walk on Christmas mornings. To be sure, the snow shortly became too deep to walk in, but when that happened, they had gazed through the windows of their warm house, and still seen the wondrous landscaping hand of God at work.

His wife had always made a big thing of Christmas, going all out to decorate the house, and to keep it filled with the delicious smells of Christmas foods. She had been nearly impossible to constrain from decorating before Thanksgiving. Once Thanksgiving passed, Christmas was there in all its glory, to be savored and enjoyed every minute until after New Year's Day. She was unfailingly saddened when the decorations had to come down, but then she was almost instantly buoyed up with her plans for the following Christmas.

Her untimely death had permanently stilled her anticipation of Christmas. Her passing followed a brief and mercifully painless illness. One moment she was here with him, and the next, she was gone.

He sadly recalled the moment of her death. They had been quietly clasping hands like young lovers, he sitting at her bedside, and she breathing with difficulty, her face glowing with dampness from the effort of those last few desperate intakes of life. Her breathing suddenly quieted, and she looked into his eyes.

"Please decorate the house for me this Christmas," she had pleaded.

"Yes, Yes," he replied, his mind growing numb at the realization she was leaving him forever.

"And please take your walks in the woods, especially when the snow comes."

"I will, I will," he had quietly responded, the tears coursing down over his lined and seamed old face.

Her grasp had momentarily tightened on his hand, as she slowly exhaled the almost silent words, "I love you." Her hand then relaxed into limpness; her eyes closed, and her face took on the peaceful serenity of restful sleep.

That following Christmas he had made an attempt to decorate the house as he had promised, but his heart wasn't in it. In his typical, masculine bumbling way, he had managed only to create a chaotic mess, rather than the loving, warm Christmas atmosphere his wife had always produced. He was infinitely saddened by his efforts. So much saddened in fact, that he had given up, and removed everything on Christmas morning. The following year he had made no attempt to even acknowledge Christmas, merely suffering through the season, if possible, sadder than ever.

"This year is going to be different," he thought, his mind returning to the present. His daughter was bringing her five year old son, Mikey, home for the winter season. Her husband was a chemist for a large petroleum company, and had accepted a very high paying assignment to the Middle East. One of the less than desirable provisions of the assignment had been a five month delay before his family could join him. And so, the Christmas season was suddenly a time to be eagerly anticipated again.

Thinking how he would make this a visit for Mikey to remember, he continued his walk through the woods, his pipe clenched in his craggy jaw. He looked around and sniffed the invigorating air, thinking, "There's a smell of snow. It won't be long now." Gazing from beneath bushy eyebrows, through amber eyes, he looked at the mountains and the pines. Striding over the beautiful tree covered land, he thought it was a good place for a young boy to grow up in; what a fitting place to grow to manhood. Without realizing it, his melancholy mood had changed to one of peace and pleasant anticipation. He seemed to draw visible rejuvenation from his surroundings, and as he walked, one could almost see his old shoulders straighten and his whole being take on an appearance of pride and vigor.

"Better get on home, and stack some firewood in the den," he thought, his pace quickening.

The next morning, he was awake much earlier than his usual early rising time. "This is the day!" he thought, springing from his bed with an alacrity that even surprised him. "Yes, this is the day my daughter and grandson arrive," he thought again.

Dressing quickly, he hastened to the kitchen for a quick breakfast of coffee and toast, his usual fare since his wife had died. Pouring his second mug of steaming black coffee, and inserting two slices of bread in the toaster, he reviewed the tasks he had assigned himself for the day. First, get a supply of firewood into the den by the fireplace. And then, clean out the damn fireplace itself. This was another chore that had gone untended for several months now. The next thing on his agenda was to clean up the accumulated stack of dirty dishes in the kitchen.

That afternoon he dressed warmly, and took up his vigil on the front porch where he could see well down the tree bordered driveway. He had lit the fire in time for it to burn down to a glowing warmth before they arrived, and just before going outside, had thrown two dry hickory logs on to add to the fire's longevity. The fire would be welcome to them because this was a chilly day, one week before Thanksgiving. "Just enough time," he thought, "For her to get organized, and cook a nice turkey dinner."

He was filling his pipe for the second time when he heard the crunch of tires on the gravel, still out of sight beyond the curve in the driveway. He lit his pipe, and watched expectantly for the car to appear. Momentarily the car came into view, a loaded down station wagon, with the baggage racks on top filled with suitcases.

Just as the car pulled to a stop beside the porch steps, the right front door opened abruptly, and Mikey fairly exploded out onto the steps, his shrill voice pealing, "Papa! Papa!" Mikey shot up the steps, and leaped into his grandfather's arms. The old man clutched the young boy with both arms in a gigantic, but tender bear hug. As Mikey smothered him with kisses, Papa managed to look around the boy, and nod a greeting to his daughter, who was walking wearily up the steps, an expression of amused pleasure on her face. When she neared, Papa managed to disengage one arm, and wrapped it around her shoulders, pulling her into the affectionate circle with Mikey.

He looked at her tenderly, thinking, "She looks more like her mother all the time."

"Took you long enough to get here," he spoke to her with mock gruffness, continuing to hold the two of them tightly.

"Well, there's a lot of traffic on the road, and as you know, you can't make much time on these mountain roads with a little boy asking with each breath when we'll get here."

"Well, you're here, and that's what counts. Better come on inside where it's warm. We'll get the car unloaded in a little while."

"Mikey, you've grown. You must weigh a ton," Papa said to the boy as he lowered him to the floor.

Mikey hadn't been here since he was a baby, so the house was a new experience for him. As soon as they were inside the door, and had taken off their coats, Mikey set off on a reconnaissance tour of the house.

Hanging their coats in the hall closet, Papa motioned his daughter into the den. Backing up to the fire, he nodded toward the bar, saying, "Help Yourself. Two fingers of bourbon with some branch for me."

"Glad you're here," he told her when she handed him his glass. "It's been too long, and too lonesome." This was the first time he had seen his daughter since his wife's funeral.

"You need some fattening up," she said, noting he had lost weight, and looked rather rundown.

"We have plenty of food, and plenty of time," he replied.

That evening, after unloading the car, unpacking, and a good meal, they all went to bed early. Papa slept better that night than he recalled sleeping since his wife died.

The days following his daughter and Mikey's arrival were the happiest Papa had experienced for a long time. They were days filled with long walks in the woods, with Mikey and Papa talking endlessly over a wide range of subjects. Mikey's mother wisely declined to take part in the walks, thinking correctly this was an excellent, and perhaps only, chance for Mikey and his grandfather to become acquainted. As the two set off for their daily walks, Papa with his pipe clamped in his teeth, and Mikey holding Papa's hand, the daughter often marveled at the striking similarity between the two, even though there was almost three fourths of a century spread in their ages.

During these walks, Papa told Mikey stories about his own younger days as a fighter pilot during the war. When he felt that perhaps Mikey was ready for a change in subject, Papa told him stories about the woods. Often they sat quietly on an old tree stump, and just looked around. Frequently, if they remained quiet, they would be rewarded with seeing deer, rabbits, squirrels, and even one time, they saw a red fox with her cubs. Mikey was at once enthralled with Papa's stories, and fascinated with his wood's lore. Mikey learned quickly that the woods belonged to the animals, and that he and Papa were the intruders.

One morning, following the first heavy snow in early December, Papa told Mikey they were going to ride, rather than walk. He then took Mikey out to the garage, and showed him a small tractor, complete with snow grip tires, and a little trailer attached to its rear.

"What's the trailer for, Papa?" Mikey asked.

"Help me load it, and you'll see," Papa replied.

They proceeded to load half a dozen five pound salt blocks, two gunny sacks of apples, a large sack of mixed corn and sunflower seed, a large bag of hickory nuts, a large bag of carrots, and finally, ten pounds of sliced, raw round steak which Papa took from a freezer in the garage.

"Mikey, we're going to feed the livestock."

With that, Papa climbed onto the tractor, and had Mikey get on the seat beside him. Papa started the tractor, drove out of the garage, and off into the woods. Driving slowly, Papa explained that during the cold winter, it was often hard for the wild animals to find enough food, so he always tried to help them a little during the winter months.

Papa had an established route he followed, with predetermined stops to offload the food. He had placed steel poles in the ground at certain places, tall enough to extend above the snow, but not too tall for a deer to reach. To these poles he attached the blocks of salt. Papa called them salt licks. Also a supply of apples was distributed here, along with a portion of the carrots, seed and nuts. Papa told Mikey the seed fed the birds, the nuts were for the squirrels, and the carrots for the rabbits. An ample portion of each food was spread around the salt licks in a large arc. The raw meat was placed at different locations. Papa explained that the meat was for the foxes. The old man tried to make a feeding trip once a week when the ground was covered with deep snow.

After they had deposited the last of the food around the final salt lick, Mikey asked Papa if they couldn't watch the animals eat.

"Sure, Mikey. I planned for us to watch. That's one of the pleasures I get out of feeding the animals."

Papa then pulled the tractor and trailer over the brow of a nearby hill, and shut off the engine. He and Mikey then walked back to the last feeding sight, and took a seat on a fallen tree. Papa told Mikey to be very quiet, and still. They sat thus for perhaps twenty minutes, then Papa touched Mikey lightly on the arm. Placing his finger over his lips, Papa motioned for quiet, and then pointed. Three doe had come out of the woods, and were cautiously approaching the salt lick. Soon half a dozen squirrels were darting back and forth carrying off the nuts. Blue Jays and Cardinals were pecking away at the seed, and rabbits were gnawing on the carrots. Papa glanced at Mikey. His eyes were like saucers as he watched the animals in wondering awe. Somewhat later, feeling the chill set in, Papa motioned to Mikey that it was time to go. They walked quietly back to the tractor, and drove home.

The daily walks through the woods had become a ritual, and were a source of pleasure to both Papa and Mikey. Papa's stories kept Mikey totally engrossed, and always anxious to set off on the walks. The two became almost inseparable, and their love for one another was a sight beautiful to behold.

It was on one of their walks that papa told Mikey about the Christmas Bugles. It was the middle of December, and they had just undergone a freak warm spell, melting most of the snow from the ground. Mikey asked Papa if there would be any snow for Christmas. Papa reassured Mikey that they would have snow and Santa's pencils.

"How else could Santa get his sleigh and reindeer to the house? And besides," Papa added, "We need the snow, angel's eyes, and the bugles to make it a real Christmas."

Papa and Mikey knew that Santa's pencils were really icicles, but it was Christmas talk they both liked.

"What are angel's eyes, and bugles, Papa?" Mikey asked, looking intently at Papa to make sure this wasn't just more Christmas talk.

"Well, Mikey, your grandmother, Omah, and I used to make it a habit to walk in the snow early each Christmas morning. If it wasn't still snowing, when the sun came up, it would make the snow flash like it had diamonds in it. Omah said the flashing light from the sun made her think of angel's eyes. When she told me that, I told her about the bugles blowing. Omah said they were Christmas bugles."

"Does everyone hear the Christmas bugles, Papa?"

"I can't answer that, Mikey, but Omah said she had heard them."

"Do you hear the bugles every Christmas, Papa?"

"No, but I've heard them on many a Christmas. The first time I heard them was the Christmas Omah and I were married. Did you know that Omah and I were married on Christmas day?"

"No, Papa," Mikey replied.

"Well, we were," Papa continued. "I heard the bugles blowing in the background as we were married. They were quietly beautiful. I didn't hear them again until your mother was born two years later on Christmas morning. That time they sounded like a legion of angels blowing beautiful, heavenly music in the distance."

Papa grew quiet as they walked. Mikey remained silent, holding Papa's hand, seeming to realize that Papa didn't want his thoughts intruded upon. After a few minutes of walking quietly, Papa resumed talking, as if there had been no pause.

"I didn't hear the bugles for quite a while after your mother was born. I guess I was too busy, off fighting wars, and making money. The next time I heard them was the Christmas after Omah and I built the house here, and moved in ten years ago. After that, we heard them every Christmas morning when we walked together in the snow. Omah really loved the snow, Mikey."

"I do, too, Papa," Mikey said. "Papa," Mikey continued, "Have you heard the bugles at any time beside Christmas?"

"Only once, Mikey," Papa replied, as he drew to a halt, still holding Mikey's hand. "It was when Omah died. That time it was different, though. That time there was only one bugle, blowing sadly in the distance. I haven't heard the bugles since."

"Will I ever hear them, Papa?"

"I'm sure you will, Mikey, but it will be at a special time, or on very important Christmas days that you'll hear them."

Thus reassured, Mikey had no further questions. They continued their walk without mentioning the bugles again, the subject apparently forgotten by the young boy.

The approach of Christmas was filled with happy activity. Mikey and his mother took the Christmas decorations down from the attic, and spent several days untangling the strings of lights, and getting the house properly decorated. Papa tried to help, but as in years past, his efforts were more hindrance than help. He was proud of his helping them with the outside lights, though. He knew for sure they would have fallen from the ladder had he not been there to climb up and install the many lights around the eves of the roof. The end result of their combined efforts was one of deep pleasure to them all. Papa said the house looked just as it would have looked were Omah still here to decorate it. Both Mikey and his mother were pleased with the compliment.

Five days before Christmas, Papa felt a little tired when he awakened. After breakfast, he and Mikey departed for their walk. Papa wasn't as vigorous as usual and finally cut the walk short, returning home early.

His daughter looked at him with a curious expression on her face, but refrained from comment.

The next morning, Papa felt decidedly worse, and begged off from the walk, saying that he was a little tired. His daughter was definitely suspicious now, especially when she noted the flushed color of his face.

"Do you feel all right, Papa?" She asked him.

"Oh, just a little run down. Getting old, I guess."

"Well, maybe you should get some rest. Why don't you lie down for a while?"

"I think I'll just sit here and enjoy the fire and the Christmas tree," he replied.

"Well, if you're no better by tomorrow morning, I'm going to call the doctor and have him come out and see you," his daughter told him.

The following morning, Papa didn't even bother to get dressed, merely putting on his robe, and walking slowly to his recliner chair in the den. As he leaned back in his chair, obviously in worse condition than the day before, his daughter watched him closely. She walked over to him, and rested her hand on his feverish brow.

"That does it. I'm calling the doctor," she announced in a firm voice. Papa halfheartedly raised his hand in objection, and then thinking better of it, didn't fuss.

The doctor arrived shortly after mid day. Walking into the room where Papa was leaning back in his chair, he asked Papa, more or less as a perfunctory opening conversational gambit, "Feeling kinda poorly today, huh?"

Papa merely nodded his head in reply, knowing full well he was going to be probed, poked, thumped, and listened to with a stethoscope. He just sat there, waiting for the inevitable.

Completing his examination, the doctor reached down and extracted a vial of capsules from his medical kit. Measuring out a supply, he placed them in a small envelope and gave them to Papa's daughter. Looking at Papa, he said, "You've got a bug. Take the medicine, get plenty of rest and liquids, and you should be on your feet by Christmas day." Again Papa quietly nodded his head in understanding. Turning to face the daughter, the doctor asked, "Is he always this talkative?"

Smiling wanly, Papa interjected, "Just didn't want to interrupt. You're the pro we're paying, so I thought I'd better listen."

Rising to his feet, the doctor prepared to leave. "I don't think there's any great cause for worry, but you should be in bed," he said to Papa. As he left, the doctor wished them all a Merry Christmas.

The next morning, Christmas eve, Papa's daughter came in early, bringing his medicine, a small glass of water, and a large mug of steaming coffee. Handing him the medicine and water, she said, "Good morning. Your pills first, then the coffee."

"Extortion," he said, downing the capsules.

Turning the table TV on, she asked, "Mind if Mikey and I have breakfast in here with you this morning?"

"I'm really not very hungry," he replied.

To this, his daughter responded, "Package deal; Mikey, me and breakfast."

"More extortion," he said, however his face showed his pleasure at the care and attention being shown him.

Mikey spent most of the day with Papa in his room, alternately talking, and watching TV. Whenever she could, his daughter came in and sat with the two of them. All three had lunch and dinner together, brought in on trays. All in all, it wasn't such a bad day, although the daughter noted that while Papa didn't look any worse, neither did he look any better. "Well," she thought, "Best to give the medicine a chance to work."

Later that evening, Mikey's mother reminded him that he should get to bed, since tomorrow was going to be an early day with Santa's visit.

"You're right," Mikey replied, crawling over the bed to give Papa a goodnight hug and kiss.

Papa held Mikey tightly for several moments, then looked him directly in the eyes. "Mikey, I want you to be sure and have a good Christmas tomorrow. Promise?"

"Yes, Papa, and you, too," Mikey responded. He then jumped from the bed and scampered off to his room, followed by his mother.

"I'll be back in a minute," she said to Papa.

Returning shortly, she sat on the chair beside Papa's bed. They talked quietly, and watched some of the Christmas programs on TV. After a while, she noted Papa's eyelids getting heavy as he began to drowse a little. Getting up, she turned off the TV, and turned to face Papa, who was wide awake now, and watching her very intently.

"Want me to turn off the lamp?" she asked.

"No, I'll get it in a little while," he replied.

When she leaned over to kiss him goodnight, Papa grasped her firmly by the shoulders, and looking her directly in the eyes, as he had Mikey, extracted the same promise from her, adding the wish for a happy birthday also. Mussing his hair affectionately, she wished him a Merry Christmas, and left the room, closing the door softly behind her.

Leaving Papa's room, she mentally reviewed the chores she had to finish before going to bed, and also in the morning before Mikey and Papa awakened. First, all the gifts had to be arranged around the tree. After the third trip to the basement, she began to realize that Papa had spent a small fortune on Christmas. Finally, the task was complete. Standing back, she surveyed the results. Gazing at the treasure trove of presents, she had a twinge of guilt for having so many material possessions. Her thoughts quickly returned to the tasks at hand.

She next cleaned the fireplace, and laid the makings for a fire to be lit in the morning. Completing that chore, she then started on the final one for the night. She completed the turkey preparations so that it could go in the oven the first thing in the morning. A 25 pound bird would take most of the day to cook, which meant she would have to put it in very early.

Making sure she had finished all she had set out to do, she shut down the house for the night, and hurried to bed, noting in passing, that Papa's bedside lamp was out. She was already tired, and she knew that tomorrow would be both early, and long. She was asleep the second her head touched the pillow.

Seemingly instantly, the alarm beside her bed was ringing intently. Turning the alarm off, she arose, and quickly dressed, not wanting any unnecessary delay, mindful that Mikey could be up earlier than usual today. Walking silently, she thought how quiet a house full of people could be in the middle of the night. She went first to the kitchen, and turned the oven on to preheat while she made coffee. She wrestled the big bird from the refrigerator, into the roasting pan, and then into the oven. Noting the coffee was ready, she drew off a mug full and breathed a sigh of relief.

Finishing her coffee, she went into the den, and lit the fire. Almost as an afterthought, she switched on the Christmas tree lights. Turning to go back to the kitchen, her attention was caught by a glinting reflection from the tree. Pausing, she looked at the tree, and saw the reflection was coming from some sort of an ornament attached to a thick manila envelope, which was resting on one of the upper boughs of the tree. Curious, she stepped closer to see what it was. She knew it had not been there when she finished placing the gifts around the tree last night. Of that she was positive.

Stepping closer, she saw that the envelope was addressed to her in Papa's handwriting. It was simply addressed; her name, Christmas, and today's date. The glinting ornament was attached to the envelope with a bright red ribbon. Straining to the tips of her toes, she reached up, and lifted the envelope from the tree. It was thickly filled with paper. The red ribbon was tucked inside the unsealed envelope. The shiny ornament was an exquisitely cast replica of a horn of some sort, perhaps a bugle, or trumpet. It was made from sterling silver, and was about two inches in length. She glanced curiously at the ornament, and then forgot it as she walked back into the kitchen.

Pouring a second mug of coffee, she picked up the envelope, and looked thoughtfully at it again. Once more she wondered how it had gotten on the tree. It was placed too high up on the tree for Mikey to have put it there, and she was sure that Papa was too sick to have done it. And besides, both Mikey and Papa were sound asleep when she went to bed last night.

Finally giving in to her curiosity, she placed her coffee mug on the counter, and extracted the contents of the envelope. She held a sheaf of legal appearing documents in her hand. On top of the sheaf was a short note to her in Papa's handwriting. It was a simple, direct message.

"All I have in the world, I leave to you, with the exceptions you will see. When appropriate, take these papers to my attorney in town, and he will help you as necessary. His fee has been paid."

Looking under the note, she saw that the first legal paper was Papa's will. It was clear, concise, and briefly written. In it, she inherited all his worldly possessions, other than those specifically named to someone else. It was signed, dated, and witnessed. The second sheet was an itemized list of his total assets. She was impressed at the length, and detail of the inventory. She was shocked when she came to the end of the list, and saw what the total cash value amounted to. She knew at once, based on the inventory, she would have no financial worries for the rest of her life. The third document was a copy of a trust Papa had established for Mikey's education. She was again amazed at the amount of money he had set aside for this purpose. Mikey would be able to attend the most expensive school in the world, if he chose, and not have to worry about a penny of the cost. Her mind was beginning to reel under the shock of the document's contents.

Reading the fourth, and final document, she was, if at all possible, more astounded than ever. This was a free and clear deed to the mountain property, and the house with all its contents, made out in Mikey's name. To this deed was attached the end of the ribbon that had the little silver ornament tied to the other end.

Carefully replacing the papers in the envelope, and leaving the little silver ornament hanging as before, she leaned back against the kitchen counter to get her thoughts in order.

"The old curmudgeon," she thought affectionately. "He didn't have to do this. He has plenty of time to get his estate settled. I think I'll go wake him, give him a kiss, and then get him to take these papers back until a later date. Besides," she continued thinking, "I want to give him his medicine. I don't want him to spend Christmas day in bed."

Picking up a small tray, she put Papa's medicine, water, and his mug of hot coffee on it. With the tray in one hand, and the manila envelope in the other, she went to Papa's room. Opening the door, she walked quietly to the bedside table, and turned on the lamp. Placing the tray on the table, she noted that Papa's facial expression was relaxed, and also the fever flush was gone. She almost decided against waking him, but then her desire to thank him won out. When her lips touched his forehead in a good morning kiss, she recoiled in horror, one hand rising to stifle a scream. Papa's brow was as cold as his beloved snow. Her eyes brimming over, she saw that he wasn't breathing. Papa was gone.

Fighting back an instinctive desire to panic, and run screaming from the room, she forced herself to stand, and take stock of the situation. Gradually, as she stared at Papa, her normal, rational thinking habits resumed control.

"Poor Mikey! This is going to be impossible for him to understand." Then, her maternal instinct asserting itself, she decided to let Mikey at least have his Christmas morning pleasure before telling him about Papa. Having thus made her rational, and perhaps, cold decision, she took the tray from the table, turned out the lamp, and quietly left the room.

"Papa would want it this way," she thought as she closed the door to his room, and in so doing, sadly, but permanently, closed the door to her childhood.

Returning to the kitchen, she placed the tray on the counter, and again stared at the envelope. She was thus engaged when she heard a slight noise. Looking up, she saw Mikey standing in the kitchen doorway, his young face wide awake.

"Mikey, did you by any chance put this on the Christmas tree during the night?" she asked, extending the envelope toward him.

"No, Ma'am," he answered, his innocent face devoid of deceit.

And then, catching sight of the silver ornament, Mikey reached out, and clasped it in his little hand. "A Christmas Bugle!" he said, his face and voice reflecting awe.

"Yes, Mikey. It's from Papa to you."

"I know, Mama."

Releasing the bugle, Mikey turned abruptly, and dashed to the back door. Turning on the outside flood lights, he stared intently through the door glass. "Oh Mama! Mama!" his voice pealed excitedly. "It's snowing, and I see the angel's eyes. Just like Papa promised! Come look, Mama."

She walked over, leaned down, and looked out through the glass. Sure enough the ground was covered with a thick mantle of snow, and more was falling heavily.

"See the angel's eyes, Mama?" Mikey asked.

She saw that the snow indeed sparkled brightly in the reflected flood light. The snow looked as if it were filled with millions of diamonds.

She straightened and thought, "Christmas Bugles? Angel's eyes? I wonder where he got those ideas."

She decided to find out. "Mikey, tell me about the Christmas Bugles, and the angel's eyes."

With no further urging, Mikey told her the story just as Papa had related it to him that day in the woods. When he had finished the story, her eyes were again brim full, but this time, she couldn't prevent the overflow of tears. Feeling the tears streaking her troubled face, she reversed her earlier decision, and said, "Mikey, Papa is dead. He died in his sleep during the night."

His response was totally unexpected. Instead of crying, Mikey replied calmly, "No, Mama, Papa isn't dead. He and Omah are walking together in the snow, and listening to the Christmas Bugles." His face showed no trace of guile, nor frivolous teasing. She knew that, in his mind, Mikey was telling her the absolute truth. Mikey then turned, and once again peered out at the snow.

For the third time that morning, her mind was assaulted with shocked surprise. And then, a frightening thought suddenly thrust itself into her mind. She was almost afraid to put it into words. Finally, overcoming her apprehension, she resolved to put it to rest.

"Mikey," she began hesitantly. "Have you . . . have you ever . . . have you ever heard the Christmas Bugles?"

"Oh yes, Mama," Mikey replied calmly and positively.

"When?" she asked.

"Several hours ago, Mama. The Christmas Bugles woke me up when Papa and Omah went out for their walk in the snow."

THE END

# GET 'EM HOME FOR CHRISTMAS

By: Dana T. Moore, II

"Merry Christmas, Sergeant," the captain said as they surveyed their new command post area.

"Bah! Humbug!" the sergeant replied, his good natured tone of voice belying his cynical response.

The first two weeks in this bitterly cold December in the Korean War were rough on the captain and his company of U. S. infantry. They had been badly mauled by a regiment of Chinese regulars. The cease fire came just in time to keep his company of doughfoot soldiers from being overrun. As it was, they lost most of their weapons platoon, leaving the company short of men, and bereft of any real organic firepower.

With the cease fire, the captain was ordered to take the remnants of his company to an area in the Demilitarized Zone, and establish a defense perimeter around a garrison for personnel involved in the cease fire negotiations at Panmunjom. The captain didn't like the tactical situation at all. His area of responsibility was a protruding salient, very vulnerable to enemy action in an attempt to straighten out the front line.

When moving into position, and requesting replacements for lost men and weapons, the captain was told this assignment was temporary before being moved farther to the rear in preparation for shipment back home; hopefully in time for Christmas. This was by way of refusing any resupply on the basis the relieving unit would be up to strength. No reason to move people forward when they were just going to be returned in a few days anyway. The captain accepted the logic with tongue in cheek.

Along with the refusal for replenishment of men and weapons, the captain was briefed on a corollary mission. A civilian party was en route to the captain's command post for a visit to the front lines. The captain was to insure their security, and brief them on the tactical situation. Good public relations for the folks back home.

And now, with increasing apprehension, the grimy, war-weary captain watched the approaching civilians. He saw a dozen American school children in the 10 to 14 age range, accompanied by two young lady school teachers. There was also a well dressed, middle-aged gentleman, followed by an entourage of six similarly dressed young men, each seeming to fall all over himself in an attempt to gain favorable attention from their mentor.

The school kids and their teachers concerned the captain. The well-dressed gentleman was a U.S. Senator from California, and politically hostile to the U.S. armed forces. Even the anticipated hostility didn't worry the captain. He was a distinguished graduate of the U.S. Military Academy, and had paid his dues, both during world war two, and in Korea. When in appropriate uniform, the captain sported some of his nation's highest medals for valor, including the Purple Heart with two clusters.

What concerned the captain was his mission, and the extremely turbulent battlefield conditions at the moment. The enemy, as usual, was taking full advantage of the cease fire opportunity to solidify and reinforce his positions along the very unstable front. This made the captain very uneasy. His forward observers were reporting constant buildup activity of the enemy's tank, artillery, and infantry forces. It was painfully obvious that a serious enemy offensive action was looming.

"So, why send a Senator, and his staff, two school teachers, and 12 American school children into harm's way?" the captain wondered. "More than likely," he thought, "the whole idea was a public relations stunt staged for the benefit of the Senator." As usual, one of the young men accompanying the senator was a photographer, and there seemed to be an unending flash of photo bulbs as the senator was photographed for posterity.

If the North Koreans decided to attack this garrison in force, as appeared to be their intent, there were enough tactical problems for the captain to worry about. He didn't need to burden himself with the safety of the civilians; in particular the children and their teachers. The senator didn't worry the captain. If the senator fell victim to enemy action, someone back home could readily be cranked up to fill his vacancy.

The senator approached the captain, and told him, along with all the other visitors, this visit to the front had been the fulfillment of one of his dreams. He wanted to see how the men were faring under conditions of extreme hardship. Another tongue in cheek statement. After a photo of the senator shaking the captain's hand, a short exchange took place. The captain informed the senator this position was at high risk of offensive enemy action at any time. He further informed the senator that he thought it would be wise to take the children and other civilians to the rear, safe from enemy action.

"Captain, you wouldn't just be trying to throw a scare into this old war horse, would you?" The Senator asked, a wry grin on his face, turning his best side to the photographer for another shot. The senator had served a short summer reserve tour in the Pentagon, qualifying himself for the sobriquet of "old war horse."

"No, Senator, I wouldn't be trying to scare you, although I wish you were scared enough to take these children out of here." The captain then went on to review the intelligence data on the enemy buildup, and the probability of heavy action at any time.

The senator looked senatorially down his nose at the captain, and then began speaking. "In the army I knew, when a visiting dignitary was expected, the commander had his men shave, don clean, new uniforms, shined shoes, and be in a spit-an-polish condition as befitted the status of the visitor. I seem to detect an attitude of slovenly, don't give-a-damn mental outlook on the part of your troops. Can't you keep 'em in line, Captain? Perhaps a good bath would do all of them a world of good, and get rid of some of the stench I smell in here."

"Senator, my men would like nothing better than a good hot bath, clean uniforms, and possibly a few hours of worry-free sleep. Perhaps then they could greet you in true rear echelon, garrison dignity, but right now, they're worried about just surviving long enough to get those benefits."

"Surviving?" the senator echoed, as if he had heard not a word the captain had uttered about the possibility of an impending enemy attack in strength. "Surely higher headquarters wouldn't permit that to happen! The Corps Commander wouldn't allow an enemy attack while a U.S. senator escorted these children and their teachers!"

As if to emphasize the senator's remarks, a loud yell was heard from just outside the company command post, "Incoming!"

A bracket of .81mm mortar, about a dozen, impacted all around the command post. Fortunately, no one was hurt. The lights on the little Christmas tree, standing forlornly in the corner on an upended ammunition box, blinked on and off momentarily before resuming their colorful illumination. Dust settled from the log ceiling. All the military assumed the face down, prone position on the floor. The civilians stood, their faces reflecting doubt of the reality of the moment.

"Incoming!"

This time, the impact was considerably closer, and everyone, including the teachers and the children, dropped to the ground. The lights on the little Christmas tree flickered, but once again resumed their seasonal illumination. Obviously the generator was not damaged.

The captain ran over to his commo sergeant, and directed, "Call S-3, and get a chopper in here pronto. We've gotta get these kids, the teachers, and the senator out of here."

The captain felt a firm grip on his shoulder. Turning, he saw the senator, a wild-eyed look on his face, and heard him shout, "The hell with these kids, and their teachers. I'm the important one. Get me and my staff out of here first!"

Shrugging off the senator's grip, the captain answered, "We'll get all of your party out of here, the enemy permitting. In the meantime, keep all these civilians down on the ground where there is less chance of them being hit by shrapnel." No one seemed inclined to stand.

"Captain, we have enemy troops crossing the field in front of the command post. Want me to give the fire order?" His ops sergeant had asked permission to shoot.

"Go ahead, Sergeant, but tell the men not to waste ammo. We've never been resupplied, so make every shot count." The sergeant passed the word via radio to his platoon sergeants. Momentarily the sound of rifle fire could be heard. The captain took a moment to squint out through a firing aperture, and saw several enemy foot soldiers fall. In a moment, the captain's few remaining .30 caliber machine guns began their stuttering fire, and more enemy soldiers toppled. After a severe bloodletting, the enemy retired to his prepared positions to lick his wounds.

During the lull, the captain spoke with his commo sergeant. "Have you told Battalion that we're under attack?"

"Yes, Sir. They've promised to get several choppers up here right away."

"Call 'em back and tell 'em to get us some ammo. We can't hold out long without a resupply of ammunition."

"Yes, Sir," the commo sergeant acknowledged.

"When you get Battalion on the radio, lemme talk to them," the captain ordered.

Momentarily, the commo sergeant handed the handset to the captain, saying, "Battalion on the line, Sir."

The captain began speaking. "We need choppers in here immediately to get the school kids, their teachers, the senator and his party out. This is an attack in force. I don't know just how long we can hold out, but we can't let these kids be blown to pieces."

At that moment, the handset was snatched from the captain's hand, and the senator began screaming, not knowing the radio mike was now off, "The hell with these kids! I'm a U.S. Senator, and deserve to get out of here first!"

"Sergeant!" the captain barked at his ops sergeant. "Get two armed men on this gentleman. Take him over in the corner of the CP. If he causes any more trouble, gag and tie him. I don't want any more interference! Understand?"

"Yes, Sir!" the sergeant replied emphatically. "You two," the sergeant barked, pointing to two messengers standing in the CP. "You heard the captain. Take charge of this civilian, and keep him out of our way!" The two armed infantry men, having heard the senator's fear driven outburst, sprang to the task with gusto.

"I'll have your bars for this, Captain," the senator yelled, hatred dripping from his voice.

A railroad-train-sound of heavy artillery shells whooshed overhead, impacting several hundred yards to the rear. The enemy artillery had not quite zeroed in on the command post. "Just a matter of a few adjusting rounds, and they'll have us," the captain thought. And then, "How in the hell are we going to get these children out of here?"

Then, a glimmer of an idea began to take shape in the captain's mind. He called his ops sergeant over. "Didn't we receive a truck load of useless tent supplies this morning?"

"Yes, Sir," the sergeant answered.

"Isn't the truck still here?" the captain quizzed again.

"Yes, Sir," the sergeant again answered. "The driver was a South Korean, and as soon as he drove the truck in here, he jumped out, and high tailed it for the rear area."

"Sergeant, that vamoosing driver just may have done us a big favor," the captain said.

"How so, Captain?" the sergeant asked.

"Let's talk a minute, Sergeant," the captain said, a calculating, cunning expression on his face.

While the captain and his ops sergeant huddled in serious conversation, more artillery rounds impacted in front of the command post.

Interrupting his briefing with the sergeant, the captain grabbed the radio headset, and called the Battalion S-3. Identifying himself, the captain began speaking forcefully. "We badly need a resupply of ammunition. Additionally, we need fire support from Division Artillery. If the enemy guns can be neutralized, and a resupply of ammo sent up, we might be able to hold out for a while. Otherwise, we're down the tubes very shortly, and I'm going to have to think of extracting my men before we're overrun. We need to get these civilians out of here as soon as possible. Over."

Battalion acknowledged his report, saying, "We'll get help to you as soon as we can. We'll lay on a fire mission with DivArty right now, and perhaps help out with the enemy artillery."

"Be sure the mission is against the enemy guns," the captain responded wryly.

Going back to the sergeant, the captain resumed their strategy talk, and in a few minutes, had a fairly workable plan for evacuating the civilians. The senator was unaware of it, but he was going to make a very heroic contribution to the scheme to get the school children to safety.

At that moment, the captain and his men heard their own artillery passing overhead toward the enemy artillery positions. One of the forward observers reported the friendly fire was right on target, and for them lay it on. The enemy artillery fire ceased.

Shortly, battalion called, and reported that one helicopter was on the way loaded with ammunition, and prepared to evacuate the senator and his staff. The school children and the teachers would be taken out on subsequent chopper evacuation flights. The captain looked at the sergeant, and they both exchanged smiles of satisfaction.

In a few minutes, the captain heard the familiar flup flup flup of the helicopter blades whipping the air as the chopper approached the command post. When the chopper approached the landing area, enemy small arms fire broke out, as well as light anti-aircraft automatic weapons fire. The chopper landed without taking any hits. The co-pilot jumped out, and ran for the entrance to the command post, shouting as he entered, "Let's get the senator on the bird so we can get out of here."

The captain noted that the crew chief was struggling to offload the ammo boxes from the chopper. Calling to his sergeant, he directed four men be sent out to offload, and retrieve the ammo.

Turning to the co-pilot, a warrant officer, the captain spoke. "You get the senator and his staff aboard. That will be seven passengers. Tell your pilot to listen up on our battalion common frequency, and we'll give him a launch signal. We'll try to get you out with as little enemy fire as possible. Understand?"

"Yes, Sir," the co-pilot acknowledged, running out of the command post, and to the right side of the chopper. Very shortly the ammo was in the command post for further distribution.

The men who carried the ammo into the CP were now charged with escorting the thoroughly crestfallen senator and his six staff men to the chopper. The captain directed the men to get right back into the CP for another mission as soon as the senator was delivered to the chopper.

Momentarily, the four men were back. "Any of you qualified to drive a deuce-and-a-half truck?" the captain asked. One man raised his hand, and said he was.

"All right, here's the plan," the captain began. I want you to get those school kids, and their two teachers on the truck. One of you drive, with one man riding shotgun. The other two men get in the rear with the passengers. All four of you draw a full ration of ammunition, and get those kids on the truck. The shotgun man carry a PRC-25 portable radio, and check in with us when you're ready to go. Understand?"

The four nodded understanding, with the driver, apparently accepting the mantle of responsibility, saying, "I understand, Captain. You going to tell us when to head out to the rear area?"

"That's affirmative, Sergeant."

"Corporal, Sir," the driver replied.

"As of now, it's Sergeant, Sergeant!"

Momentarily, the sergeant checked in on the radio, saying they were ready, and waiting for the start order.

"Standby," the captain directed.

Calling the chopper pilot, the captain told them to launch, and wished them a good flight.

"Roger," the pilot replied, and the chopper began lifting from the ground. Almost before it was clear of the ground, the pilot turned the chopper to a southerly heading, and began to head out on a knap-of-the-earth flight to safety.

"Launch!" the captain told the truck driver.

Keeping close watch on the chopper, the captain observed it taking heavy automatic weapons fire. The pilot immediately attempted to land, succeeding in making a forceful emergency landing. The landing gear beneath the helicopter squashed outward from the landing impact. The whirling blades bent downward, striking the ground, instantly shearing from their mounts. As the helicopter began rolling slowly onto its side, the aircrew, and three of the senator's civilian staff jumped from the door, and ran toward the company command post. Almost before they had gone 50 yards, the helicopter exploded in a giant, orange fireball. The aircrew and the three civilians were hurled to the ground, but almost immediately were on their feet, and completed their escape to the command post.

"Sergeant, did the truck with the school kids get away?" the captain inquired.

Yes, Sir," the sergeant replied. "The chopper effectively decoyed the enemy gunners," the sergeant continued.

"Apparently the senator and three of his staff were killed either by enemy fire, or the crash. We'll make out a report to battalion on their heroic sacrifice," the captain commented.

"I think, Sir," the sergeant replied, "we'll have to make a pretty good case for the senator volunteering to draw enemy fire while the school children were allowed to escape."

"Yes, Sergeant. A truly dedicated public servant, with nothing but the welfare of his constituents in mind. Very noble!"

"Yes, Sir. Very noble!" the sergeant agreed.

"Captain," the commo sergeant called, Battalion is on the line. S-3 wants to speak to you."

Slipping the headset over his head, the captain identified himself. The S-3 began speaking. "Get your troops ready for departure. Your relief is on the way by motor convoy. You and your men are scheduled for air evac to Japan tomorrow. We have orders here reassigning your company to the States, with each man getting a 30 day leave. You will be in Japan for approximately three days to draw new uniforms, clean up, and be flown back to the States. Merry Christmas!"

Turning to his ops sergeant, and anyone else listening, the captain jubilantly said, "There is a Santa Claus! We're out of here today and on to Japan tomorrow. Then we're flying back to the States in time for Christmas. Merry Christmas to all!"

# NELL'S DOG CHARLEY

## BY: DANA T. MOORE, II

Ecstasy! Sheer Ecstasy! Nothing else could come close to describing the expression on our daughter's face. Nell was without doubt in her Seventh Heaven. To understand this projection of absolute delight, you would have to place yourself into the mind of a ten year old who wants something more than she has ever wanted anything in her entire life. This desire is all consuming, almost unbearable. Then, when this wanting has reached the height of its intensity, the object of this immeasurable craving is suddenly presented to you. The childish prayers of your wildest dreams are abruptly answered in their entirety. Wonder of wonders! Now you can hold, feel and smell this priceless thing you have wanted for an eternity. The ecstasy of possession is more overpowering than the pain of desire. This was how Charley Brown came into our lives.

When I say, "Came into our lives," it is slightly misleading. Actually, Charley took us into his life. He was a black and tan, male, eight week old Airdale Terrier. No doubt he was the most perfect dog ever to stride the earth. When the Good Lord made Charley, He immediately destroyed the mold, thereby assuring that no duplication would take place. To Nell, Charley was everything. To me, Charley was the culmination of a sucessful, and very cleverly waged campaign. I was the vanquished, and Nell, with the aid of her mother, Joanne, was the victor.

It all started a few months previously. We were living in Germany at the time. I was the USAF Liaison Officer to the West German Army, with duties involving frequent absences from home. Leaving my wife and daughter alone in a foreign country caused them more than a little concern. Never failing to spot an opportunity for advantage, Nell had seized upon this as justification for a dog. And so, she casually announced at dinner one evening that we needed a dog. When I responded to this proposal with nothing more than a noncommittal grunt, Nell and Joanne resorted to an alternate plan of attack.

A few days later, the house began to blossom with all the appearances of dog presence. I found a dog bone on the floor in the den. A leash was draped conspicuously over the back of my favorite easy chair. A six pack of dog food inexplicably appeared on the kitchen counter. A dog bed, complete with cedar chip mattress, mysteriously materialized in Nell's bedroom. The intent of this undeclared war was unmistakably clear. I was in for it.

I was outgunned, outflanked, outmaneuvered, outweighed, and outsmarted. I finally hauled down my colors in defeat. As I faced my victorious opponents, I wondered dejectedly what the terms of surrender would be. Unconditional! Giving in completely, I inquired in a pleading tone of voice, "A small dog?"

"Yes, a small dog," replied Nell, facing me with arms akimbo. "A small Airdale puppy," she continued.

"An Airdale!" I echoed in dismay. "He'll eat us out of house and home. Do you realize that an Airdale will be dragging in bones, cats, dogs, shoes and Volkswagen cars?"

"An Airdale," repeated Nell forcefully. One look at the implacable expression on her face served to reinforce the terms of unconditional surrender. Thus, we found ourselves a few days later in the small village of Holtzapple. This was the home of one of the better known Airdale kennels, the owner being highly recommended by the Frankfurt Terrier Klub. When the kennel master answered his doorbell, and we made our intentions known, his face lit up with anticipation. Here was a wealthy American family to buy one of his Airdales. The kennel master's obvious delight sparked an equivalent level of apprehension in me.

We stepped inside his home, and entered into a discussion of price. After a few minutes of halting German on our part, mixed with an equally halting dose of English on the kennel master's part, we settled upon a price. 400 Deutche Marks! Or 100 dollars. I groaned, mentally equating a one hundred dollar Airdale to a like amount of good bourbon. However, there was no evading the issue. Nell's appreciation for Airdales exceeded, if possible, my appreciation for good bourbon.

We then followed the kennel master's beckoning signal, and walked out to the wired enclosure of the kennel in the rear of the house. Approaching the kennel, all I could see was a seething, yapping mass of black and tan animal activity. The kennel was divided into two sections, with the adult males separated from the females and puppies. All the dogs were making an equal cacophonic contribution of sound. Speaking soothingly to the dogs in German, the kennel master walked over, and unlocked the gate to the section housing the females and puppies.

As the gate swung ajar, Nell, in the flick of an eyelash, was through the entrance, darting directly for the puppies. Simultaneously, a partially grown puppy emerged from the squirming, wiggling, furry collection of heads, legs and tails, and ran toward Nell. Almost within Nell's reach, the puppy jumped from the ground. In one swift movement, Nell caught the puppy in midair, then clasped, and hugged it to her bosom. Joanne, the kennel master, and I just stood with mouths agape, staring at the scene before us. The puppy licked Nell about the face and ears, its little clipped tail wagging in a blur of motion. Nell grinned, and laughed, her now moist face glowing with rapture. It was obviously a case of mutual adoration at first sight. It was also obvious that Nell wasn't about to release the dog.

The kennel master then walked over to them, grasped the puppy's tail, and held it rigidly erect. Pointing, he said, "Boy dog." Since we had specified a male, he was merely confirming that the dog was indeed a male.

Returning to the house, the necessary pedigree papers were completed, and authenticated with a stamp similar to a notary seal. The papers were handed over to me, along with a recommended diet and a booklet on how to raise champion show dogs. Then it was time to pay the man. With a sigh, I handed over the 400 Marks. Doing so, I had a mental picture of quart after quart of good bourbon stretching out into the distance, slowly evolving into an endless line of dog food cans. With a shrug of resignation, I suggested we go home.

Nell sat in the back seat with the dog, which she now addressed as

"Charley." Oblivious to Joanne and me, she carried on a non-stop conversation with Charley all the way home.

Nell's life with Charley was idyllic. They were virtually inseparable. Since we lived in an all German community, and Nell attended German public school, I think Charley made up for the childhood companionship that Nell sorely missed. She didn't even want to go to school without Charley. Naturally we couldn't allow him to accompany her to school.

When Nell left for school in the morning, Charley took on an entirely different personality. He would settle down into a subdued, pattern of quiet, watchful waiting. To be sure, he was interested in Joanne and me; however, it was plain to see that Nell was the very center of his existence. Sometime around two in the afternoon, Charley took up a position by the front door, and at this time, we could see a definite change in his demeanor. He then assumed a very pronounced appearance of vigilance. How he knew it was time for Nell to return from school, we were never able to determine. But just as regularly, and just as accurately, as if in obedience to some inner clock mechanism, he would move to the front door shortly before Nell was due home.

With Nell's appearance at the front door, pandemonium broke loose. Charley jumped at Nell, licking her about the face, all the while barking, almost as if to say, "Where were you? I'm glad you're home. Now we can play." Nell responded with peals of happy laughter. Then Charley would break into a mad gallop through the house. In his exuberance, his rear quarters almost got in front of his front legs, at times causing him to seem to run sideways. On each lap he jumped at Nell, and then continued his frantic dash around the house. Never mind the bumped furniture, or the scrunched-up carpets. On his third or fourth lap, he invariably picked up his favorite toy, stopped abruptly in front of Nell, and with hind quarters wagging briskly, and an expectant look on his face, gently lay the toy at Nell's feet. Then followed a session of throw and fetch, or run and chase. Joanne's ultimate appearance upon the scene always served to restore order.

Then Nell would have her after school snack, sharing equally with Charley. No matter what she had to eat, Charley ate the same. The snack was always followed by an extended play period. This time, in self defense, Joanne required them to play outside in the yard. This pattern of affection, love and play continued throughout the remainder of our stay in Germany.

In early summer of the following year, I received orders transferring me to the United States, and simultaneously, authorizing my voluntary retirement from the Air Force. Charley was then ten months old. Since we were to fly home, Charley was unable to accompany us. I had him sent home separately. I shipped him via commercial air freight. It cost more for me to send him to the United States than it did for Uncle Sam to ship my automobile home. However, fly home he did.

Settling into civilian life. We enrolled Nell in public school. At first, the routine with Nell and Charley went unchanged. As time passed, however, an almost imperceptible change began to take place. Nell made new friends among her schoolmates, and frequently, some of her friends came home with her after school. The presence of strangers inhibited the after school play periods. There was no lessening of love and affection between Nell and Charley; just an interference with it. Charley still maintained his afternoon vigil by the front door. He was just as unaccountably accurate in his timing. But regardless, there was a change.

With this change, a change occurred in Charley. He began to show more and more affection for Joanne and me. Whenever Joanne had cause to be out of the house during the day, she encountered the same affectionate display from Charley on her return. Joanne circumvented the play period by substituting a piece of candy, or some other tidbit of food. When I returned from work late in the afternoon, Charley now barked and jumped at me. He still reserved the offering of his favorite toy for Nell. As for me, it was sufficient for him if I rubbed his head and ears, and just talked to him while he rubbed against my legs.

When Nell entered high school, there was a definite change in her relationship with Charley. Nell's interests appropriately shifted elsewhere. This was a natural part of her growing process. At first, Charley still maintained his front door vigil, but as was more and more frequently the occasion, Nell perhaps didn't return home until dinner, or occasionally, with our concurrence, didn't return until early evening. When she did return, Charley was waiting faithfully for her. Now, though, the riotous play period was a thing of the past. Nell had other things on her mind; studies, boys, dates, dances, and other school activities. To adult humans, this development was natural.

To a devoted pet, it was a painful transition. Transition it was, though. As a result of this change, Charley became more and more devoted to Joanne. I think this was a natural result of her being home most of the time. I still rated a vigorous show of affection upon my return at the end of the day, but Joanne was now the inseparable companion. Nell was by no means cut off from Charley's display of love. He merely ceased his front door vigil. When Nell came in, Charley instantly appeared, ran and sat anxiously in front of her, his face aglow with love. Now however, he received only a preoccupied, perfunctory greeting from Nell. Joanne and I could see the dismay and hurt on Charley's face, but nothing could be done. It was an inevitable evolution of growth and expanding interests for Nell. When Nell graduated from high school, she applied for, and was accepted in college. She departed for school that fall and embarked upon a four-year quest leading to a degree in nursing.

In the beginning, as is usual with first year college students, Nell came home at every opportunity. She was away from home for the first time, and was naturally lonesome. During this short phase of her life, she and Charley resumed their very close relationship of affection, love and play. Again however, the inevitable began to manifest itself. As Nell grew accustomed to college life, and spread her wings in her new environment, her visits home grew more and more infrequent. As she progressed into her fourth year in college, her visits home were limited to holidays such as Christmas, Easter, and between semester breaks. On these visits, Nell was either accompanied by one or more girl friends, or in the absence of visiting girls, a bevy of admiring boys was present. In either case, Charley was now relegated to a passing pat on the head when Nell arrived home. As Nell grew more distant in her association with Charley, he grew ever closer to us, and we in turn, closer to him.

Charley was now getting old. He was in his twelfth year. The once tan muzzle of his proud, square, Terrier head was streaked with gray. His hearing had noticiably diminished. Those once limpid, brown eyes were clouded with cataracts. He suffered from arthritis. Occasionally we heard him whimper in pain when he climbed onto the living room sofa, or up into his favorite easy chair. Lately, it wasn't unusual for one of us to walk into the living room, and find him standing in front of the sofa or chair, obviously wanting to climb to his comfortable resting place, but because of the pain involved, just standing there and looking. On these occasions, Joanne or I would help him to his favorite spot.

Of late, Joanne and I had reluctantly acknowledged that time was running out for Charley. But knowing it as we did, neither of us could bear to even utter the thought that he might have to be put to sleep. After all, he was an integral part of our family, and we loved him. His death would cause us to die a little, too. And so, we closed our minds to his ultimate passing. Instead, we tried to make his life as pleasant as possible. Joanne prepared his favorite food. I gave him candy whenever he wanted it. He was never scolded for any reason. He slept more and more of each passing day. When I was home, he positioned himself beside my chair, within easy arm's reach. Frequently I would reach down, and rub the inside of his ear with the knuckle of my forefinger. This always brought forth groans of pleasure.

One cold winter night in early March, we went to bed around eleven. Charley's bed was now at the foot of our bed. As had been the custom for quite some time now, Joanne tucked Charley snugly into his bed, covering him with his favorite wool blanket. Some time later, I was awakened from a sound sleep by a cry of pain, mixed with a thrashing sound. I turned on the bedside lamp, and looked at Charley. He was half in, and half out of his bed.

His rear legs were jerking in a spasmodic fashion. All the while he was making an intermittent, whimpering sound, obviously suffering considerable pain. I quickly awakened Joanne, jumped from bed, and rushed over to Charley. He looked at me with an expression of, "Please make it stop!" I sat down on the floor, cradled his head in my lap, and began to rub the inside of his ear. He was breathing with great difficulty.

I turned, and saw Joanne sitting on the edge of the bed, her face a picture of abject sorrow. Still stroking Charley's head, I said to Joanne, "Honey, I believe his time is here, and I don't think we should let him suffer. Would you go call the vet?" Joanne pulled on her robe, and started for the bedroom door. Pausing in the doorway, she turned and looked at Charley. The tears were streaming freely down her face. Turning abruptly, she disappeared down the hallway to the phone.

I continued to stroke Charley's head, and speak to him in a soothing tone.

In a few minutes, Joanne returned, and sat once again on the edge of our bed. Charley had stopped whimpering, but was still breathing with a rasping sound. He lay there, looking up at me as if he were trying to permanently affix the sight of me on his brain. Perhaps he was attempting to store up a final image for eternity.

This scene continued for a few minutes. And then, as I became aware of a decrease in the weight of Charley's head on my lap, he raised his head part way toward my face. I paused in stroking his head. Charley's eyes abruptly became very clear as he stared intently into my eyes. The only sound was that of his labored breathing. We were frozen in this tableau for a full half minute; as if time had stopped. Then, as the full weight of his head again settled onto my lap, his eyes clouded over, and he stopped breathing. Charley was gone.

Once again, alternately stroking his head, and rubbing his ear, I turned absently mindedly to Joanne. "Perhaps, if you call the vet, you can catch him still at home, and save him a trip over here." Nodding her head, she turned to the phone on the bedside table. No need to conceal the call from Charley now.

As Joanne placed the call, I suddenly realized something she didn't know, and something Nell would never know. In those last few seconds of life, as Charley had stared intently into my eyes, he had silently asked me a question. There was no doubt of it. It was as unmistakably clear as if spoken aloud. In a beseechingly pathetic plea, coming from his ever devoted heart, Charley had asked, "Where's my Nell?"

# BEEN THERE BEFORE?

By: DANA T. MOORE, II

Deja Vu! "I swear I know that guy!" "That song sure sounds familiar." "I think I've been here before; everything looks so familiar." Do the foregoing statements ring a bell? Are they also familiar?

Who remembers Bridey Murphy? Back in the mid-50's, a series of articles about Bridey Murphy appeared in True Magazine, a periodical devoted to publishing only true material. Bridey Murphy was a young lady who, under deep hypnosis, revealed having lived in centuries earlier, former life. However, Hollywood hokum, and the Madison Avenue urge for a fast buck, cast serious doubt on the validity of the tales of Bridey Murphy, and the excitement generated by the articles soon dropped into the same limbo as her former lives.

Have you been there before? Have you been recycled? Do you think it's possible to recycle the soul? Do you see a connection between environmental and spiritual recycling? Does nature possibly point the way? What, or who is nature? Is God synonymous with nature?

Young people, under 40, take everything for granted; good health, youthful beauty, a Stradivarius, bacon and eggs, the Grand Canyon, and not the least, a perfectly assembled, normally functioning baby. But, once on the far side of middle age, some begin asking questions about eternal life. Answers, if any, are purely deductive. Strengthened devotion to religious beliefs satisfies many. But, in a way, this is a form of shoulder shrugging, in effect saying, "What will be, will be." The questions plague me; the answers elude me. Nevertheless, I would like to project my hypothesis.

Since most of the questions impinge upon the area of "Divine Mysteries," factual answers are notably absent. True, many see the answers in their particular religious practice. Still, I am mindful that we humans are great rationalizers; we convince ourselves to see and hear only what we want; ignoring that which fails to conform to our preconditions. How else explain so many broken marriages and families; so many abused and cruelly raised children; so many lives lost to narcotics?

Nature could well be synonymous with God. Who else controls the earth and all the universe? We call it nature. So be it. Take a look. Everything created on this earth eventually returns to the earth. NASA may have some plans we aren't aware of yet, but nothing living permanently escapes earth; at least not to date. If a tree eventually crumbles into dust, and is absorbed into the earth, providing humus for growth of future trees, is not that recycling? At death, all living organisms biodegrade to their basic chemical constituents, returning to the earth, thus providing a never ending source of those essential elements to support new life. Recycling?

If all deserving people, "The Elect," go to heaven at the end of their mortal sojourn, it will be a crowded place. What about those living before recorded history, and thus, before recorded religion? Were they excluded from heaven by chronological prematurity? I doubt it. Could not God, in His infinite wisdom, recycle souls into new carriers? What is a human body, if not a carrier? If so, then why not repeatedly recycle souls?

Recycling souls should provide an endless opportunity for cleansing, or refining out undesirable qualities. Refining souls, like steel, should eventually produce purity meeting God's stringent requirements. If, as is often the case, the carrier, with its soul, stumbled during a life passage, gathering immoral impurity, then subsequent recycling should provide further refinement. This process could also serve as a never ending source of souls.

"Surely, someone must go to heaven before the biblical end of time," one might insist. I am confident this is true. Jesus was the supreme example. All the canonized saints are probably more examples. "Well, then," one might ask further, "if everyone is eventually pure enough for God, what about those who seem so evil they could never go to heaven?" I am also confident, God can, if He chooses, dispose of an unworthy soul just as the steel refiner sifts and disposes of the impure flotsam bubbling at the top of the crucible.

I see indicators in nature that all living matter, including humans, may well be the subjects of a Divinely ordained continuing chain of life; recycling. Examine the food cycles, with foods, animal and plant, originating in the earth, maturing, consumed, and ultimately returning to the earth to repeat the process. Recycling?

Think of the potential for divinely directed replacement of talents like Mozart, Martin Luther, Einstein and Eisenhower, to name a few. Potentially great people, possessed of learning capacities far in excess of normal, may be recycled into the mainstream of human life. Things we take as fortunate breakthroughs, such as the cure for polio, heart transplants, blood transfusions, and many others, could be the results of a recycled soul merely continuing along his God directed path toward the discovery of these "Miracles."

If, at least for the moment, we could accept the possibility of a divinely managed, never ending cycle of life, would that not perhaps be the answer to, "I've been here before. It sure looks familiar." "Hey! I've heard that song before!" Could it be that some previous life experience might be seeping through to the current life? It might also explain the merged personalities of two people deeply in love, frequently seen in couples living to old age together. Possibly they have unknowingly gone down life's road together before. Would that not be reassuring when one loses a beloved husband or wife?

When a loved one dies, we choose to believe that we will one day be reunited with him in heaven. This may well be true, but we aren't absolutely sure, since no one has been there, and come back to tell us about it. Death is the supreme unknown. Coupled with the instinctive fear of death, is the human desire for immortality. We know we cannot live forever, but we are taught, in heaven, we live eternally. I would not deny that, however, would not recycling through a mortal existence add to eternity? I think so. Something else to consider. If, by way of recycling, our souls are refined to a continually greater degree of purity, would we not be better prepared to enjoy the grace of heaven?

This concept in no way denies the philosophy of Christianity. It may well enhance it. Nothing in the endless process of recycling seen in nature denies the possibility of everything taught in Christianity coming to pass.

BEEN THERE BEFORE?

# THE DIVINE PARALLEL

## BY: DANA T. MOORE, II

The mathematician defines a parallel thus: Lying evenly everywhere in the same direction, but never meeting, however far extended.

In His infinite wisdom, God placed Jesus on earth to provide a means of salvation for man. This salvation was not to be limited to any particular group, but was to be available to all mankind. Further, the history of Jesus, starting with the immaculate conception, and continuing through His birth, life, death, and resurrection, was in accordance with a divinely ordained schedule of activities and results. Jesus knew the purpose of His mission on earth, and was aware of the cause and effect of His actions, and therefore, certainly aware of the consequences resulting from those actions.

God chose to have Jesus carry out His mission in a dual role. He was simultaneously both mortal and immortal. Had He been cast singularly, as merely mortal, or a totally divine being, His accomplishments would have been, at best, somewhat less significant. As a mortal, He would have been accepted as such, and most likely have been remembered as a superbly accomplished and dedicated evangelist. On the other hand, as a divine being, the true Messiah, the effect would have been to force the ultimate outcome by the sheer magnitude of His overwhelmingly divine presence.

The duality of Jesus is evidenced in the immaculate conception and virgin birth. In choosing to begin Jesus' life thusly, God assured that He was at once of God and of man. This gave Jesus both a mortally humble, and a divinely magnificent beginning.

The Synoptic Gospels are notably lacking in pertinent information concerning Jesus' childhood. There is however, one significant incident indicating that Jesus was probably aware, even then, of His divine mission on earth, with all its ramifications and consequences. When Jesus, at the age of 12, was taken by Mary and Joseph to celebrate the Passover in Jerusalem, He was inadvertently left behind on the return trip to Nazareth. After discovering His absence, and returning to Jerusalem to search for Him, Mary and Joseph found Jesus in the temple participating in a very learned discussion with the temple teachers. When they remonstrated with Him for His apparent lack of consideration for them, He replied, "How is it that you sought Me? Did you not know that I must be in My Father's house?"

Again, little information is available in the Gospels from which to draw any conclusions as to Jesus' appearance and physical impression as a man. However, from His manner of speech, His dealings with the disciples, the Pharisees, Pontius Pilate and the Devil, and His obvious concern for the poor in health, a reasonably accurate personality picture can be drawn. He showed Himself to be an even tempered, dedicated, intelligent man; a man with compassion, and yet, a man who was also firm and decisive.

Further reinforcement of Jesus' duality of purpose is reflected in His insistence upon baptism by John the Baptist. His baptism established the requirement for the initial cleansing rite of baptism before salvation, and in so doing, provided for Christians the symbolic point of departure upon the path to eternal life. Also, baptism enhanced Jesus' earthly role, thereby encouraging His identification with man.

In order to provide the means for man's salvation, Jesus' ministry was aimed at two major objectives. First, He had to proclaim, and convince man of the coming of The Kingdom of God. Secondly, He had to evoke man's consuming desire to enter The Kingdom of God. To attain these objectives, Jesus utilized two avenues of approach. He taught and explained the Kingdom of God, including qualifications for eternal life. Secondly, He was the living example of the philosophy He was teaching.

Knowing, as He did, the immediate results of His ministry, Jesus saw the need for carrying on His work after His death. He also saw the need for continuity based on first hand experience and participation in His work. To accomplish this, He selected the initial cadre of 12 disciples. While His ministry was for all who "had ears to hear," His efforts at enlightenment were directed primarily to the disciples. After His death, they were to become the founders of Christianity, and would devote the remainder of their lives to this end.

Throughout the conduct of Jesus' ministry, two recurring themes appeared; the eruption of the Kingdom of God, and Jesus' eschatological philosophy. He emphasized in His teachings that the Kingdom of God was present, and was at the same time a condition of the future, extending beyond the end of time. In presenting the Kingdom of God as He did, Jesus saw Himself as an instrument of its inauguration.

In order to increase His effectiveness, Jesus employed the use of parables as a teaching device. In so doing, He was not attempting to couch His message in confusing, or secretive form. The parables presented His message in terms understandable by men of all time, and conveyed His teaching in a manner that avoided both simplification and complication. At the same time, the parables were used in an effort to convey Jesus' meaning by use of analogies drawn from the everyday world of that time.

In performing miracles, Jesus wanted a touch of divine authority, but did not want to be seen as a magician, nor a mystical performer of the supernatural. This divine authority was necessary to instill faith and confidence in Him by His followers; not faith in Himself as the panacea for all man's ills, both spiritual and physical, but rather faith in the Kingdom of God as Jesus presented it. Further, the miracles emphasized the compassionate quality of God. Additionally, the miracles enhanced the necessity for voluntary acceptance by man of the validity and importance in the message Jesus delivered; the Kingdom of God is now and forever.

That Jesus knew of his impending crucifixion, death, and resurrection there can be no doubt. He acknowledged this Himself at the last supper when He told the disciples, "Truly, I say to you, I shall not drink again of the fruit of the vine until that day when I drink it new in the Kingdom of God."

Now, why would Jesus place Himself in a situation that He knew would surely result in His death? Again, this was part of His divinely ordained plan, and as such, served the purpose of obtaining God's forgiveness for all men; all men living in a state of sin.

Jesus was probably condemned to death by the Jewish authorities, The San Hedrin, then turned over to the Romans for trial and conviction. This lent an aura of legality to the proceedings, and at the same time, shifted the perceived responsibility to the Romans. At this trial, which today we would call a hearing, Jesus had ample opportunity to avoid conviction. Pilate was not unsympathetic. However, to carry out his mission, Jesus refused to avail Himself of any opportunity to be found innocent. In fact, as shown by the Gospels, Jesus adopted a rather taciturn position during the proceedings. Finally, Pilate symbolically "washed his hands" of the whole affair and allowed the rabble of Jewish observers to decide the issue.

Jesus must have indeed been a lonely individual during His final hours of earthly existence. He was betrayed by one of His select disciples; thrice denied by His favorite disciple, Peter, and then finally renounced by His own people. And then to be taunted and belittled during the agony on the cross was to deny Him the smallest shred of dignity even in death.

And now, Jesus' most significant act during his entire sojourn on earth: the resurrection. The significance of the resurrection was Jesus' victory over death. The resurrection served to unite the disciples as never before, but more than that, the resurrection served to set the Christian example of life after death for those who accepted Jesus' teachings. It was vivid proof of the eternal validity of those teachings. Finally, the resurrection prepared the disciples for their final charge, which Jesus then gave them. Jesus instructed His disciples: "Repentance and forgiveness of sins should be preached in His name to all nations, beginning in Jerusalem." Then He led them out as far as Bethany and, lifting up His hands, He blessed them. While He blessed them. He departed from them.

The Parallel had converged!

A parallel is defined thus: Lying evenly everywhere in the same direction, but never meeting, however far extended.

With God, all things are possible!

# FOLLOW ME

By: DANA T. MOORE, II

The past six weeks had been rough as hell on him. His name was Earl Jackson, and he was a pilot, as well as squadron maintenance officer in Fighter Squadron 33, a shipboard squadron of Carrier Air Group Six, presently embarked aboard the aircraft carrier U.S.S. Intrepid, CVA-11. The air group was given a no-notice deployment order one morning back in mid-November, and moved aboard ship.

The deployment order caught the whole air group unawares, and somewhat less than prepared. They had been returned, less than a month, from a six month cruise in the Mediterranean. Their planes were in bad shape, and his squadron was in the throes of repair and retraining. There were many new pilots, and all old planes. Additionally, a large portion of his maintenance men had been replaced with new people; the older, more experienced personnel having finished their four year sea duty tour, and transferred to shore duty.

Normally, upon return from an extended sea cruise, the men were all given a couple weeks leave; the old ones left for new assignments; the new ones worked into the squadron routine, and the planes either replaced with more airworthy machines, or a priority given to repair and updating them. This generally took eight to ten weeks, during which the squadron could expect to be allowed to train, and repair up to expected standards. Added to this was the similar turnover of pilots, which in itself involved considerable training.

In theory, all newly assigned pilots and maintenance personnel were thoroughly trained and ready for duty upon assignment to a sea going fighter squadron. In practice however, this was rarely the case. People had to be trained in a myriad of routine procedures; even to the point of learning where the heads were located. Overlaying all this was the central problem of getting the planes back into top notch condition. Some of them were in such bad shape they couldn't be flown off the ship upon return from the recent cruise. They had to be offloaded by crane at pier 12 in Norfolk, and brought to NAS Oceana on a flatbed truck.

The normal shore station compliment of planes was 18 to a squadron. Because of physical space limitations, this number was reduced to 12 when aboard ship. Upon receipt of the recent deployment order, Earl could only count on nine planes being combat ready, and one more barely flyable; not even able to retract the landing gear. This one had to be flown to NAS Norfolk with the landing gear down. Nothing looks more ungainly than an F8-U Crusader jet fighter flying around with the wheels down, and the variable incidence wing in the up position for landing. Nevertheless, Earl did manage to get ten of his planes loaded aboard the carrier.

The deployment order was issued as the result of a political upheaval in the Dominican Republic. The political chaos in itself was serious enough, but of prime concern was the large community of American nationals working and living in the Dominican Republic. These people had to be assured of their safety, and if necessary, safely evacuated should the political crisis become sufficiently severe, which it did. Thus, Earl's air group was deployed aboard ship, and sent swiftly off to the Caribbean, along with a ship load of helicopters and Marines, and the various support ships necessary to keep this small task force operational.

Everyone thought this would be no more than another routine United States show of force, with the carrier steaming around just off the coast of the Dominican Republic, conducting flight operations. This generally had a stabilizing effect on active political instability. Just seeing the powerful United States flexing its military muscle was enough to sober, and settle most of the banana republics in the Caribbean area. Not so this time, though. The political conditions worsened considerably in the time it took Intrepid to make the trip into the Caribbean from Norfolk. By the time Intrepid arrived on station several miles south of Cuidad Trujillo, the local conditions had degenerated into an outright rebellion, with active combatant confrontation and bloodshed the order of the day.

While the administration in Washington tried in vain to apply diplomatic pressure to the adversaries in the Dominican Republic, the air group was directed to conduct training flights within easy view of the inhabitants. This failed in its desired effect, since the severity of the rebellion increased. Washington finally decided to take a much more positive approach. A reconnaissance flight was directed, with the pilots ordered to fly over the capitol at low altitude, in plain sight. This was an unheard of, unauthorized violation of the sovereign airspace of a foreign nation. Nevertheless, the mission was laid on.

Eight A4-D, "Scooter," attack aircraft were to fly over in loose formation, with four F8-U, "Crusaders," flying top cover. Since no targets were designated, nor any offensive action authorized, no ordnance was carried. The internal 20 mm. cannon were loaded, but this was nothing more than a passive token to defensive capability for the planes. After all, no hostile action was even remotely anticipated during the flyover. The aircrews were all briefed that the mission would amount to nothing more than an airshow, demonstration type of flyby.

During the pre-flight briefing in the squadron ready rooms, the pilots were jocular, and in a festive mood. This was really a chance for them to show off a little, and in so doing, let off a little steam. Everybody likes an airshow. Those pilots not selected for the mission, were envious of those who were, chiding their more fortunate chums for getting a lucky break. The briefing called for launching the eight Scooters, followed by four Crusaders. The eight attack aircraft were to join up in a loose formation at 5000 feet, and when the Crusaders had assumed a covering position 5000 feet above, the Captain would issue final mission clearance. The flyover was to consist of one pass at cruising speed from sea to shore, carried on through inland. After a leisurely 180 degree turn, the planes were to fly back over the capitol, heading out to sea, and completing the flight as a training mission. It was sure to be a pleasant, harmless milk run.

The launch, joinup, and clearance were uneventful. During the initial flyover, there were even some casual comments over the radio about the peaceful beauty of this Caribbean city. The mighty United States was telling its southern brethren to straighten up and get their affairs in order. Just as the planes were over the northern outskirts of the city on their outbound pass, all hell broke loose!

A veritable wall of flak erupted! Numbers three and four Scooters in the first flight were literally blown out of the sky. Where the two planes had been moments before was now nothing but a large ball of black smoke, and orange flame, with bits and pieces of debris showering earthward. Number four in the second flight took a critical hit, and immediately burst into flame. This plane was still barely flyable, and headed forthwith for the Intrepid, the pilot ejecting alongside the ship. One of the Crusaders took a hit, and instantly began streaming fuel and black smoke. Another Scooter began trailing smoke and fire from a hit.

The airwaves, moments before carrying light banter about the peaceful, pretty city below, now crackled with excited shouting.

"Did you see that!"

"Three and four just disappeared!"

"Number two is on fire, and headed for the ship!"

"Let's get the hell outta here!"

"Look at that Crusader! He'll never make it! Probably blow before he makes it back to the ship!"

"Let's go down and straffe the hell outta those bastards!"

Finally, an authoritative voice intervened. "This is Atlas. Knock off the chatter!"

"Atlas" was the radio call sign of the Intrepid, and when the pilots heard this call, they knew they were being spoken to by the Captain, through his primary flying control officer in the tower, normally referred to as "Prifly."

The radio chatter stopped. The planes continued their path out over the water. The flak stopped; the targets were now out of range.

"This is Atlas. I want an immediate battle damage report!"

"Roger, Atlas," the mission leader replied. 'We lost three Scooters. One Scooter and a Crusader are inbound to you with critical damage. The Crusader's radio appears to be out, since I can't raise him. They'll need a ready deck as soon as you can have it."

"Roger, Lead. Take your undamaged planes overhead at 20 thousand. Your signal is Dog. Remain on this channel for your Charley." Prifly had told the mission leader to take the remainder of the flight to the overhead orbit point, and hold for landing instructions.

Prifly then continued, "Sick Birds, this is Atlas. We're turning into the wind, and executing an emergency pull forward. You will have a ready deck in five minutes. Your Fox Corpen is 270 degrees." Prifly had made a blind call to the pilots of the damaged planes, telling them that Intrepid was turning into the wind for landing, and was pulling all the aircraft forward to get a clear deck for landing, with a landing direction and time of 270 degrees, and five minutes.

Earl was in his maintenance office on the hangar deck when the announcement about the damaged planes came over the ship's public address system, followed by the orders for the emergency pull forward. He was talking to Chief Thompson, his Maintenance Chief, when the P. A. System abruptly shattered their conversation. The two men glanced wordlessly at one another, then bolted for the flight deck.

"Shades of Korea!" Earl thought, running for the flight deck. "Battle damaged planes in peacetime? What the hell's happened?"

Sprinting through the island door onto the flight deck, Earl saw a fever of activity. Plane captains were pushing planes by hand. Other plane handlers were pulling planes forward with tractors. Each plane had a brown shirted plane captain sitting in the cockpit riding the brakes. Prifly was bellowing on the bullhorn to move this plane here, and that plane there. It looked as if pandemonium prevailed. In actuality, this was a well rehearsed, smoothly orchestrated function. The flight deck had to be readied for landing in minimum time, five minutes, in order to take the damaged planes aboard. While this emergency activity was being carried out, the carrier was turning into the wind, accelerating as it turned. The carrier needed at least 35 knots wind across the flight deck to recover the fast, heavy jet fighters as they plummeted into the arresting wires.

As Intrepid rolled out of its turn into the wind, and the last aircraft was pulled across the foul line marking the landing area, Prifly bellowed, "Standby to recover aircraft!"

Moments later, Prifly announced, "Heads up! We have a battle damaged Scooter in the groove for landing!"

All eyes on the flight deck stared aft to the landing area. Earl saw the damaged plane on final approach, about a quarter mile behind the ship. The plane was trailing a thick, black coil of smoke, and small tongues of flame were darting intermittently from its starboard side. The landing gear, flaps and tail hook were all down. Earl saw "Paddles," the Landing Signal Officer, standing on his platform on the port side of the landing area. The tension was so thick as to be nearly strangling.

"Get a good wire," Earl pleaded silently, watching the damaged A4-

D approach. As the plane quickly overtook the carrier, Earl could see that the nose gear was cocked off at an angle, the strut obviously damaged. This would normally result in a wave off, but before Paddles could flash the red wave-off lights, Prifly bellowed, "Trap him, Paddles!"

The little "Scooter Bomber" came right down the groove, flying a perfect three wire pass, coming in like a homing pigeon. Approaching the touchdown point, the tail hook engaged the number three wire, and the plane slapped onto the deck in a normal carrier landing. The damaged nose gear strut however, snapped off at impact, allowing the severed nose wheel to bound down the flight deck, and over the side into the water. The nose of the plane slammed down onto the flight deck. The plane skidded forward, then was brought to an abrupt halt by the arresting wire. The pilot slumped forward in the cockpit, blood staining his right shoulder.

Prifly bellowed, "Get that pilot out of the plane!" This was a redundant command, as plane handlers, firefighters, and flight deck personnel converged on the stricken plane. "Get a tractor on him!" Prifly continued, "We have a hurt Crusader to take aboard."

The firefighters, clad in asbestos suits, smothered the fire with foam. Two of the flight deck personnel disengaged the now slack arresting wire from the tail hook. Three plane captains struggled with the canopy to get it open. Earl dashed over to the plane, and unlatched the canopy via the external access release. The three plane captains reached in, unsnapped the unconscious pilot from his safety belt and parachute harness, and lifted his inert body from the cockpit. At the same time, a tractor was attached to the plane, and dragged it out of the landing area.

"Look alive!" Prifly again bellowed. "We have a damaged Crusader in the groove."

All eyes on the flight deck again turned aft, staring intently at the F8-U approaching the carrier from astern. Earl could see that the Crusader, as did the A4-D, trailed smoke. The smoke was less dense, and there were no flames. The plane was flying slightly sideways. Alternately the pilot straightened its path, and the left wing dropped. Earl could see why. The landing flaps on the left wing were either missing, or were in the up position, creating an asymmetrical lift and drag factor on the plane. When the pilot attempted to straighten the flight path, the left wing dropped. He instinctively compensated with right rudder, and then the plane was again flying slightly sideways, like a sand crab on the beach. The overall effect of the missing wing flap was an erratic approach, with a higher approach speed to make up for the lost lift. Added to this was the apparent radio failure in the plane, no one having had heard a word from the pilot after the plane was hit with flak.

"He's too fast," Earl said to Chief Thompson. Too fast meant the plane would either snap the arresting wire, or pull the hook from the rear of the plane. The plane would then either skid off the flight deck, drop into the water and sink, or, with the sideways touchdown, be thrown into the ship's island superstructure. Both options held equally fatal potential.

"Wave him off, Paddles!" Prifly bellowed.

Paddles flashed the red wave-off lights, and the Crusader pilot responded by adding power, and climbing away from the ship. As the plane passed about 30 feet above the flight deck, Earl could see that the left flap was missing completely, leaving a jagged hole in the rear of the left wing. The trail of smoke was issuing from the gaping hole where the flap had been. Earl could also see numerous torn holes in the left wing, and bottom of the fuselage. The pilot climbed his damaged plane up to the downwind leg, and resumed his approach for another landing attempt.

Commander Dickson, Primary Flying control officer, picked up the phone in the tower, and spoke directly to the Captain, on the bridge. "He's too fast, Captain. Can we get any more wind across the deck?"

"We'll have it, Dick," the Captain replied. "Take him on the next pass." The Captain turned to his Officer Of the Deck on the bridge, and spoke to him. "Tell Engineering I want every knot this ship can make. We're going to trap that boy on his next time around."

"Aye, Aye, Sir," replied the OOD, turning to pass the Captain's instructions into the phone connected with the Engineering Officer.

Very shortly, Intrepid could be felt to quiver and shake as she began to put on more speed. It was obvious the "Old Fighting I" was giving her all, and doing quite well considering she was of World War Two vintage, her keel having been laid in 1941.

"Paddles," Prifly said, "We've got 42 knots across the deck. Can we trap him this time?"

"Affirmative, Prifly. He'll be on the high side, and we may have to change a wire, but we can get him," Paddles answered into his microphone. All eyes were again locked onto the Crusader as the pilot began his second approach. The approach was the same as before; fast, and erratic. Earl sweat for the pilot. He knew the pilot was well aware of the high speed arrestment risks. Earl also knew, since he was a Crusader pilot himself, the pilot was slowing his plane to the absolute minimum speed possible that would still allow him to control it. As the plane approached the landing area, Earl could see the rudder, elevator, and the ailerons all working simultaneously as the pilot strove to maintain control. Crossing the stern, the left wing started to drop. The pilot compensated with right rudder, electing to land sideways, rather than on one wheel, depending on the arresting wire to straighten the plane in its 190 foot roll out.

The tail hook caught the number two wire, and the Crusader slapped onto the deck. The left main wheel tire blew out on impact, but the arresting wire brought the plane to a safe halt. Coming to a stop, the pilot shut the engine down, and opened the canopy. While the flight deck crews converged on the plane, the pilot disengaged himself from the cockpit straps, and climbed out, obviously unhurt. The plane was quickly hauled from the landing area. Walking briskly toward the island, heading for the ready room below, the pilot passed by Earl, who said, "Welcome aboard, Sport."

The pilot replied, "Thanks. Glad to be here. Some milk run, huh?" he muttered, and then added, "We get all our people back?"

"All but the two lost over the beach, and the one's waiting overhead for their Charley signal," Earl answered.

The remainder of the airborne aircraft were recovered, and the task force retired south to lick its wounds.

The next day, the headlines at home were full of the story of the "Unprovoked" attack on the U.S. Navy. Public outrage was at an all time high. Ambassadorial notes were exchanged. The U.N. was called into emergency session. The administration was subjected to extreme public pressure to take some positive action. The public dither continued for three days as the hue and cry increased. The U.N. fumed and fussed. The Russians looked for something to veto. Finally, the President had his fill. He decided to act unilaterally.

The Marine contingent was ordered into the Dominican Republic to evacuate the American nationals. The airwaves were thick with operations orders, and counter orders. Gradually, a pattern of intelligence emerged. The Marines were to land in the harbor of Cuidad Trujillo, and set up a perimeter defense around the harbor. A small combat force was then to go into town, collect the Americans, and escort them to a helicopter pickup point. The Dominican Republic was urged to observe a temporary cease fire while the evacuation took place. The air group aboard Intrepid was ordered to fly armed reconnaissance. Top cover would be provided by the Crusaders.

The assault landing by the Marines was carried out by helicopter. As soon as the troops were ashore, with their organic fire support and surface vehicles, the helicopters were ordered to return to the ship, and await orders for evacuation duty. The operations plan looked foolproof on paper. In practice, as is almost always the case, it proved to be less than perfect. The major flaw was the native combatants. They completely ignored the plea for the cease fire. The Marines were caught in the resultant cross fire. Apparently everyone in the Dominican Republic involved in the rebellion, used the U.S. Marines to vent their pent up wrath upon. When neither side could find lucrative targets, both would open fire on the Marines. Added to this problem was a firm restriction issued from Washington. The Marine Commander wasn't allowed to return the hostile fire. All the Marines could do was take cover from the incoming fire, and wonder who the enemy really was; The Dominican Republic; the rebels, or the administration in Washington.

This situation made evacuation of the Americans too risky to carry out, so any positive action by the Marines was held in abeyance until Washington could muddle through with directions. Finally, after diplomatic efforts proved fruitless, the President ordered the sources of hostile fire, both Dominican Republic and rebel, to be neutralized by air attack. This decision was received with glee by the pilots aboard Intrepid, and by the Marines ashore.

Very soon thereafter, the air group was assigned targets, and given a launch order. Earl's planes, the Crusaders, flew top cover, an apparently unnecessary luxury, since the Dominican Republic had no aircraft capable of mounting any hostile counter air action. The Crusader pilots were authorized, if necessary, to lend a helping hand to the attack pilots strafing ground targets, but this authorization was mixed with a strong admonition to refrain from needless bloodshed. The pilots all agreed about the needless bloodshed, especially if it happened to be their own.

The fire suppression missions went well. By morning of the second day's air operations, most of the hostile fire was extinguished. The pilots could see the Marines moving out in their small convoy of surface vehicles, heading for the pre-arranged pickup point where the Americans were awaiting. Things went well enough, so that by the third day, the entire operation was moved on into town to a large hotel where the Americans were directed to assemble. The evacuees were picked up there by helicopter, and flown directly to the waiting ship. By the end of the fourth day, most of the Americans were evacuated, and it was time to begin withdrawal of the Marine contingent.

Late that afternoon, Earl's squadron commander directed him to fly the Crusader, repaired after the first day's debacle, on the last top cover mission of the day. The damaged plane had been hastily repaired with new flaps, and aluminum skin patches, but there had been no time to paint the repair work. The olive drab primer paint of the repaired areas contrasted vividly with the grey paint of the rest of the plane. An anonymous plane captain, with a keen sense of humor, had stenciled the name "Patches" in brilliant red on each side of the cockpit of the repaired Crusader.

"Earl," the Skipper said, "I want you to give Patches a good checkout on this flight, and report back to me when you return."

"Yes, Sir," Earl replied, wondering why the special emphasis on Patches. It had flown several times since the repair work was completed.

Earl flew the mission, and as he would have anyway, checked Patches out thoroughly. The plane was completely airworthy, as Earl already knew. When he returned from the flight, Earl found the Skipper waiting for him in the ready room.

"How's Patches, Earl?" the Skipper asked.

"Four-O," Earl replied, indicating nothing was wrong with the plane. "Good," replied the Skipper. "I have a special mission for you tomorrow, to be flown with Patches."

"What's that, Skipper?" Earl asked.

"Take her to the beach, and bring back a replacement plane."

"Why not keep Patches here, and have someone fly the replacement plane out from the beach?" Earl asked, remembering he was short two planes. "There's more to it than a routine replacement, Earl," the Skipper replied, a twinkle in his eye.

Earl stood silently, waiting for the bomb. The Skipper continued, "The President wants some photos of the damage to the plane. Its part of his public relations program to enlist support of Congress and the

American public for his unilateral actions here the past few days. He wants a combat plane, and a combat pilot for some P.R. pictures, and press releases. You're it, Earl."

Earl felt a little uncomfortable at the thoughts of the P.R. work, but at the same time, he was grateful for a few days off the ship.

"Where am I taking Patches, Skipper? N.A.S. Key West?"

"No, Earl, you're taking her home to Oceana."

Earl felt a surge of elation. At least he would get to spend some time with Joanne and the kids.

"Earl, I'm going to contact Commander Dace, Skipper of the replacement air group at N.A.S. Jacksonville, and have him put up an A4-D tanker. You can air refuel en route, and not have to stop until you arrive at Oceana. I want your flight plan by breakfast tomorrow. Give me your rendezvous point, time, and required fuel off-load to get you into Oceana. You'll be launching with the 1900 twilight mission tomorrow evening. You can proceed with the top cover flight, then detach and fly directly over the Dominican Republic, and be on your way. That should put you on the ground no later than 2330 tomorrow night. Any questions?"

"Yes, Sir. When do I return?"

"You'll have about three days there," the Skipper answered.

"Aye, Aye, Sir," Earl acknowledged, and turned to leave. "Earl," the Skipper continued, "Do you know what tomorrow is?"

Earl paused, and as he looked intently at the Skipper, his mind went blank. He had been so busy flying, and working, he had lost all track of time. His facial expression must have been equally as blank as his mind.

"It's Christmas Eve, Earl," the Skipper said, the twinkle in his eyes growing even more pronounced.

"Well, I'll be damned! So it is," Earl replied, his feeling of elation changing to one of warm anticipation at the thought of spending Christmas with his family. "I had completely forgotten," he continued.

"Get me your flight plan by breakfast, Earl," the Skipper reminded.

"Yes, Sir!" Earl replied, a wide grin spreading over his face.

The following morning, Earl submitted his flight plan to the Skipper, and once approved, a copy went to Combat Operations for transmittal to the appropriate shore installations. The Skipper made the necessary arrangements for the refueling rendezvous. Patches was kept off the flight schedule for the day, in order to insure her readiness for the flight home.

"Mr. Jackson's going home for Christmas!" The word spread through the air group like wildfire. Numerous Christmas presents began to accumulate in the maintenance office. Bags of Christmas mail began to pile up. Chief Thompson had the chore of stuffing all this Christmas cheer into the cramped space of the Crusader. He finally solved the problem by removing all the 20 mm. ammunition containers from the plane, and using that space for the Christmas mail.

Two hours before launch time, Earl, accompanied by Chief Thompson, walked out onto the hangar deck to load his baggage onto Patches. As the two men approached the plane, Earl noticed that almost all of the squadron enlisted men were standing in front of the plane. When they drew close, the men stepped aside, and Earl was amazed at what he saw. Boldly emblazoned along both sides of the fuselage were the bright green and red letters of "Ho! Ho! Ho! And a Happy Christmas to All!" On each side of the nose section were stenciled three small reindeer, with the reins painted back into the cockpit. On the canopy rail, where the pilot's name was normally printed, was the name, Santa Claus.

Earl, normally an unflappable individual, not given to visible emotions, suddenly had a large lump in his throat. These grimy, sweaty, tired, and overworked men had stayed up all night to give him this Christmas present. He knew they had worked hard to do it; cutting stencils, spray painting several coats, and treating the entire process with infra red heat lamps in order that it would properly dry before flight. This was why Chief Thompson had asked that Patches be left off the flight schedule today. Earl looked silently at each of the men standing expectantly before him.

"What a crew!" he thought. And then, swallowing the lump in his throat, he said, "Thanks, troops. I wish I could stuff all of you in the plane, and take you home with me." He then turned to Chief Thompson, and shaking his hand, said, "Thanks, Tommy. I really appreciate it." With that, the tension released, and the men broke into a lusty "Merry Christmas!"

"And the same to you," Earl warmly replied.

That evening, the launch was routine, although Patches received more than its usual share of attention from the flight deck crews before launch. Immediately following the catapult shot, while raising the landing gear and flaps, Earl heard over his radio, "Merry Christmas, and a good trip, Patches."

Earl grinned to himself, pressed the mike button on the throttle, and replied, "Thanks, and a Merry Christmas to you, Atlas."

Earl then joined up with the four Crusaders going on patrol, and the five planes climbed out toward the Dominican Republic. Arriving at the northern end of the patrol area, still climbing, Earl pressed his mike button, and called, "This is Patches. I'm detaching now, and heading on out."

"Roger, Earl. Have a good trip. See you in a few days," the flight leader replied.

With that, the flight began a slow climbing turn to the left, and Earl continued his climb on course to the Northwest. An hour and forty five minutes later, Earl switched his radio to the pre-briefed refueling frequency, and called his aerial tanker. The Tanker pilot replied with his altitude, heading and location. Earl spotted the tanker's refueling lights, and joined up. They were at 40,000 feet altitude, approximately 50 miles off the coast of Cape Canaveral. Earl extended the refueling probe, and plugged into the trailing, flexible refueling basket behind the A4-D tanker. Some 20 minutes later, approximately 50 miles Northeast of Jacksonville, the tanker pilot called Earl, and informed him he had to turn around, and head for home. Earl acknowledged with, "Roger. I have a full load. Thanks, and a very Merry Christmas."

Reducing power, Earl allowed the Crusader to disconnect from the refueling basket. Retracting the probe, he took up a heading for landfall at Savannah. Switching his radio over to Jacksonville Center, he called in his position, and asked for the current weather at Oceana. Jacksonville informed him Oceana was at minimums, but his alternate airfield was still in good shape. Oceana was having intermittent snow showers, with a ragged ceiling, and variable visibility conditions. Earl acknowledged the weather report and continued north. As long as his alternate was in good weather conditions, Earl had no cause to worry. He was a highly qualified, professional pilot, and cracking a minimum ceiling at night was nothing new to him. And besides, he was glad to hear that he would have a White Christmas.

At a point 75 miles south of Norfolk, Earl was directed over to Washington Center frequency. Washington Center verified his position by radar, then handed him off to Norfolk Approach Control. By the time he was firmly established under Norfolk's radar control, and had finished the numerous radio channel changes, Earl looked around, and noticed he was flying in a thick, white cloud layer. Norfolk Approach Control updated the Oceana weather with essentially the same conditions Jacksonville had given him earlier, but with one minor change. The alternate airfield was now at minimums for use as an alternate. Earl weighed the various factors, and chose to continue to Oceana. Norfolk then cleared him to the 35 mile fix on the Oceana Tacan, and also to descend to 20,000 feet prior to arriving at the fix. Descending toward 20,000 feet, Earl noted he was now flying in very thick, dark clouds, with heavy snow spattering his windshield.

Approaching the fix at 20,000 feet, Earl reported to Norfolk, who replied by clearing him to descend to 5,000 feet on the 180 degree tacan radial. He also cleared Earl to contact Oceana GCA. Earl switched channels, and called Oceana GCA, who came right back, and confirmed that he was painting Earl's plane clearly on his radar scope; directed him to continue his descent to 1,500 feet, and requested him to report arriving at 1,500 feet altitude, and ten miles out. Reaching 1,500 feet at 15 miles, Earl leveled his plane, and continued to slow to approach speed. At the ten mile point, Earl reported to GCA as level at 1,500, ten miles out, and gear and flaps down for landing. GCA directed Earl to continue his heading, maintain altitude, and to stand by for the final approach controller. Earl again acknowledged. Momentarily, the final approach control radar operator came on, established radio contact, then instructed Earl not to acknowledge any further instructions.

GCA then directed Earl to begin a 500 feet per minute rate of descent, and to maintain his heading. Shortly, GCA said he could see that Earl was descending on the glide path, and on center line, eight miles out. A minute later, he repeated the transmission, amending the distance to six miles.

Then, Earl heard an unusual, dull popping noise in the cockpit, not coming through his headset. The radio went dead, and the cockpit lights went out, accompanied by an instrument panel warning light telling him he had just had an electrical failure. Earl quickly grabbed his penlight from his sleeve pocket, turned it on, and grasped it between his right forefinger, and second finger, clutched around the control stick. Complete electrical failure! All the gyro instruments on the panel, other than the turn and bank instrument, were inoperative. Earl knew the turn and bank instrument had about three minutes useable time before its internal gyro ran down from lack of power. Then aircraft attitude control by instrument reference would be impossible.

Earl quickly calculated, "120 knots; two miles per minute; six miles out; three minutes until touchdown; provided he could find the runway in this blinding snow storm. No choice. Climb on out, and head inland for either a clear weather area, or a safe ejection area." He knew that blundering around at night, with an electrical failure, and no instruments with which to fly the plane in this foul weather gave him no choice. "Continue to try and land, and I'll be an unexplained statistic on some accident board's report. No way!"

All this thought process took only a moment of time. As Earl, his decision made, started to advance power to climb setting, he halted when his eye was caught by a lighted image on the windshield. He stared momentarily at it, maintaining control using the limited instruments illuminated by his penlight. He delayed adding power.

The image on the windshield was an almost perfect replica of the GCA final approach controller's radar panel on the ground. Earl saw a miniature, lighted runway, with a small duplicate of his Crusader superimposed on the extended center line. The miniature Crusader was the only difference from an actual radar presentation. Right beside this image on the windshield was a vertical presentation, showing the glide path to the runway, and the same little airplane superimposed on that as well. The entire visual image was shining in a subdued, green and white light.

"What the hell?" Earl wondered. He knew there was no such electronic equipment available today, and if it were, he knew positively his Crusader was not so equipped. Gingerly rocking the wings of his plane, he noted the wings of the miniature Crusader on the windshield rocking similarly.

"I can try it down to 100 feet," Earl thought. Noting the little Crusader was slightly above the glide path now, Earl reduced power slightly, and saw the plane on the windshield image slowly return to the glide path.

Earl continued his approach. He brought the windshield visual presentation into his instrument cross check as he changed power slightly to keep the plane on the glide path, and made slight turns to remain in the projected center line. Passing through 100 feet on the altimeter, he continued his descent, thinking, "This is it. I'll either land, or splatter all over the country side." Earl was mindful the allowable error in the altimeter was 50 feet, plus or minus. He could be skimming the trees right now, and not be able to see them. Obviously the weather had deteriorated considerably during the time elapsed since he departed the fix.

Earl sensed, rather than saw, the green runway threshold lights pass under his plane, followed momentarily by the welcome impact with the runway. The runway lights gave off a dull halo glow through their snow covering, but were more than enough reference for Earl to keep his plane rolling straight down the middle of the runway. The deep snow shortened his rollout, and slowed him to taxi speed very quickly.

Approaching a taxiway dully lighted by snow covered blue lights, Earl added power to keep Patches moving in the snow, and turned off the runway toward the parking area. Abruptly he saw a different image on the windshield, another presentation he knew also his plane was not equipped to receive. In place of the runway, glide slope image, Earl now saw the sad, gaunt face of a man, illuminated in the same subdued green and white light. The face on the windshield was bearded, with high cheekbones, and long, dark hair. He seemed to be wearing some sort of a cowl collar garment, gathered thickly under his long hair. The face on the windshield was saying something, repeating it over and over, apparently a short phrase. Earl stared intently at the image, trying to decipher the soundless phrase the image was repeating. Earl almost had it when his thoughts were interrupted by the appearance of the transient alert jeep that had come out to lead him to the parking area.

"Follow Me! That's it!" Earl thought excitedly.

The alert vehicle had a large sign mounted on its rear, with large, lighted neon words reading "Follow Me" facing the following plane. Its purpose was to lead unfamiliar pilots into the parking area.

The image on the windshield was gone now. The soundless phrase it had repeated was "Follow Me." Earl shook his head in confusion, and disbelief. Was it the image, or the sign on the rear of the alert vehicle? Earl tried to get his thoughts in order as he followed the alert jeep into the parking area. Parking Patches in front of Base Operations, Earl shut down the engine, opened the canopy, and handed the alert crewman his helmet and knee pad, saying, "No service, please. I have some mail in the ammo compartment. Would you get it out for me, along with my baggage?"

"Aye, Aye, Sir. We'll take care of it," replied the enlisted man.

Earl climbed from the cockpit, glad to be home, and even more glad to be on the ground in one piece. While he filled out the flight logs, one of the enlisted men asked him, "How did you find your way in here tonight, Sir?"

Earl pointed to the paint job on Patches fuselage, and said, "The reindeer led me in."

The crewman looked at Patches in disbelief, and then, under his breath, muttered, "Smart assed pilots."

Finishing the flight write-up, Earl tossed the flight log into the cockpit. Turning to the enlisted men, he said, "Just tie her down for the night. Someone will be here for her tomorrow or the next day. If you will, please, take my baggage and mail into base operations, and put it by the street-side door."

"Aye, Aye, Sir," replied the crewman, still looking at Earl with a funny expression on his face.

Earl walked into base operations, taking delight in the crisp, cold night air, and the snow pelting him in the face. Stepping up to the counter where the duty officer, a young Ensign, waited, Earl noted the Ensign had a surprised, quizzical look on his face.

Handing the Ensign a copy of his flight plan, Earl said, "Please close this out for me."

The Ensign replied, "Yes, Sir. But where did you come from?"

"The U.S.S. Intrepid," Earl answered.

"Isn't she in the Caribbean, Sir?" asked the Ensign, the questioning look on his face becoming more pronounced.

""Affirmative," Earl confirmed.

"We didn't have a flight plan on you," the Ensign said. Before Earl could reply, the Ensign continued, "How did you find your way in here tonight, Sir? We're well below minimums."

"Why, GCA, of course," Earl replied, a note of irritation beginning to sound in his tone of voice.

"Whose GCA, Sir?" the Ensign continued.

Before Earl replied, he noticed the transient alert crew standing quietly off to one side, listening intently to the conversation.

"Your GCA! Oceana GCA!" Earl snapped, definitely irritated now.

"But, Sir," the Ensign replied, an incredulous tone in his voice, "Our GCA has been off the air since sundown today. With the bad weather, no inbound flight plans, and Christmas Eve, we put the GCA crew on 30 minute standby status at 4:30."

"No GCA?" Earl repeated, a dumbfounded look on his face now.

"That's right, Sir. Our GCA has been shut down since 4:30 this afternoon."

Earl's mind reeled under the impact of what the duty officer was telling him. Mentally reviewing the situation, Earl thought, "No GCA; weather below minimums; electrical failure on GCA final; radio out; the visual GCA presentation and the sad face on the windshield . . . . then how?" Earl wondered if he might be succumbing to combat fatigue. He quickly rejected that explanation, knowing full well he was mentally sound. He realized if he told the duty officer, and the listening alert crewmen, what had happened to him, they would think he was crazy. Earl also knew that finding the runway under the existing weather conditions, with no aid from ground based navigational facilities, was virtually impossible.

Realizing the duty officer was looking expectantly at him, waiting for a plausible explanation, Earl snapped out of his mental holding pattern, and said, "Well, I must have been working with Norfolk RAPCON." Earl had evaded the answer by alluding to Norfolk Radar Approach Control having directed him to the end of Oceana's runway. This could be done, but not under the current weather conditions.

The answer apparently satisfied the duty officer, and the curious alert crew, since they all relaxed, and appeared to accept the only logical explanation possible.

Earl turned, and walked over to the phone at the end of the duty counter. Picking up the phone, he dialed his home. His wife, Joanne, answered. "Merry Christmas, Honey," Earl said.

"Earl! Where are you?" Joanne shrieked into the phone.

"I'm at base ops. Can you pick me up?"

"Yes. Yes, I will! How did you get home? Why didn't you let me know? This is the best Christmas present ever!" Joanne said, the excitement obvious in her voice, her words tumbling out in a rush.

"What about the kids?" Earl asked. "Are they asleep? Can you leave them alone?"

"Chet and Peggy are here, helping me put the Christmas toys together. The kids are sound asleep. They sure are going to be happy when they wake up in the morning," Joanne answered. Chet and Peggy were good friends and neighbors from down the street. Chet was also an airline pilot, contributing to the close association between the two couples. When Earl had to be away from home for extended periods, they took Joanne and the kids under their protective surveillance.

"Joanne," Earl said, looking at his watch, "If you hurry, we can make it to the Christmas Eve services at the base chapel. Do you think Chet and Peggy will mind?"

"No, they won't mind. In fact, they had planned on a couple more hours anyway to help me put these toys together. Actually, they'll probably get home earlier now that you're here, and can take over. I'll be there in fifteen minutes."

"Good," Earl acknowledged. "I would like to give my special thanks for being here tonight."

"Me, too. I'll be right there," Joanne said, before hanging up the phone. Earl replaced the phone on its cradle. Walking toward the door from Base Operations, he turned, and looked at the men behind the duty counter. "Merry Christmas," he said.

Walking out the door, Earl stopped to wait where Joanne could see him when she arrived. Standing in the cold, night air, Earl looked at the dull, snow shrouded lights of the air station. Gazing into the falling snow, Earl knew, as he saw once again the image of the sad, gaunt face from the windshield of his plane, saying, "Follow Me," this was going to be the best Christmas ever.

THE END

# HOLLY AND MISTLETOE

BY: DANA T. MOORE, II

Santa felt depressed. He knew this was not going to be one of the happiest of his annual Christmas trips. As usual, he had received many Christmas gift requests, but none seemed to express anything but thoughts of self from the young people sending them. No one this year had asked for anything for someone else. None of the gift list originators seemed to have the slightest idea of the reason behind Christmas giving.

"Maybe it's time for me to pack it in," Santa sadly surmised. "No one seems to appreciate Christmas anymore. What are the children being taught about Christmas, these days?" Santa wondered sadly. Continuing, he thought, "Too bad Maw and I don't have any children of our own. Be nice to have an understudy to take over with this annual round-the-world trip. Probably, because of the lack of appreciation, I'm getting burned out. The trip has to be made, though, and no one seems likely to take over." With that, Santa put the unsettling thoughts out of his mind, and returned to the more pressing problems of preparing his sleigh for the grueling, all night Christmas Eve trip. "Must be sure and feed the reindeer extra rations, too," he thought. As daylight dwindled on Christmas eve, Santa made a thorough last-minute check of the sleigh. It was fully packed. His brownies and elves had spent the day checking the packing list against the gift lists, and seemed to have gotten everything aboard.

Back in the house, Santa dressed quietly, Mrs. Claus standing silently by, handing him his various articles of cold weather clothing as he needed them. He had on warm, fleece lined underwear, heavy, lined red trousers, a warm knit sweater, his fur lined black boots, and his heavy ermine trimmed red topcoat, buttoned to the chin. He then added the thick, black belt, with the gleaming brass buckle. Finally, he donned the red cap with the white tassel hanging over his shoulder.

Surveying himself in the mirror, Santa asked, "How do I look, Maw?"

Laying an affectionate hand on his shoulder, Mrs. Claus replied, "You are the fulfillment of any child's dreams, Santa. I know there will be many happy children in the morning."

Thus reassured, Santa clasped his gift bag in hand, kissed Mrs. Claus goodbye, and walked jauntily to his sleigh, gaily whistling "Jingle Bells." The reindeer, already hitched to the sleigh, catching sight of his approach, began to stamp their hooves, and snort in happy anticipation of their impending round-the-world trip.

Santa was under way at sundown, the reindeer pulling swiftly along the world wide trip. Most of the homes visited were warm and inviting, with Christmas trees gaily lighted, stockings hanging from the fireplace mantle, and all the inhabitants soundly asleep. A few homes had cookies and milk left out for Santa, and even in an occasional one, Santa found dried corn for the reindeer.

In a few of the homes, thankfully very few, Santa could hear the raucous sounds of loud shouting and argument. Obviously the people living there had been partaking of a little too much bottled Christmas cheer, and were giving vent to their frayed tempers. "Poor children!" Santa thought of the unhappy children in those houses, diverting his sleigh away, and continuing on his route.

As the gift load diminished, and the delivery trip grew near its finish, Santa had the deer land near one isolated, dark home where all the lights were out. Shouldering his heavy gift bag, Santa tried the front door, and found it ajar. There were a few subdued lights on inside, but no human sounds, nor any other perceptible activity. Entering the living room, Santa saw the Christmas tree, lights all smashed, on its side on the floor. Christmas gifts were strewn about, some opened, and others crushed as if stamped upon by angry feet.

Gaining the impression the house was abandoned, Santa began a slow exploratory walk through the home. The first bedroom obviously the master bedroom, had clothes scattered around, the bed unmade, and was in a condition of general disarray. Moving on to another, smaller bedroom, Santa found it unused. Coming next to a bedroom that was undoubtedly the nursery Santa saw two infants, a baby girl, and a baby boy, in twin baby beds. Walking closer, Santa was shocked to see neither of the children, twins, were breathing. In fact, they were in the early stages of death. Touching each of the twins, Santa discerned they were still warm, but not breathing. They had been abandoned, just as had the home.

Grasping his gift bag, Santa rushed outside. Throwing the bag in the rear of the sleigh, Santa paused. Momentarily, he kneeled, and with one hand on his forehead, began a fervent prayer. "Heavenly Father, I don't know what took these children's lives, but I am sure they didn't deserve to die at this early age. Would you not be so kind as to give them back? I know you wanted your son back after his brief sojourn on earth, but not these little children! Not at such a young age!"

Pausing momentarily, Santa continued, "Please, Heavenly Father, if you will give them back, I will take them home, and raise them in a family of eternal love. They will never want for anything. They were entirely too beautiful to have their innocent lives end so early!"

Shuddering slightly, Santa stood, reached into the back of the sleigh, and picked up a shovel. Accepting the finality of the twins' death, Santa thought, "At least I can give them a decent burial."

Dropping the shovel by the front door, Santa sadly returned to the nursery, and took another look at the twins before picking them up to carry outside. Seeing them move, Santa shouted for joy, "They're living! Oh, thank you Father! I'm taking them home straight away. Thank you for giving them back!" Large tears of happiness coursed down Santa's old, lined cheeks.

With that, Santa rushed around the house, found the kitchen, and retrieved some baby formula from the pantry. He then located four baby bottles, and put the formula on the gas stove to heat. While the formula heated, he found warm clothing for the babies, and even located a stack of diapers. Cleaning the twins, and changing their diapers, and in response to their healthy squeals, he fed each a bottle of now warm formula.

Bundling the twins warmly in thick blankets, along with several bottles of warm formula, and picking up his shovel as he left the house, Santa strode swiftly to the sleigh. He placed the twins in the sleigh, just under the dashboard where they would be protected from any wind blast. Tossing his shovel into the gift compartment, Santa climbed into the sleigh, and shouted, "On Donner! On Blitzen! Away! Away! Now we'll have the happiest Christmas of all!"

Arriving at his North Pole home, Santa reined in the deer by the back door. Carrying the twins carefully into his house, Santa yelled, "Maw! Come here! Look at our Christmas present!" Mrs. Claus peered at the twins, her face stupefied in awe.

Finally regaining her composure, Mrs. Claus asked, "Whose are they, and what on earth are you doing with them?"

Santa then related the entire episode of the twin's discovery. He told Mrs. Claus of his very pleaful prayer, his acceptance of their death, and his response of sheer delight upon finding them alive when he returned to the house to take them outside for burial. The Almighty had answered his prayers. "Besides," Santa said, "I couldn't leave them there alone in that cold house on Christmas; a house that was undoubtedly abandoned. If I had not brought them home, especially after our Lord had returned them to life, they would surely have died again, and this time, there would have been no second chance for them."

"Santa," Mrs. Clause began, "this isn't the same as bringing home a pair of puppies. These are two humans. They belong to someone."

"Maw, they belong to us, now," Santa answered.

Taking the twins, Mrs. Claus said, "Let me see to their needs, and you take care of the reindeer." Santa knew that once his wife held those two beautiful children in her arms, there would be no talk of returning them.

"Yes, Maw, I'll go out, and put the deer up for the night."

Walking ahead, Santa, and a number of his brownies led the deer, with the sleigh still attached, into the barn. The deer were then unhitched, led into their stalls, given a large portion of food, and as they ate, a brownie rubbed each one down, and brushed him with a soft brush.

One of the brownies, with a calculating look in his eye, stepped up to Santa, and asked, "What was the special gift we all received for Christmas, the one you brought home in the sleigh?"

"The reindeer have been talking, huh?" Santa then related the story of the dead twins in the abandoned house, and the favorable answer to his prayers. He went on to say, "Now we have two new members in our family. I know that all the brownies and elves will make them welcome."

"When can we see them, Santa?" the brownie asked.

"Any time. Right now, if you wish," Santa answered.

With that, Santa led the brownies, and the elves into his house. They all went to the bedroom now designated as the nursery, and saw Mrs. Clause putting the twins in their new beds. Mrs. Claus' face was radiant. The twins were smiling happily, now that their little tummies were full, and they were in a warm, soft bed. They were responding as expected to the all embracing love so evident in the entire family.

Upon catching sight of the twins, there was a chorus of "Oohs," and "awhs." "Aren't they beautiful!" one of the elves commented. "Are they going to stay with us, Santa?"

"Definitely," Santa replied. "They're part of our family now. I know all of you will love them just as much as we will."

"What are their names?" one of the elves asked.

Santa stepped up to the bed, and placed an index finger on the brow of the little girl. "Holly," he said. Turning, he placed his other index finger on the little boy's forehead, and said, "Mistletoe." Pausing momentarily, Santa then said, "Holly and Mistletoe. Our Christmas twins."

## MERRY CHRISTMAS!

# KATIE'S CHRISTMAS CANE

## BY: DANA T. MOORE, II

The old man walked slowly toward the front steps to his house, his old border collie following loyally at his heels. Pausing before the house, he looked intently at the sky. It was late afternoon on Christmas eve. The sky was leaden, and swollen with the promise of winter's first snow.

Too bad Oma wasn't here to see what was sure to be a white Christmas. Oma dearly loved Christmas, and she particularly loved it when there was a fresh, pristine snowfall just before Christmas. She had coined the phrase, "Diamonds in the snow," when she once looked at a bright sun shining on the new fallen, white snow, reflecting the sunlight. "Yes," he thought, "too bad she won't be here."

The old man frequently thought it too bad that Oma wasn't going to be here to share Christmas with him as they had shared and enjoyed so many during their 45 years of married life. Two years ago Oma developed cancer, and before they were hardly aware of the enormity of the problem, she was gone. Blissfully, she hadn't suffered, but he had. When he thought of her, which was almost constantly, he settled into despair. He knew he would never again experience joy. His despondency had not lessened one bit since she died. This year he had not even bothered to drag out any of the Christmas trappings. He had tried it alone the previous Christmas, and found that at best, he had made a miserable mess of the decorations, and the holiday season.

Ordinarily, in times past, Oma would have the house decorated almost before the Thanksgiving turkey had cooled after dinner. She exuded the spirit of Christmas, turning the house from a place to live into a home to enjoy. Of course, she did that all year long anyway, but the holiday season was especially warm and pleasant because of Oma's abiding love for Christmas.

And now, this season was going to be worse than ever, if possible. A few months before Oma died, their daughter, living in California, had given birth to a daughter. The grandchild was named Catherine, called Katie for short. Neither Oma nor he had seen the child. Living in the mountains of North Carolina, and the new baby being in California presented travel problems too difficult to surmount. Age and economics prevented him from going to California. His daughter was too involved with her work to make the trip back east. The inability to visit with one another was not really the cause for his unusually sad state this Christmas.

Katie was born with a defect in her left leg. It was slightly shorter than the other. At first, this was not a cause for great concern, but when she grew old enough to begin walking, she refused to walk. No amount of coaxing, nor pleading could get her to walk. An orthopedic surgeon was consulted. He was opposed to any surgery, preferring to wait and see if Katie might not learn to walk anyway, then she could be fitted with a brace for her short leg, and thus prevent any permanent damage to her spine. However, damage to her leg muscle structure did occur. The leg muscles didn't develop as the ones in the good leg did, appearing to suffer from atrophy, giving the leg a deformed appearance. The overall effect was one of infinite sadness for the old man. First Oma's death, and then the magnitude of Katie's deformed leg.

"If there was only some way I could restore Katie's leg to normal," he thought. No matter how hard he pondered the subject, he could devise no solution to the problem. "I would gladly trade her one, or both of my legs," he mused wistfully. "At my age, good legs are no longer an asset," he acknowledged.

"Well, Cole," he spoke to his dog, "Let's go on in and fix something to eat." The dog wagged her tail as if she understood exactly what he said.

The two entered the mountain style house he had built for his wife and himself. The house was located in the mountains of the western Piedmont region of North Carolina. At this time of the year, when snow fell, the house took on the appearance of a Swiss chalet. The design was very amenable to a Christmas motif, which was one of the reasons he and Oma loved the home so dearly. Added to this was the abundance of deer and other wildlife. He cultivated the wild animals by placing food out for them during the cold months. He and Oma had spent many a happy hour watching the animals feed on the food they had placed in the woods.

Following a somewhat skimpy evening meal, he took the dog out for a walk before closing the house for the night. It was dark, and though he couldn't see them, he could feel the snowflakes hitting him in the face. The falling snow, combined with the lowering temperature, left him no doubt the ground would have a thick, white cover by morning.

Following the evening walk, the old man and his dog returned to the warmth of his house. He placed a long compact disk on his CD player, and settled down in his recliner to listen to the Christmas music. His dog stood patiently before him, begging for her nightly snack. He gave her two pieces of candy, a chew stick, and four dog biscuits. She settled gleefully on the floor to devour the manna. The nightly walk, followed by the treasured snack was a routine originated by Oma. Every night along about bed time, she would walk Cole, then give her the goodies. The dog would prance around in circles, excitedly anticipating the savored end-of-the-day ritual reward. Now, with Oma's passage, Papa gave the dog her evening walk and repast shortly after the evening meal.

Leaning back in his recliner, Papa listened to the Christmas music playing softly in the back ground. The light in the room was dim, coming from a single night light. Cole now lay quietly at the foot of his chair. Gradually, the old man's mind wandered back into happier times. He recalled his youngest daughter's diagnosis, and prescription for a dead sparrow she and some of her playmates had found in the back yard. As the children intently examined the dead bird, his daughter was overheard by a group of ladies at a luncheon hosted by Oma. In a clear, and authoritative voice, the youngster was heard to say, "Just give it a shot of bourbon, and it will fly away." Oma received a razzing from her lady friends about that astute analysis.

Another pleasant memory drifted almost wraithlike into mind. One year, his older daughter had received a near life-size doll for Christmas. The doll was named "Emma Em," after a candy with a similar name. Not too long afterward, the older daughter was heard to scream in terror. Apparently Emma Em's head had come off during some vigorous play. Papa came to the rescue. Deftly snapping the doll's head back into place with its retaining ring, Emma Em was like new, and tranquility was restored.

Then there was the time when his son had received a very extensive train layout for Christmas. The youngster was fascinated with the train set. Everything had run like clockwork with the new train until a neighbor had come over, and volunteered to teach his son how to run the train. After several circuits of the train around the track, his son had picked the train's engines off the track, causing a train catastrophe. This was repeated several times until a pause in the train play was called. After the time out, and upon return to the trains, neither his son, nor the train engines were to be seen. Apparently his son had solved the possession problem by going to bed, and taking the engines with him, nestling cozily next to them on the pillow beside his head.

Papa's mind once again returned to Katie. "What to do about the deformed leg?" he wondered for probably the millionth time, and again, he came up with the same answer, "Nothing!" He settled farther back into his recliner, and became more absorbed in thoughts about Katie. After a while, the CD player finished the record of Christmas music, and automatically shut itself off. Papa didn't even notice the enveloping silence. He continued to descend deeper into thoughts about Katie. He was unaware of the passage of time and of the approach of Christmas day.

And then, for no obvious reason, Papa slowly sat ramrod straight in his chair. His face took on a subtle glow, and at the same time, a benign expression of understanding and satisfaction settled over his craggy old features. Cole abruptly lifted her head, and looked adoringly at Papa. Papa nodded his head as if in response to a clear instruction, and a smile spread slowly across his face. He leaned back in his chair, and his expression took on a peaceful, serene look of complete relaxation. At the same time, Cole's head settled to the floor between her forepaws, and her eyes gently closed.

Several hours later, in California, Katie's mother was wakened by an insistent telephone jangling. It was just before dawn on Christmas morning. She picked up the phone receiver, and spoke sleepily into it. "Hello," she said.

A man's voice spoke from the phone. "Ma'am, this is Patrolman Raymond of the North Carolina Highway Patrol in Alamance County. Does your father live alone on Cane Creek Road?"

As the cobwebs cleared, the young woman replied, "Yes, he does. Why?" she asked apprehensively.

"Ma'am," Patrolman Raymond continued, "I hate to be the bearer of sad news, and especially so on this the happiest day of the year, but I'm afraid I have to tell you that your father is dead. I received a call a short while ago from the hospital lifeline service. Your father didn't answer his daily lifeline call this morning, so I was called to go check on him. When I got there, the house was dark, except for a small night light, and the house was quiet. I got no response to the doorbell, so I tried the front door, and finding it unlocked, went in. I called out to your father, and still got no reply. Turning on the light, I saw your father relaxed in his recliner chair. He appeared to have died in his sleep. And most unusual, his old border collie had also died. She was on the floor at his feet."

After a significant pause, Patrolman Raymond continued, "Ma'am, I need some instructions as to what funeral home to send your father to, and what to do with the dog."

Shaking her head in shock, she finally roused and told the patrolman which funeral home to handle the arrangements. She then instructed him to have the dog's body prepared for burial in a similar fashion as a human preparation. She concluded her response to the patrolman by telling him she would call the funeral home and alert them. She then thanked him, and replaced the phone on its receiver.

She sat by the phone table, absorbed in thoughts of her father. She was filled with sadness. Now, both her parents were gone, and neither had ever seen Katie. Infinitely worse, Katie would never see them. She desperately wished she had made the time to take Katie back east to see her parents. They were both her and Katie's link to the past. Now it was too late. Her sad reverie was interrupted by Katie's voice. "What's wrong, Mama?"

"I just had a phone call from North Carolina," she answered. "It was a highway patrolman. He told me that Papa had died during the night. Also, Cole died," she finished the sad summary of the phone call.

"Oh, no, Mama, they aren't dead," Katie answered. "They were here a while ago," she continued.

"What do you, mean, Honey? Who was here a while ago?"

And then, abruptly, before Katie could reply, the woman exclaimed, "Katie! You're not upstairs in bed! How did you get down here? And you're standing!" she continued in shocked surprise.

"Oma, Papa and Cole were here, Mama," Katie answered. "I walked down here. Oma and Papa came upstairs, and when I woke up, they were standing by my bed. Even Cole was standing there, wagging her tail," Katie concluded.

"I still don't understand how you got down here," Mama said. "Did Papa carry you?"

"No, Mama. He picked me up, and said, "Katie, you didn't know your leg got well during the night, did you?'"

Mama continued, in shocked disbelief, "But, Honey, I just had a call from the police in North Carolina telling me that Papa and Cole had died during the night."

"Mama, they were here," Katie insisted. "Papa fixed my leg, even though he said it got well during the night," she concluded.

"I don't believe it!" her mother stated.

"Look, Mama!" Katie said excitedly. She then scampered up the stairs, disappearing from sight. Momentarily she reappeared, skipping lightly down the stairs. Her mother noted that the child gripped a stick, or some object in one hand as she approached.

"What's that, Katie?" her mother asked, still in a state of near shock.

"It's a Christmas Cane, Mama. Papa gave it to me. He said he made it for me for a Christmas present." Katie extended the cane to her mother.

Accepting the cane, Katie's mother examined it closely. It was a walking stick, with an exquisitely carved Christ Child's head on the top. On the side of the cane, near the head, was carved, "From Papa to Katie." Approximately midway down the shaft of the cane was carved the name, "Katie." The cane was just the right length for a child Katie's age.

Still trying to sort out what the child was telling her, Mama asked, "Where did Oma, Papa and Cole go when they left here, Katie?" She hopefully wanted the child to tell her that her parents were staying in a nearby hotel, thereby discrediting the phone call from the patrolman in North Carolina.

Katie's answer dislodged any hope the phone call was in error. "I asked them where they were going, Mama. Papa told me they were going to see a little Baby in a manger in a place called Bethlehem. What is a manger, Mama?" Katie ended her answer with a question.

"It's a box to hold hay for cows and horses to eat, Katie. It's usually found in a barn where livestock sleep for the night. The Holy Bible tells us that the Baby Jesus was born in a barn, and had to sleep in a manger because there was no room in any of the inns in Bethlehem."

Katie accepted her mother's answer. But her mother still had trouble accepting the fact that her parents, along with their dog, were here on Christmas Eve, and that Katie's deformed leg was now cured. That, coupled with the phone call from the patrolman, was too much for logic to accept.

Believable or not; logical or not, two facts were inescapable. Katie's deformed leg was deformed no longer, and she was the proud possessor of a cane carved for her by Papa.

"Come here, Honey," she said to Katie. As Katie walked into her mother's outstretched arms, her mother said, "Katie, I think we owe a prayer to the Little Baby in the manger. I think we should thank Him for the wonderful gift He gave us on His birthday. You can walk normally now, and Papa brought you one of his canes carved especially for you. This is no doubt the most wonderful Christmas anyone could have, Katie. Merry Christmas!"

She knew, in the midst of her collision of emotions, even though her link to the past through both her parents was now gone, Katie had a strong link with the future forged through their visit.

"Merry Christmas to you, too, Mama," Katie replied. She did not mention it, but resolved to ask later in the day why her mother's eyes were brimming over with tears. She couldn't understand why grownups cried when they were happy. But one thing her young mind did understand. She and her mama were both very happy, and she knew it had something to do with the Baby Jesus, Papa and her new Christmas Cane.

MERRY CHRISTMAS!

# GET THAT MOUSE

## BY: DANA T. MOORE, II

A number of years back, as a young Army Major, I had occasion to encounter a very memorable occurrence. My mother-in-law, a tiny dynamo of energy, topping the scales at an impressive 90 pounds, was visiting my family at Fort Benning, Ga. My wife, children, dog, and I came inexorably under her very persuasive influence.

The occurrence I make reference to took place on one of those routine, dull days, frequently following an evening involving a mild overdose of Martinis before dinner. It all started after I had gone to the office.

It seems that . . . .

"Granmere," Lisa said, "Wouldn't you prefer a cup of hot coffee to that cold beer?"

"Child, don't be persnickety with your Grandmother. I've been around long enough to know what's best."

"Okay, Granmere," replied the budding young thirteen year old, wondering at the wisdom of adults.

Sitting quietly in the kitchen, Granmere sipping her beer, and also wondering how in the hell her daughter had gotten hooked up with such a screwball bunch, and Lisa wondering how her mother could have evolved from such an inscrutable woman, Lisa casually glanced through the kitchen door into the dining room. Her eyes idly recorded a little gray mouse darting around in the dining room. Abruptly, Lisa's mind registered what her eyes were observing.

"Granmere! A mouse!" Lisa shouted excitedly.

"Where?" asked Granmere, steely glint of battle clearly evident in her eyes.

"In the dining room," answered Lisa.

"Now, child, don't be alarmed. I'm an old hand with mice. Gimme the broom." Lisa dutifully complied, uneasy about the impending events.

"Now, child, go in the bedroom, and get me a pair of your dad's jump boots."

"Why, Granmere?"

"I don't want that mouse running across my bare feet," Granmere replied. Lisa again complied.

Thus accoutered with boots, long bathrobe, beer in one hand, and broom in the other, Granmere sallied forth to scourge the house of the mouse. Lisa timidly followed, fully aware of Granmere's philosophy of overkill.

"Where is he, child?" Granmere demanded briskly.

Lisa, with an intuitive feeling of impending disaster, looked apprehensively about. "There, Granmere, under the bookcase."

Taking one aggressive step forward, and dropping her can of beer, Granmere drew back, and let go with the broom, muttering, "Get that mouse!" The mouse casually evaded the attack, and scornfully darted under the dining table.

"There he is, Granmere," shouted Lisa, pointing under the table.

Granmere unleashed another mouse mashing blow with her broom. Thwarted by the table, the death dealing broom struck the table top, glanced off, and landed squarely against Lisa's chest.

"Thwack!"

Lisa sailed cleanly across the living-dining room area, and landed on her backside, snug up against the coffee table.

"Get that mouse!" Lisa heard, blinking her dazed eyes.

"Oh, My Gawd! Breast Cancer!" Lisa thought, gingerly feeling her training bra. "Breast cancer, and at my age, too!"

"Crash!" Lisa heard, becoming aware of the ensuing conflict. Her mind however, was riveted on one thought; "Breast cancer!"

"Get that mouse!" was the battle cry.

"Crash! Crinkle!" went the fine crystal glass on the buffet. The mouse disdainfully ran back under the now demolished book case.

"Get that mouse!" shouted Granmere, winding up for another blow.

"Oh, My Gawd! Breast cancer!" came the plaintive background lament.

"Shatter, Crash!" went a beautiful Dresden lamp, giving up the ghost to the scythe like strokes of the broom. "Gotta get that mouse!" shouted Granmere.

Just about this time, the Moore's little, 70 pound Airdale Terrier, "Boo-Boo," ambled sleepily from the bedroom. Surveying the increasing disarray of combat, Boo-Boo wondered, "What the hell's going on?"

"Mouse, Boo-Boo!" shouted Granmere.

"Mouse?" thought Boo-Boo, his licorice nose beginning to quiver.

"Over there, Boo-Boo," yelled Granmere, pointing with her broom.

Boo-Boo, the curley black and tan hackles of his back beginning to rise, gleefully joined the fray. Boo-Boo caught a fleeting glimpse of the now worried gray mouse as it scampered under an expensive Grand Rapids chair. Boo-Boo followed.

"Swish," hissed the broom.

"Growf," growled Boo-Boo.

The mouse darted safely out the other side as the chair rocketed skyward, and crashed through a picture window.

"Get that mouse!" shouted Granmere.

"This is fun. Wish she would visit more often," thought Boo-Boo as he cheerfully pressed the attack.

"Oh, My Gawd! Breast cancer! I wonder if surgery would help?"

While all this household mayhem was underway, Joanne, Lisa's mother, was finishing her morning shower. Briskly toweling herself, and looking intently into the mirror to insure she had emplaced enough hair curlers, she became faintly aware that all was not as it should be. When the mirror began to shake, she decided to find out what was going on.

"That damned Boo-Boo again!" she thought, hastily flinging a bathrobe about herself, and striding purposefully into the living room. She was instantly confronted with a living, panoramic display of efficient destruction in process. Her mind was shocked by the scene of a gray mouse darting across the dining room floor, followed by a happily yawping Boo-Boo, in turn followed by a determined Granmere, clutching a tattered broom. Lisa was propped against the coffee table, moaning, "No man would marry a woman who had lost her breasts." Additionally, Joanne's shocked mind registered the fact that her normally well kept living room had been reduced to something worse than shambles.

"Get that mouse!" resounded the battle cry.

"Under the dining room table, Boo-Boo," shouted Granmere.

The dining room table seemed to defy gravity as it flew upward.

"Crash! Crunch! Tinkle! went the rare collection of Japanese porcelain, as Granmere's perpetually moving broom took its toll.

"Get that mouse!" repeated Granmere.

"Oh hell! Why couldn't I have been a Nun?" thought Joanne as she pursued Granmere, thereby unwittingly joining the destructive caravan. Sobbingly in the background, "No breasts! Oh, My Gawd! Breast cancer!"

"Bing, Bong, Bing," chimed the doorbell. Joanne was dimly aware of the chimes in the background. "Perhaps," she thought, "If I ignore it, they'll think no one is here, and go away." Realizing that no one in his right mind would think the house unoccupied, Joanne disengaged herself from the pursuit, and walked to the door in answer to the insistent doorbell.

Jerking the front door open, she was confronted by two glossy booted, sunglassed, burly Military Police, complete with armbands and .45 automatic pistols.

"Lady, we've had reports of a fight going on here."

"No, Sergeant, we're only trying to kill a mouse," replied Joanne. Unfortunately, at that moment, Granmere, in the process of scaling an overturned chair, with her broom inadvertently placed between her legs, passed momentarily into the Sergeant's view.

With bulging eyes, and an incredulous look on his face, the Sergeant said, "Lady, you're practicing witchcraft here. I just saw one fly by."

"Now, Sergeant, you're imagining things," Joanne responded placatingly.

Perhaps timely, or otherwise, Granmere, on her next pass around the room, spotted the two MP's. She slid to an abrupt stop. With a haughty look upon her face, broom clutched offensively in hand, and unlaced combat boots slapping noisily, she marched over to the front door.

"Officer! Come in here!" Granmere demanded imperiously. "I'm only a Sergeant, Ma'am."

"Never mind that, Officer. Come in here, I said!"

Turning to his partner, the Sergeant said, "Bill, you stay out here. I'm going in. If I don't make it back, you call for reinforcements."

"Are you sure, Sarge?" Bill asked apprehensively.

"I'm sure. After all, we've got to maintain law and order on this post," replied the Sergeant, taking a tentative step by Joanne, standing in the doorway, disheveled hair awry.

"Crash!" went an instantly worthless piece of furniture inside the house. Boo-Boo had struck again.

"Come on, Officer," said Granmere, gripping the Sergeant firmly by the arm.

"Sergeant, Ma'am," replied the Sergeant, moving briskly into the room, propelled by Granmere's firm grasp.

Granmere said to the Sergeant, "We have a mouse in here. We've got to get that mouse." As if ordained by Divine Authority, the mouse chose this instant to dart across the dining room floor, disappearing under the buffet.

"Swish! Thump!" Went Granmere's broom as she took an ineffective swipe at the mouse. The Sergeant's garrison cap and sun glasses disappeared under the impact of the broom.

"Officer, gimme your pistol!" demanded Granmere. Somewhat shocked by the blow from the broom, and the request for his gun, the Sergeant nevertheless refused. At that particular moment, the mouse darted from beneath the buffet, scaled the wall, and disappeared behind an oil painting of the Alps.

"Thump!" went the broom.

"Crash!" went the painting, plummeting to the floor. Granmere had struck again! The mouse scampered back to the safety of the buffet.

"Now, lemme have that pistol, Officer!"

"Sergeant, Ma'am. No, but I'll shoot him for you, if you wish."

"I wish," replied Granmere. With that, the Sergeant drew his pistol. Granmere said, "Right there! Shoot right there!" pointing at the buffet.

"In the middle of the buffet, Ma'am?" asked the disbelieving Sergeant.

"Yes, By damn! We've got to get that mouse." affirmed Granmere.

Shrugging his shoulders, the Sergeant took aim with his leveled gun, and fired into the middle of the buffet. "Blam!" Bits and pieces of wood, glass, newspapers, and other odds and ends issued from the gaping hole in the buffet. The mouse darted from beneath the smoking buffet, and dashed to the safety of the living room sofa.

While this activity with the Sergeant took place, Boo-Boo momentarily tired of the chase, was sprawled on the floor, tongue lolling from one side of his toothy mouth. He viewed the Sergeant with dislike, remembering, "That's the S-O-B who chased me away when I had those cats cornered." He therefore kept a rather limpidly alert eye on the Sergeant. Boo-Boo didn't trust the man with the glossy boots.

"Officer!" said Granmere, "If my son-in-law didn't soldier any better than you shoot that pistol, he would have been fired out of the army years ago."

"Sergeant, Ma'am. All I am is a Sergeant."

"Oh, My Gawd! Breast cancer! I wonder how much longer I have!"

Boo-Boo, now aware that the Sergeant had somehow interrupted the happy chase, and knowing the mouse was safely ensconced under the sofa, decided to get things back in motion. Gazing thoughtfully at the Sergeant's sharply creased army green trousers, Boo-Boo thought with anticipation, "Halfway between the knee and the hip!"

While Granmere engaged in heated verbal exchange with the Sergeant, Boo-Boo rose languidly to his feet, tongue now safely between his gleaming white teeth, a vengeful look on his hairy face, and walked slowly up behind the Sergeant.

"Officer, as I was saying," continued Granmere.

"Sergeant, Ma'am."

"Growf! Riiiiip!" And thus a gleaming white thigh was exposed.

"He bit me!" shouted the Sergeant.

"Why not, Officer. You missed the mouse."

"Well, I won't miss him! exploded the Sergeant, swinging his pistol toward Boo-Boo.

"Swish!" went the broom. "Thunk!" went the pistol as it landed in the corner of the living room. The mouse, as if on cue, darted from beneath the sofa. Boo-Boo, in full cry, happily resumed the chase. Granmere followed, shouting, "Get that mouse!" The Sergeant joined in hot pursuit.

Joanne, still standing in the doorway, pushed a curl of dark hair from her eyes, and moaned, "Oh no. Not him, too."

Now, while all this was taking place at home, Major Moore was suffering at work. The overdose of Martinis from the night before was still taking its toll.

"Perhaps the quiet and tranquility of my peaceful home, combined with a cold beer, might serve to resurrect the day. I really don't have much to do here at the office, anyway," he rationalized. "Might as well cool it at the house for a while." And so, Major Moore headed unknowingly for home.

Driving into his parking area, the Major noted an MP jeep sitting there, with an MP leaning against it. Pulling up beside the jeep, Major Moore climbed from his car, nodding to the MP.

Saluting, the MP said, "If I was you, Major, I wouldn't go in there. All hell has broke loose."

"Whattaya mean?" asked Major Moore, the beginnings of apprehension stirring his stomach, still unsteady from last night's Martinis.

"There's one hell of a fight going on in there, Sir. I've already called for reinforcements."

"In my house?" gasped the Major, voice rising with incredulity.

"Yes, Sir, if that's your house. Not only that, Sir, but there's a witch in there, raising pluperfect hell!"

"Granmere!" Major Moore sprinted up the sidewalk to his front door.

Stepping by his wife, and through the doorway, Major Moore was confronted with total chaos. Joanne stood in the doorway, hair mussed, holding her head in her hands, moaning, "Oh, no!"

Major Moore caught a glimpse of a gray streak as the mouse dashed across the living room, followed by a gleefully yawping Boo-Boo, now clad in sun glasses and garrison cap. A broom swinging Granmere ran a close third, shouting, "Get that mouse!" This rapidly moving stream of household destruction was rounded up by an angry, raggedy trousered MP shouting, "He bit me! Gimme back my gawddamned hat and glasses!" In the background, "Oh, My Gawd! Breast cancer!"

"Maybe," thought Major Moore, "If I close my eyes, it will all go away." He momentarily clenched his eyes tightly shut. However, just to dispel any doubt, another beautiful lamp sailed across the living room and crashed sickenly into the wall.

"Get that mouse!"

"Growf!"

"Gimme them damned glasses and hat!"

"Oh, My Gawd! Breast cancer!"

"I'll be damned," thought Major Moore. "The last time I saw anything like this was on D Day, during the Normandy invasion.

"Gestoppen! Halten Sie! Stop, Damnit!" shouted the Major, availing himself of the only two languages he knew. The tumult continued.

Spotting the Sergeant's pistol in the corner of the living room, Major Moore dashed over, scooped up the gun, and with one fluid motion, raised it, and fired a round into the ceiling.

"Kerblam!"

The result was like a stop action shot on TV. Everything ceased abruptly. "All right, someone tell me what in the hell's going on here!" shouted Major Moore. No response.

"What about it, Sergeant?"

"Officer, Sir," replied the Sergeant, a glazed expression on his face.

"What about it, Granmere?"

"This damned officer couldn't even shoot a mouse!" said Granmere, pointing to the Sergeant.

"He's a Sergeant, Granmere," Major Moore corrected.

"Officer, Sir," said the thoroughly brainwashed Sergeant.

Ignoring Granmere and the Sergeant for the moment, Major Moore spoke sharply to his daughter. "Stop that moaning, Lisa. You have to have breasts before you can have breast cancer."

"Are you sure?" sniffled Lisa, clutching her training bra.

"Well," said Major Moore, glancing around the wrecked living-dining room area, "Enough has been done here; enough to last a lifetime." Pausing, and then extending the Sergeant's belongings to him, Major Moore continued, "Sergeant, here's your cap, glasses, and gun. Tell your partner to call off the replacements."

Holstering his pistol, and replacing his cap and glasses, the Sergeant walked over to the front door, followed by Major Moore, Granmere, Boo-Boo, and Lisa.

"I'm okay, Bill," shouted the Sergeant. "No need for help." Joanne still stood in the doorway.

And then, a surprising thing happened. The mouse, giving up his sofa sanctuary, sauntered casually out the open door. As everyone stared in disbelief, the mouse stopped, turned, and looked disdainfully at the gathering. Then, he very impudently shrugged his shoulders, turned once again, and strolled leisurely away across the lawn.

THE END

# THE MOUNTAIN THAT WASN'T THERE

BY: DANA T. MOORE, II

He could tell this was going to be one of those days; one of those days when things start badly, and then get worse. Beginning with a roaring start, he had "busted" the launch. Busting a launch is that highly undesirable situation aboard an aircraft carrier when no more than half of the squadron's scheduled planes remain in commission for launch. In this case it was particularly bad since it was the first launch of the day, often called the "First Light Go." Busting a launch tends to get people in a bad humor. His Commanding Officer, or "Skipper," was scheduled to fly the first light go, and his was the first plane to abort. That in itself was enough to spoil the day. The Skipper didn't like to get up at 0400, brief, strap in, start up, taxi forward to the catapult, and then have his plane not check out for flight. In naval aviation jargon, this is known as "going down." The plane was down. This was especially disconcerting when the skipper of one of the rival squadrons, turning up on the parallel cat, gave his skipper the finger just before giving the okay for the cat shot. Yes, as maintenance officer, he would hear about that from the skipper when he got back to the ready room.

There were others who tended to have their disposition disturbed by having a plane go down on the cat. The Captain of the carrier, a person endowed with godlike characteristics and authority, had a tendency to temper tantrums when this happened. A down plane meant a delayed launch, which in turn meant steaming into the wind at higher power longer than the Captain thought necessary. For one thing, this carrier, the USS Intrepid, CVA-11, was of world war two vintage, and turning up enough power for air operations put a strain on the old lady. Not that she couldn't take it, but like an old war horse, there was no point in making her work too hard for her oats. Added to this was the fact that charging through the water usually resulted in getting the ship a long way from its assigned station. This required a hurried run back to designated waters. Inevitably this resulted in some caustic comments from the bridge, spoken over the bullhorn so that everyone on the flight deck knew who the offending maintenance officer was, along with some frequent information pertaining to his ancestry.

And then there was the flight deck officer. This poor soul often caught hell from every senior officer on the ship, from the captain on down. His job was to coordinate all activities on the flight deck before, during, and after the launch. His was the responsibility for providing the necessary deck personnel supervision to insure all launches and recoveries proceeding with clockwork precision. When a plane went down in the midst of launch, it invariably caused a delay, and added to the flight deck officer's gray hair. If this delay occurred while planes were airborne, awaiting recovery, usually low on fuel, the result of a delay in launch was guaranteed to give him a severe case of falling hair, stomach ulcers, and nightmares, frequently followed by fits of foul mouth. Naturally, he would then seek out the offending squadron maintenance officer, and divest himself of his anxieties and tensions. No one is as adept at unburdening himself as colorfully as a flight deck officer. Very few people possess such a vivid collection of blue adjectives.

Yes, this was going to be one of those days.

Mr. Moore was the aircraft maintenance officer in fighter squadron thirty three, or in Naval parlance, VF-33. He was also, among other things, a USAF fighter pilot on exchange with the U.S. Navy for two years of carrier duty. As maintenance officer he was required to look after the status of his 13 shipboard jet fighter aircraft, supervise some 200 enlisted men, stand scheduled bridge watches, and all the while function as a full time fighter pilot in the squadron. As maintenance officer, he was the one who had committed the aircraft to the operations section for today's flying, and it was his job to deliver. He had not delivered today. Even the spare aircraft went down.

It was standard procedure to position a spare plane and pilot on the flight deck for each launch. Since this morning's schedule called for six planes and pilots, seven of each had been readied for flight. To Moore's dismay, the spare, and one primary had gone down on the engine start order. Added to this was the Skipper's abort on the cat. If the Skipper had gotten airborne, things wouldn't have been so bad. Mr. Moore learned long ago that a good flight makes a happy skipper, and a happy skipper makes happy people. Right now, Moore felt like strapping his own backside to the catapult, and having the cat officer shoot him off the bow into the water.

Proceeding below to the hangar bay, Mr. Moore reflected on the Skipper's safety policy. The Skipper had often told the pilots, "If the plane isn't okay, don't go." After all, a lost flight is a small concession when compared to a pilot and plane in the water, a situation not recommended for longevity. Once the catapult fires, pilot and plane are going, regardless. If the plane isn't airworthy, and the pilot accepts it anyway, he has just bought himself a lot of problems, not the least of which might be a watery grave. The pilots in the down planes this morning were merely following instructions, and good judgment.

"Well," he thought, "better get on with it." The Skipper is going to want some answers. Mr. Moore walked briskly aft along the starboard side of the hangar deck. Approaching the maintenance chief's office, he spotted Chief Petty Officer Thomas, his maintenance chief, and right hand man. Before Moore could open his mouth, Chief Thomas said, "Have a mug of coffee first, then I'll brief you."

Thomas handed him a mug of steaming, black coffee, and drew one for himself. Moore then said, "Okay, Tommy, give me the rundown."

"To begin, Mr. Moore, the Skipper's plane sheared the afterburner pump drive shaft. Material failure. The spare had corroded wires in the starter switch. The other primary couldn't get any nose wheel steering. This was all the result of our extended stay in Naples. Remember, I asked you if we could turn up each plane just once during that 10 day port period." The request had been refused because engine noise would have disturbed the sensitive ears of the Neopolitans.

"Thanks, Tommy. I've gotta get on up to the ready room for a little arse-chewing exercise. The Skipper has had enough time to get ready for me." Chief Thomas shook his head in an exaggerated gesture of mock sympathy.

Stepping into the ready room, Mr. Moore caught sight of the Skipper talking with a small group of squadron pilots. The Skipper, seeing him, nodded his head, and continued his conversation. Moore walked over to the ever present coffee pot, selected his personal mug from a wall peg board, and poured himself one of the many mugs of coffee consumed during the course of the day. He often thought the Navy sailed on coffee, rather than salt water.

Momentarily, the Skipper detached himself from the group of pilots, and with a serious expression on his face, walked across the ready room toward Moore.

"Here it comes," thought Moore.

"Tell me the story of the broken airplanes, Bluebelt." The nickname, alluding to Moore's USAF uniform, didn't conceal the gravity in the tone of voice.

Without wasting words, Moore repeated Chief Thomas' earlier explanation for the poor showing this morning, being sure to remind the Skipper of the refused request to authorize an engine turnup while in port. Much to Moore's surprise, the Skipper received the explanation without comment, making only a noncommittal grunt of acceptance.

The Skipper was silent a few moments, and then, "I hope you can glue those birds back together for the rest of the day's schedule, and keep them that way. We were just committed to launch four on the twilight go tonight. You'll be on that schedule."

"We'll make it, Skipper."

Mr. Moore received the news of the scheduled night ops without a change of expression. He did, however, view it with a feeling of mixed emotion. He shared the opinion of the naval aviators about night ops from a carrier. He knew it was necessary, but also considerably risky. He often thought of it as, "Flying around in a bottle of ink." Simultaneously he felt a flush of pride in being on the night schedule. Because of the limited capability of the day fighters at night, and the inherent risk involved, the Skipper had restricted the number of squadron pilots authorized for night ops. Moore was one of the six pilots so cleared. It was an acknowledgement of his professional skill as a pilot.

With considerable effort, Chief Thomas and his maintenance men hung in and met the remainder of the day's operational schedule.

As Chief Thomas and Mr. Moore observed the last day recovery around 1700 hours, or 5:00 p.m., they were both thinking of the night schedule. "Tommy, those damn planes are just like people! The longer they sit, the slower they are to get off their butts. Just to make sure for tonight, put two spares on deck for the launch. If the four primaries get off, you'll already have two up for tomorrow's first go." Thomas nodded agreement, mentally calculating the number of men who would draw short rations on sleep tonight.

Observing the last plane taxi out of the arresting gear, the two men headed below to their respective dining areas. They didn't have long to grab a quick meal before night ops commenced. After a hasty meal in the wardroom, Mr. Moore hurried to the ready room for a detailed, but routine pre-flight briefing. He was to fly number three in a flight of four, led by the Skipper. The mission called for a join up right after launch; a climb in battle formation to 35,000 feet altitude, and then a separation into two sections of two planes to practice shipboard radar controlled intercepts. After the intercept portion of the mission, the flight was scheduled to separate into singles for the remainder of the flight, with each pilot to make an individual shipboard radar controlled recovery.

Weather was briefed as an insignificant factor for the evening, although by recovery time there was to be multiple layers of clouds from 3,500 feet up to 25,000 feet. This entailed an instrument approach through the clouds, but at night, all approaches to landing aboard ship were under instrument conditions anyway.

The carrier was to operate in an area 50 miles west of the coastal city of Livorno, Italy. Except in emergency conditions, the planes were not allowed to come within 10 miles of land. All flying over sovereign territory, without prior arrangement and approval, was prohibited. Surface winds were from the west, dictating a recovery from the east, near the coast of Italy. The combination of surface winds, the carrier's location, weather aloft, recovery procedures, and proximity of the land mass was going to produce a totally unexpected, unexplained and unusual situation later in the evening.

The launch, join up, climb out and intercept portion of the mission went according to briefing. The last intercept was completed just as darkness closed in. Each pilot was then assigned an individual altitude, radio frequency, and approach time. After individual check in with the shipboard radio, the flight separated, each pilot proceeding on his own.

Nearing his approach time, Moore headed toward the general area of the recovery fix. He contacted the carrier, and requested recovery directions. He was told to report arriving at the 35 mile fix, 090 degree radial, at 20,000 feet. Translated, this meant, call in on the radio when he was inbound 35 miles east of the carrier, on a radio track of due west at 20,000 feet altitude. This was standard procedure. The thought of miles, carrier location, and his assigned position of 35 miles east told him that he was left with only a 15 mile buffer separating him from land mass overfly.

"Cutting it pretty close," he thought. He was confident, however, that the people aboard ship knew what they were doing. Besides, in following their instructions, he was technically absolved of any responsibility associated with an inadvertent penetration of sovereign airspace. He knew also that recoveries tonight were going to be on a westerly heading, which would be taking the entire operation away from land. Without further concern, he headed for the assigned fix.

Approaching the fix, Moore mentally prepared to make his radio report. One mark of the professional pilot was to keep radio chatter to a minimum. Say what you had to; no more, and no less. Arriving at the fix, he pressed the mike button on the throttle, and transmitted, "Atlas, 204 at the fix." This simple declarative statement said a lot. He had, addressing the ship by call sign, given his call sign, and told them he was over the fix. No more, and no less!

"Roger, 204. Cleared for an approach. Check through ten, five, gate and 500 feet." The ship had told him a lot also. He was to call when passing through ten thousand feet altitude, five thousand feet, passing a point 15 miles astern of the ship, and when level at 500 feet above the water.

Prior to descending to 20,000 feet, he had been flying in bright moonlight, with a full moon reflecting off the clouds below him. At 20,000 he was in and out of the clouds. This was no problem to an experienced pilot. In fact, he thought, it was, "Like shooting fish in a barrel." Just a routine, straight ahead descent.

He reduced power to descent setting, lowered the speed brakes, and started down, holding a constant 250 knots on the airspeed indicator. He noted that he was descending through multi layered clouds with breaks in them. These breaks in the clouds allowed the bright moonlight to illuminate the clouds around him. Passing through these intermittent openings, he cast a quick glance ahead, and then returned his eye scan to the instrument panel upon reentering the clouds.

Descending through 13,000 feet, he passed into one of the moonlit breaks. Glancing ahead, he was shocked to see a mountain in the middle of his flight path. "Damn!" His reflexes taking over, he simultaneously hauled back on the control stick, jammed the throttle to full power, and retracted the speed brakes. His little fighter responded like the thoroughbred she was, rotating abruptly, and shooting skyward like a rocket.

He didn't know how close he had come to hitting the mountain, but judging by his sphincter tension, he hadn't missed by far. Within seconds, he popped out on top of the clouds. He began to feel that old, familiar stab of pain in his lower back, indicating his adrenalin pump had gone into overdrive. Were it not for that beautiful patch of moonlight, he would have been another of the all too common "Unexplained accidents" in the statistical data of the safety magazines.

His reaction was to call the ship, and give them a piece of his mind for not warning him about the mountain. Getting his temper under control, he kept his silence, and headed back for the fix.

"Atlas, 204. Do you have me under positive radar control?"

"Affirmative, 204."

"Atlas, 204, since you almost ran me into a mountain, I'm at 25,000, and headed back for the fix."

"Negative, 204. There are no mountains in your vicinity. You're over open water," came the laconic reply. "Call at the fix."

Moore returned to the fix, repeated the check in procedure, and received the same infuriatingly impersonal instructions. Once again he established his plane in the prescribed descent configuration, and started down. This time he resolved to be considerably more alert outside his plane than he was before. He'd be damned if he was going to come that close again. One thrill like that per flight was more than enough.

The cloud and moonlight conditions were unchanged. Descending through 15,000 feet, he became even more alert. Passing through 13,000 feet, he was once again momentarily bathed in moonlight, and again there was that plane snaring, death dealing mountain. As before, his reflexes took over before he could will himself to act. His luck held, but he could have sworn he passed even closer to that mountain than before.

This time, when Moore called the ship, the dialogue was a little more terse. He was forbidden by regulation from giving vent to his wrath over the radio, but there were other, more subtle ways to get his feelings across. When the radar operator again informed him that he was flying over open water, with no mountains in his vicinity, Moore thought he detected a note of bored unconcern in the detached voice coming through his headset. This was tantamount to being told he didn't know what he was doing, and had probably allowed his normal apprehension of night flying to cause him to conjure up an imaginary situation that didn't exist.

"Atlas, 204. I'll make an approach from overhead the ship this time. In the meantime, perhaps you ought to make sure you haven't spilled your nice hot cup of coffee all over your radar scope."

"Roger, 204," came the even more impersonal reply. Moore felt better. He had gotten his meaning across.

The situation was now beginning to be a little sticky. The two aborted approaches, coupled with the high power setting used to avoid hitting the mountain, had bitten into his fuel reserve. His fuel wasn't critical yet, but it was down to the level where, along with the game of mountain tag, it was a pucker factor to be considered.

Reaching 20,000 feet, he throttled back to minimum power, and headed directly for the carrier, homing in with his radio navigation equipment. Passing over the ship, he called in over the radio that he was beginning his recovery descent, and began a descending left turn, heading out to a point 10 miles abeam. When he was on the opposite heading from the ship, he shallowed his turn in order to maintain the 10 mile separation he wanted.

Just as forecast, the bottom of the clouds was at 3,500 feet. Below, the black ocean waited to embrace him with its deadly, moist grasp. He leveled at 1,500 feet, and slowed to approach speed, continuing to turn back into the carrier. Completing his circling descent, he lowered his wheels, flaps, and tail hook. He continued his descent to 500 feet.

"Atlas, 204 five miles astern at 500 feet, with all down for landing."

"204, Atlas. Roger your position. This isn't your night, 204. The landing mirror just crumped. What are your intentions?"

That unforeseen emergency! The landing mirror was a device mounted on the left rear of the flight deck. It gave the pilot a visual flight path to follow down to the 50 foot target area where the arresting wires were strung to catch the plane's tail hook, snatching it to a halt, and thus converting it from a jet fighter at 160 mph, to a waddling duck on the flight deck. This arrestment took place in a scant 190 feet. Without the mirror, the odds were that he would miss the arresting wires, and shoot off the deck, and back into the air, or worse, into the sea.

"Atlas, 204. My intentions are to land this plane on that carrier on this pass. I don't have the fuel for a divert to the beach."

"Roger, 204. You're cleared to land."

Mr. Moore knew that landing a jet fighter aboard a carrier was a matter of constants, and when to apply them. He knew the proper rate of descent for landing was 1,200 feet per minute, with the approach speed held steady. The trick was in knowing when to start the prescribed rate of descent. The point for starting down was approximately 500 yards astern. This was one of the visual aids provided by the landing mirror. The mirror automatically compensated for the speed of the carrier, the speed of the aircraft, and the necessary angle to assure that plane and carried arrived at the same position at the same time. The rest was mechanical. Once the pilot placed his plane at the right spot at the right time, with the correct approach speed, the hook engaged an arresting wire, and the plane was jerked to an abrupt halt.

Now! His instinct told him to start down. He could see the little dustpan lights imbedded in the carrier's flight deck. They outlined the landing area.

He thought, "Now is the time, if there ever was one, to be steady." He jacked the throttle slightly while concentrating on keeping both the speed and the rate of descent pegged. His eyes flicked back and forth between the dustpan lights, and his plane's instruments. As the first dustpan lights flickered astern, he felt the familiar impact of the wheels with the flight deck. Instantly jamming the throttle wide open, standard procedure on a carrier landing, he was already prepared for the plane to bounce back into the air. Instead, he was subjected to that welcome lunge into the shoulder harness as the arresting gear pulled his plane to an abrupt halt. At the end of the runout, where he could see nothing but the blackness of the greedy ocean, the arresting gear completed its function by jerking his plane backward for 50 feet of recoil. At the same time, he pulled the plane's throttle to idle.

Raising his tail hook, folding his wings, and taxiing out of the arresting gear, he gave vent to a long sigh of relief, and muttered a short prayer of appreciation. "Thanks, Lord. I'll take over now."

Following a mug of coffee in the ready room, Mr. Moore walked aft to the Combat Intelligence Center, or CIC. He wanted a word with the radar operator who had worked him during the "Mountainous" approach to the ship.

Stepping into the dimly lit room with its rows of green tinted radar scopes, and sounds of communications equipment, he asked, "Who worked 204 on the last recovery?"

"I did, Sir," came a reply from the dim recesses of the radar scopes.

Stopping beside the controller, a young ensign, Moore asked in a rather belligerent tone, "Where in the hell did you get that mountain?"

"Sir, there was no mountain there."

"I'll be damned! There sure was a mountain there! I had ample opportunity to look at it. How far was the ship from the coast?"

"We may have been a little inside the 50 mile zone, Sir, but I know there was no mountain anywhere near you on your approach."

The concession of possibly being a little too close to shore was plaintively made, but the statement concerning the absence of any mountains was made with the self assurance of certainty.

"Sir," the ensign continued, the plaintive tone returning, "if the captain finds out about your problem tonight, I'll be in charge of the bilge detail for the rest of this cruise."

Moore felt an immediate sympathy for the young man. He knew how swift, and sometimes painful, disciplinary procedures could be aboard a naval vessel at sea. He had no desire to get the ensign into difficulty.

"That's okay, Son. Just let someone else find that mountain the next time. It will take a gallon of Colorback to get my hair back to normal now. The next time I may not have any hair left."

Moore knew that his successful landing, despite the mirror failure, far overshadowed any problems he had on the approach phase, and if he kept silent, no one would know about it.

Turning to leave CIC, Mr. Moore halted abruptly, leaned down, and stared intently at the radar scope.

"Nope. Don't see any coffee on it."

With a trace of a grin on his face, and glancing sidewise at the ensign, Moore walked out of CIC. He had had the last word.

Walking to the maintenance office to check on the aircraft status for tomorrow's schedule, Moore kept pondering the mountain. He knew damn well he had almost flown into a mountain. There was no doubt in his mind. The ensign had seemed equally as sure the mountain wasn't there. Possibly the ship had been closer to shore than any of them realized. Possibly his airborne navigation equipment was faulty. He recalled not being able to see the ground, nor the ocean from 25,000 feet. Regardless, there was a mountain there. While thinking it over, an oft repeated statement his mother used to make in times of crisis, popped into his mind.

"God looks after fools, babies, and drunkards."

He was too old to be a baby. Naval regulations prohibited alcohol aboard ship. He knew the category that left for him.

# MUTE MATE

## BY: DANA T. MOORE, II

Placing the last dish in the dishwasher, and slowly drying her hands on a towel, she walked into the living room, pleasantly anticipating an enjoyable respite, watching her favorite soap opera. She was not a person addicted to watching television, especially during the day, but there was one hourly program to which she treated herself. She looked forward to it each day during the work week, secure in the knowledge she was neither a wastrel, nor a slothful housewife.

Her anticipation was heightened by two significant facts. This was a Friday in the Christmas season, and her soaper was approaching a Christmas crisis. The second factor was the recent purchase of a new, wide screen, color television, complete with remote control tuner, and channel changer, containing an invaluable muting device, used to silence the sound of the set; a particularly handy feature during commercials. This new television was an agreed upon Christmas gift, from her husband, and from her, to each other. They had ordered the new set delivered early in order that they could enjoy it for the entire holiday season.

"Damnation!" She nearly burst out.

Sprawled in her favorite recliner chair, beer clutched in hand, eyes locked onto the television, was her husband, intently staring at a wrestling match in progress. She had forgotten that, as a school teacher, he was home from work on Christmas vacation.

"Double Damnation!" she continued thinking. "Why doesn't he watch the television in our bedroom? That was the purpose in having two sets." She was convinced, even if there was only one channel to watch, they would disagree on the selection of a program.

"Well, this is my time. I'm gonna watch my program on the new television, and if he doesn't like it, he can go watch wrestling on the set in the bedroom. Or better still," she mentally amended, "he can go jump in the lake." With that, she walked to the TV, and changed the channel to the one featuring her program.

As she turned to demand her husband surrender her chair, he casually flicked the remote tuner, and returned the selection to the wrestling program. Now she was boiling mad inside.

"One hour a week, and I have to give that up to watch a pair of fugitives from weight watchers obscenely grappling one another around the ring in an obviously faked contest! Hell! I'm not gonna!" she thought determinedly. Once again she turned, and changed the channel selector. This time she stood before the television, rendering the remote tuner ineffective by the obstruction of her body.

"Owww, Honey, I wanta watch wrestling," her husband wailed, his tone of voice plaintively pleading.

"Well, I don't," she replied, her lower jaw protruding pugnaciously. "You get to watch everything you want. This time, I'm gonna watch my program on the new set. You can go watch wrestling on the one in our bedroom. It's also in color, and has an excellent picture." With that, she turned, and standing with arms akimbo, her body still obstructing the tuner, stared belligerently at her husband.

His facial expression was now equally belligerent.

Walking to her husband, she reached out, and took the remote tuner from his hand, then said, "My chair, please."

He stood, and stepped aside.

Ignoring him, she sank into her recliner, and tilting it back to a comfortable position, fastened her attention on the tense action in her program.

"By Gawd! I don't know if I'm gonna take this," her husband began, his chest puffing in righteous, male indignation, belt dropping slightly with the upward shift in center of gravity.

"Go away," she responded absent mindedly, attention riveted on the tense domestic drama unfolding on the TV screen, ignoring the domestic disruption building beside her.

"I'm telling you, I'm not gonna take it!" he yelled louder. "You can't push me around like this. I have rights, too."

Still gazing intently at the TV, but in a casual, ho-hum manner, she aimed the remote device toward her husband, and depressed the "Mute" button. What followed was a welcome surprise. It was all of half a minute before she realized her husband was still spewing vitriol about her brash takeover of the viewing menu, and even worse, in his mind, because of her calm disregard of his displeasure. Finally, becoming aware of his unbroken tirade, she returned her fascinated gaze to him.

Her response to what she saw was surprise, then shock, and finally, disbelief. Her husband was talking, at least that's what his mouth indicated, but there was no sound. It was exactly as if she had turned his voice off with the muting element of the remote unit. Apparently, she quickly deduced, he was unaware of his silence, as verified by his red face, the veins standing out on his neck, and his brow deeply knit in anger. His jaw moved just like the mouth of a ventriloquist's dummy, without benefit of the "thrown" voice.

Hastily pressing the mute button on the remote unit, she was relieved to hear, ". . . ., and I'm telling you, I'm gonna have my say in what we watch on the TV in this house from now on."

Depressing the mute button again, she was rewarded with husbandly silence, accompanied by the apparent automatic mouth movement. The only sound was that coming from her TV soaper. She darted a glance at the TV, then returned her gaze to her perturbed pedagogue.

Pressing the mute button, it was an on-off switch, she again heard her husband's voice resume, ". . . ., and I think, as master of the house, that chair should be mine, too." She quickly hit the mute button, and was again rewarded with the silent harangue.

Not daring to believe her good fortune, she quickly ran through a mental review of the current "dummy" act being carried out before her. If what she thought happened, had actually happened, then she had stumbled upon a treasure trove beyond comprehension. Think what most housewives would give for the controlled capability of temporarily tempering a tyrannical husband; especially when the toning down would be at a critical time such as this.

"What the hell!" she thought, "Friday afternoons are crisis times in the lives of us soaper saps, sufficiently so, as to disallow disruption by disgruntled husbands. The muted mate is an unlimited, undisguised blessing."

However, all thoughts of her soaper evaporated in the face of this overwhelming development. She had to think it over, and do a little research. Pointing the remote unit toward the TV, she changed the channel back to the wrestling, and stood from her chair, saying, with mock meekness, "All right, Dear, you may have the chair, and watch your wrestling."

As her husband sank into the comfortable recliner, facial expression bright with male dominance, she unobtrusively directed the remote unit at him, and pressed the mute button. Sound once again issued from the unbroken flow of the macho, masculine motor mouth.

Stepping slightly out of her husband's line of sight, and in a tone of feigned female fragility, she asked, "Why are those wrestlers so mean to one another?"

When her husband replied, in a tone of masculine superiority, she heard, "If you would watch more, and talk less, . . . .," the mute button interrupted the rest of the peremptory putdown. When his mouth stopped, and he was once again absorbed in the wrestling, she "unmuted" him, and left the room.

In the kitchen, she mentally recapped this amazing situation. "I can turn his voice off and on at will, whether he is speaking or not. Apparently he is unaware that he has been muted, since he keeps right on talking, even though I hear nothing. Also, there seems to be no physical damage involved, so it's safe to turn him on or off." Reviewing that last thought, she chuckled aloud. "Hell, I've been turning him on and off for years, and he's never known that, either. It's truly a woman's world," she concluded, secure in her new found power.

"I need to do a little more research," she continued thinking. "I should find out if I can mute anyone else, and if it will work against me." With that, she began murmuring in a barely audible tone, and while doing so, aimed the remote unit at herself, and pressed the mute button. Her voice continued, "But I'm really not sure if anyone else can hear me or not. What I need is someone I can trust to give me a little help. Who?"

Abruptly, she broke into laughter. "I know who'll help me. Granny! She'll get a kick out of the whole thing, and I know she'll keep it to herself. She'll really enjoy seeing my husband's mouth turned off for a change. I'll give her a call." Granny was the family's affectionate name for her mother.

Dialing the phone, she heard Granny's voice, then asked, "Hello, Granny, can you hear me?" She remembered she had not lifted the self-mute condition.

Hearing Granny's repeated, "Hello, Hello," she aimed the remote at herself, and pressed the mute button.

"Can you hear me now, Granny?" she asked.

"Of course, I can hear you. Why shouldn't I?" Granny replied.

"I wasn't sure," she answered, then continued, "May I come over for a few minutes? I have something to discuss with you."

"Anything wrong?" Granny asked.

"No. Nothing at all. Just something I need to talk to you about. I'll be right over."

"I'm going to Granny's for a while," she called to her husband, certain he didn't hear a word she said, and equally confident he didn't give a damn anyway. The wrestling match took care of that. Donning a coat, and stuffing the remote unit in her purse, she walked out the back door to the garage. Following the two block drive, she knocked, and opened the front door to her widowed mother's home.

Granny met her in the foyer with, "Are you sure there's nothing wrong?"

"Positive, but let's have some coffee, and I'll tell you something out of this world."

"Come on in the kitchen," Granny said, leading the way.

Minutes later, seated at the kitchen table, each with a steaming mug of black coffee, she related the tale of the remote unit.

"Incredulous!" Granny said, "This I've gotta see. For once I want to see that overweight, overbearing, overconfident, over-the-hill Lardbutt with nothing but the real thing coming out of his mouth: hot air!"

"Now, Granny, he isn't all that bad."

Casting a jaded glance at her daughter, Granny was silent for a moment, then, "I do think we ought to check this out a little further. We should find out if it works on anyone other than Lardbutt."

Ignoring her mother's favorite disparaging title of her husband, she acknowledged the need for further investigation of the muting capabilities she had stumbled upon.

"You haven't tried it on anyone else?" Granny asked.

"Only on myself. I muted myself before I called you on the phone a while ago. That's why I asked if you could hear me. I wasn't sure whether the muted person could hear himself, or at least thinks he's hearing himself when he's been muted. I need to try it on a third person just to make sure. Want to volunteer?"

"You don't think it's dangerous?" Granny asked, her tone of voice wary.

"No. Let's try it."

"Okay, if you're sure," she answered, obviously not sure herself.

"Well, you want to see my husband muted, don't you?"

"Yes, I certainly do," Granny answered, unaware the remote unit was aimed at her. "I'd like to see Lardbutt expending his stock in trade; hot . . .," the mute button terminated the sentence. Granny continued talking, her facial expression changing in context with her comments. ". . . that big boob with the only thing he really has, nothing, coming out of his mouth," resumed the voice, now released from the muting constraint.

"Could you hear yourself all along, Granny?"

"Why, yes, of course." Then, realization dawning, "Did you do it to me?" she asked, astounded at the thought.

"Yes, and you didn't even know it. It's obvious the muted speaker doesn't know he's had his sound turned off."

"Well, I'll be damned! Let's go try it on Lardbutt."

Shortly later, with Granny watching in the background, and the wrestling match still captivating her husband, she dared to ask another frivolous, feminine question. "Don't those big, ugly men ever get tired of throwing each other around on that dirty canvas?"

"That's what they get paid for doing!" barked her husband, annoyed at the interruption. "If you'd keep quiet, and . . . .," the voice stopped, leaving only the raucous sound of the cheering fans on TV The remote tuner still worked. In a moment, his voice returned, once again released from muting. Granny's face showed pure rapture.

Young Son's face, observing unbeknownst to the three adults, showed eager anticipation. The cat was out of the bag!

Two days later, just before soaper time, the phone rang. Before she could get to it, her husband answered on the living room extension. After a few minutes of increasingly loud conversation, he confronted her in the kitchen doorway.

"Can you imagine that? he asked. "The manager of What's

Department Store at the mall called and told me our son had muted their Santa Claus. Said the old duffer was talking to a bunch of kids, and during a long Ho-Ho-Ho, he was cut off in mid-Ho. Nearly had apoplexy before he could talk again, and then the happy Ho-Ho-Ho's changed to unhappy obscenities. Said our son used a TV remote tuner to mute Santa. Can you believe such nonsense? What're the merchants gonna think up next to get a little publicity? At least they oughta leave Santa alone." Shaking his head in disbelief, he returned to his program on TV

The cat was indeed out of the bag, and apparently Santa was in the bag.

She resolved to have a talk with her son as soon as she could find him. Fate must have been reading her thoughts, since her son walked in the back door at that moment.

Grasping him by the arm, and propelling him ahead, she swiftly walked out the door to the garage. "All right, Young Man! Tell me about it! What've you been doing to Santa at the mall?"

Laughing, her son replied, "I saw you and Granny turn Dad off the other day when he was watching the wrestling match. I wasn't sure I'd really seen it, so I decided to try the tuner out on someone else. You should've seen Santa when he couldn't talk!" The memory drove her son into a fit of gleeful laughter. He continued, "I thought Santa was going to explode!"

"How'd he know he was muted," she asked.

"A little girl on his lap started to laugh, and told him he wasn't making any noise with his mouth. Then a group of kids started to laugh. I guess Santa knew something was wrong. I gave him back his voice then, and the kids laughed even more, and asked him to do his 'Dummy Act' again. That's when he really got mad, started cussing, and yelled for the manager."

"How'd you explain it? she asked.

"Hid the tuner in my coat pocket, and played dumb. I think the manager thought Santa was drunk, because he talked to him, then let me go." With that, Son began to laugh again.

"If I ever hear of you doing that again, or for that matter, using that remote tuner on anyone again, I'll tan your bottom so brown you won't be able to sit for a month." Gathering momentum, she continued, "And you'd better remember, this is Christmas time, and I happen to know you're expecting a home computer. You better mind your P's and Q's, and not a word of this to anyone. You hear me?"

He heard. He was crestfallen, and ashamed, not to mention a little apprehensive over the computer. Nodding vigorously, he replied, "I won't use it again, Mom. I promise. And I won't tell anyone, either."

"If you know what's good for you, you'd better keep that promise!"

Pausing a moment, she was struck with a sudden apprehension. "And, my Young Disturber," she resumed speaking, "have you used the tuner on anyone else?" she asked, almost fearful of the answer.

Looking downward, and beginning a nearly imperceptible shuffle, he stammered out a reply. "Well, I, uh . . ., I sorta, . . ., I used it a couple more times, but it was more funny than bad," he finished lamely.

"Damn! I knew it," she thought.

"All right, who else did you use it on?" she asked, fearful resignation in her tone of voice.

Glancing up, and with guilt spread on his face like jam, he slowly worded a reply. "I sorta quieted down a group of Salvation Army singers on the corner of Main and Maple Streets." Pausing, he darted his gaze around the garage, stopping first here, and then there; anywhere but where he might meet his mother's penetrating stare.

"All right, all right!" she exclaimed impatiently, "Let's have the rest of it! Go on! Who else?"

Shoulders slumping, Son answered again, "Well, there was one of those weirdos preaching the end of the world outside What's Store at the mall. He really looked funny after I turned him off. He stood there, mouth running, long hair and long toga waving in the breeze, arms flapping like a bird, until people started to laugh at him. I gave his voice back then, and the crowd really howled."

Suppressing a grin, she spoke, "It may have been funny, but it could be dangerous. I don't know what would happen if you left someone muted. I don't know if he would remain mute, or if the voice would return after a few hours. I don't think we ought to play with this, Son."

He nodded in agreement.

"Where's the tuner now?" she asked.

"I left it in the living room by your chair," he replied.

"Good! See that it stays there!" Then placing an arm around his shoulders, she continued, in a lighter vein, "So Santa was upset, huh? Well, let's not ruin his image before the children again. Okay?"

"Okay, Mom, but he sure was funny," he replied.

That evening, over the phone, she related to her mother the story about her son's escapades with the various victims he had chosen. They both had a big laugh out of it, but agreed the tuner had to be kept under close control. If the story got around, there was no telling what might happen. The potential for mischief was unlimited. They also agreed that the longer before her husband found out about what had taken place, the better it would be for all concerned.

Several days followed, with no further disturbances resulting from the remote TV tuner, other than a few calls from Granny wanting to put the zap on Lardbutt.

Holiday tension was building, but should be considerably more eased later this evening. Tonight's schedule involved mid-night, Christmas Eve services. All the family would attend together, thereby providing the volatile ingredients for a real brouhaha, should in-law antagonism run too high.

"Surely," she thought, "if Granny behaves, none of the rest of the family would spoil Christmas with a fight tonight." Nevertheless, she couldn't dispel a feeling of low-grade apprehension. "Everything will be all right once we get home from church. We'll all be looking forward to opening our Christmas gifts then." Thus reassured, she put aside further worries as unnecessary.

Granny arrived in time for a cup of eggnog before leaving for church. It was readily apparent she had done somewhat more than a little eggnogging prior to leaving home. Never mind, most everyone enjoyed a little bottled frivolity during the holiday season. Finally, laughing, and exuding steam in the Winter chill, they all squeezed into the family car, and with Lardbutt driving, launched for midnight church services.

Some time later, too much time in the minds of quite a few, heads were nodding, low volume snores were beginning, church programs were alternately fanning to disperse the collective human odors, and pausing before mouths to conceal recurring yawns, while the seemingly endless sermon droned on and on. Hellfire and Damnation were being ladled upon the defenseless congregation in such volume as to inspire repeated silent thanks for a once a year limit to the Yule celebration. "There may or may not be an eternal hereafter," Granny thought, but one thing is for damn sure; this sermon is eternal." Granny's eggnog was beginning to assert itself.

Shortly later, in the midst of a damnation threat, the minister's voice stopped abruptly. It was a tribute to the anesthetic qualities of his sermon that the vocal cessation went unnoticed for several moments. Finally, Lardbutt leaned over, and whispered to his wife. "Hey! Look at the preacher! He's talking, but I can't hear him!"

"Huh?" she said, eyes opening fully, awareness of the silence penetrating her sermon lulled mind.

"The preacher's preaching, but I can't hear him!" her husband stage whispered in her ear.

Looking around, she saw others undergoing the same awakening. "The tuner! That damned remote TV tuner! Who?" she wondered desperately, looking first at her son, head bowed in slumber, and then at Granny, face wreathed in an expression of daffy delight.

"Granny! Gimme that damned tuner!"

Nodding negatively, Granny's mouth opened in a silly grin, as she eased sideways, and slowly raised the tuner. "Want me to zonk everyone in here? I'm already zonked anyway. Might as well have more company." With that, she leaned forward, and pointing the tuner, said, "Banish thy hot air voice, Lardbutt. Get thee with yon noisy preacher."

Face showing alarm, his mouth began moving, but no sound emitted. Now aware something was wrong, he turned, and yelled at his son, who obviously heard nothing. He then shook his son rudely, shouting silent deprecations. Son awakened, and took in the situation at a glance.

Looking at his mother, Son mouthed the question, "Who?"

Now in the pits of dejection, his mother merely jerked a thumb at Granny, peaked out on eggnog and exultation, sappy grin spread across her face.

"Oh, no! We're in trouble, now!" Son thought, knowing full well Granny's capacity for wreaking havoc when she was so inclined. With her eggnogging, she was definitely so inclined.

Standing abruptly, Son walked swiftly to the rear of the church, crossed to the aisle next to the wall, and returned to the pew behind the one occupied by his family. Excusing himself, he threaded his way over knees and feet to a point behind his thoroughly happy Granny. By now, most of the congregation had its collective eyes zeroed in on this area of the church.

Son reached over, and in a surprise move, plucked the remote tuner from Granny's hand. Quickly, he turned to his father, and squeezed the mute button. In a likewise quick motion, he did the same for the minister, who remained in frozen, silent shock at the goings on in his church.

With no prompting, his mother stood, and grasping Granny by the arm, began to lead the family from the church. At the rear of the sanctuary, as all eyes in the congregation strained to look to the rear, Granny, with her daughter supporting on one side, and her grandson on the other, turned, and in a loud, eggnog voice, shouted, "Merry Christmas, and Peace on you all!"

Lardbutt, in a benumbed behind position, turned a dazed look toward the front of the sanctuary, then, apparently gathering his wits, and with his face showing the beginnings of understanding, mumbled "Merry Christmas," turned, and followed his family from the church.

"And peace on you, Lardbutt!" wafted Granny's receding eggnog voice from the foyer, disdainfully slurring the word "peace" to a pronunciation with a more liquid intent.

MERRY CHRISTMAS!

# PUNKY'S PRECIOUS PUPPY

BY: DANA T. MOORE, II

"Oh, you poor little thing!" Punky was shocked. She had just discovered the little dog in the corner of their open garage. Apparently the animal had dragged itself into a corner of the garage to die of its miserable injury, and the cold.

The little dog, possibly a combination of poodle, beagle, and other nondescript breeds, was wet, muddy, bloody, and streaked with automobile oil. As Punky leaned over to see if it were alive, the little dog whimpered lowly, more a painful sigh than a true whimper. It was plain to see that it's strength was rapidly running out. It was also plain to see that it had been run over by an automobile.

Abruptly, Punky bolted into the house, yelling at the top of her lungs, "Mama! Mama! Come quick! Something terrible has happened!"

Punky was the 12 year old daughter of a female non-commissioned officer in the navy. They were stationed on the west coast, just outside Seattle. It was the middle of a rainy winter day, with the temperature hovering just above freezing. Punky was also an animal lover, as was her mother. The poor, little injured dog could not have chosen more receptive people to hear her plea for sympathy and succor than Punky, or her mother.

"Hurry, Mama!" Punky wailed.

"What is it, Honey?" her mother asked.

"Hurry, Mama," Punky pleaded, grasping her mother by the hand, dragging her through the kitchen, and out the door into the garage.

"Look, Mama!" Punky said, her eyes as large as saucers, and the expression on her face one of extreme concern. She pointed at the little dog in the corner by the kitchen door. The dog was now shivering softly, and emitting a weak whimper of pain.

"Punky, run get a thick blanket from the linen closet. We have to keep it warm, and try to keep it from going into shock. Hurry!" Mama concluded emphatically.

When Punky returned with the blanket, she saw that Mama had slipped a thin plywood board under the dog. Covering the animal with the blanket, the two then picked up the board, and slid it into the back seat of the car.

Hurrying into the house and quickly grasping her purse, Mama and Punky then got into the car, and drove swiftly to the local vet. Punky rode in the back seat, murmuring to the little dog. Rushing into the vet's office, Mama told the lady behind the desk they had a badly injured dog in the car, and asked if they could bring it in.

"Yes," replied the attendant. "Bring it to the emergency room. I'll get the doctor."

By the time Punky and Mama carried the softly whimpering dog into the emergency room, the vet was there waiting. "Put it here on the table," he directed. "Leave her on the board for a few minutes." He went swiftly to work, examining the dog carefully.

"Will she live, Doctor?" Punky asked, her face lined with sorrow and concern.

"Right now I give her a 50-50 chance," the vet answered. "She's pretty badly injured," he went on.

"Oh, Mama," Punky moaned, large tears welling from her eyes. The vet continued, "Perhaps you should wait in the reception room. I'll have to get my assistant in here, and we'll go to work. I think the dog needs surgery."

"Yes, Doctor," Mama said, "whatever it takes. We'll wait." With that Mama and Punky walked back to the reception room, and took a seat.

Some time later, the lady behind the reception desk looked at Mama, and said, "It's going to be a while yet. Wouldn't you like to go get something to eat, and come back?"

Mama looked at Punky, who nodded in the negative. Punky's face was a study in sorrow and concern. She unconsciously chewed a fingernail. "Do you think she'll be all right, Mama?"

"Punky, let's say a prayer. Maybe God will let the little dog live, and make a complete recovery from her injuries."

Punky lowered her head in silent prayer.

Following what seemed like an interminable wait, the vet approached, surgical mask hanging to one side, and an expression of satisfied relief on his face. Punky and Mama looked expectantly at him.

"I think she'll make it. She'll be here for a few days, then she's going to need a lot of tender loving care."

Mama and Punky both seemed to deflate in response to the good news. "Punky, looks like you've got a dog," Mama said. "Will you take good care of it?"

"Oh yes, Mama," Punky replied, her face now a vision of happiness.

"Punky, maybe you ought to say a little prayer of thanks," Mama said.

Again Punky's head lowered in a moment of prayerful thanks.

Four days later, Punky and Mama went to the vet's, and after paying their bill, took the dog out to the car. The little dog was still weak, but all in all, one hundred per cent better than when Punky first found her. Gently placing the dog in the car, still on the same plywood board, Punky and her mother drove home. Punky gently stroked the dog, and crooned a low, toneless tune to it. She said to the dog, "You're precious." Following that observation, Punky turned to her mother, and announced, "Mama, since this dog is so precious, I want to call her 'Precious.'"

"Sounds like a proper name to me," Mama answered, keeping her eyes on the road as she drove.

In the months following surgery, Precious made a complete recovery. She was vivacious, and full of life. She and Punky were inseparable. Punky played with the little dog at every opportunity. There was no worry about being hit by a car again, since their home had a fenced in back yard, and being nearly an acre in size, with lots of trees, Precious could run and play to her heart's content. At night, Precious slept on the foot of Punky's bed. Precious was an ideal house pet. She was short haired, little, and very clean about herself. She was already house broken, so there was never a moment of worry over dirt, or mess in the house. At one time in her unknown past, she had been neutered, so there was never any worry about that problem. She was, in fact, an ideal house pet, and both Punky and her mother loved the little dog dearly. Little did they know that Precious was shortly to prove her worth more than could ever have been contemplated.

One night, when everyone was in bed asleep, Mama in her room, and Punky, with Precious on the foot of her bed, both asleep, Punky awakened to the sound of Precious growling. Turning on her bedside light, Punky saw that Precious had her ears laid back, and the hackles on her shoulders and neck were standing up. She continued a low growl. Abruptly, a shadow appeared in Punky's bedroom doorway, and at the same time, Precious let out a battle cry, and leapt from the bed. Punky screamed, "Mama!"

A man appeared in the full light of the bedside table lamp. He was dressed like a bum, with long, dirty, shoulder length hair and a high collared coat turned up around his neck, and in front of his face. What Punky could see of his scowling face revealed not a beard, but what appeared as an unkempt need for a shave. But worst of all, he grasped a long, wicked looking, gleaming knife! The look on his face left no doubt as to his intent to use the knife.

Precious launched herself at the intruder, sinking her teeth into the man's calf. The man gave a vicious kick, and at the same time, chopped at Precious with the knife. The little dog was propelled across the room by the force of the kick, causing the knife to miss. However, as Precious flew across the room, her head struck the corner of a chest of drawers, and she then hit the wall with a sickening crunch.

"I'll kill that little bastard!" the man with the knife muttered venomously. "And then, I'll kill you," he said with a no nonsense threat in his voice as he looked at Punky.

"If anyone is to be killed, it's going to be you," Mama said from the doorway. The man turned abruptly, brandishing his knife. Mama held a .38 revolver in her hand. She always kept the weapon in her bedside table for just such emergencies as this. In her other hand, Mama grasped a police billy club.

"I'll kill you first," the intruder said, advancing toward Mama, with his knife pointed threateningly toward her.

"Far enough!" Mama said. The man continued toward her.

Mama carefully squeezed off a round. The bullet struck the intruder in the knee. He went down, screaming an obscenity.

Mama was surprised to see the man still struggling to try and get within knife range of her. With that, Mama raised the police billy club, and cracked the would be assailant a vicious blow to the bridge of his nose. That put him to sleep.

"Punky! Go call 911, and have the police come! Hurry! We may have to take Precious to the vet!"

Punky edged around the man on the floor, and ran quickly to the phone to do as Mama had bid.

Returning to her bedroom, Punky saw that her mother had removed the knife from the intruder's slack grasp. Grabbing an extension cord, Mama tied the man's hands behind his back. She then walked over to Precious' inert form.

Leaning over the dog, Mama felt for a pulse, and then placed the back of her hand before the dog's nose. "She's still alive, Punky, but she's badly hurt. We'll have to call the vet, and see if he'll meet us at the vet's hospital."

Just at that moment, the police arrived. Briefly, Mama explained what had happened. She then told the police officer that they had to get their dog to the vet, or it would die.

"Yes, Ma'am." the officer nodded. "Could you come by our office when you finish at the vet? We need a more detailed, and signed statement. In the meantime, we'll get this loser some emergency medical attention, and then lock him up. We know him. He's done this before. We already have a warrant out for his arrest for assault with a deadly weapon, and attempted murder. This time he's not going to get away just because some slick lawyer gets him off. We will see you later. Good luck with the little dog."

Mama then called the vet. He agreed to meet them at his office. Mama and Punky put Precious, again on the same board, into the car, and drove swiftly to the vet's.

After a careful examination, the vet talked to Punky and Mama. This time, there was no good news. With a sad face, and tears in his own eyes, the vet told them that Precious had a broken neck from the blow on the her head as she flew across the room. She had just died. It was very clear the vet felt as bad about Precious' death as they did.

Looking at Punky's tear streaked face, Mama, herself crying, said, "Come on Punky. We'll take Precious home." As they walked to the emergency room, Mama asked the vet what the charge was. He told her to forget it. He was an animal lover, too.

In the car, Punky stroked Precious' now serene face, telling the little dog how much she loved her. She then asked her mother, "Mama, why did God let Precious die? Precious never hurt anyone, and was such a good dog." Tears continued coursing down Punky's face, dripping from her chin.

"Punky, I think I know the answer," Mama said. "I think God has an Angel about your age who had a little, loving dog for a pet. He borrowed Precious to send her to us to save our lives. Now He's taken her back to return her to her Angel. This way, Precious will live forever in heaven, and will be looked over by her own personal guardian Angel. When the time comes for you to go to heaven, Precious will be there waiting for you."

"Mama, do you really think that's the answer?" Punky asked.

"Yes, I do, Punky," Mama replied. After a pause, she continued, "I think God wanted Precious in heaven, and I'm sure He will keep her for you to be with at some time in the future. You should feel good that Precious has had a chance to be with two Angels; you and the one already in heaven."

Punky thought it over, and then nodding her head in agreement, said, "We'll bury her in the back yard, and that will remind us of where she really is, Mama."

"She will always be with us, Punky. And she will also be with God. Nothing could be better than that."

# THE RECTOR AND THE ERECTOR

BY: DANA T. MOORE, II

The Reverend Theo Elysium had a problem. No doubt about it. He was being hassled at every turn. The vestry was after him to bear down on the parishioners to contribute more money for the proposed new wing to the parish school. The parish program committee was hounding him to generate more funds for classroom materials. At the same time, the Minister of Music was bugging him for new choir robes, and new hymnals. Money! Money! Money! The root of all evil—the absence of it, that is. Theo was then stricken with a momentary mood of contrition, thinking of Jesus' admonition, saying, ". . . it is easier for a camel to pass through the eye of a needle than for a rich man to enter the kingdom of God." And then, returning to the pragmatic perusal of his parish problems, he thought, "I'm the camel trying to get through this needlelike dilemma, and I'm truly hung up on my hump." Being thus distressfully disposed, Theo felt as if his hump was being needlessly needled; periodically pricked by the piercing prongs of the fulminating factions within his church.

Sitting at his desk, pondering the problems of his church, Theo was a study in concentration. Theo was the rector of the largest, and wealthiest Episcopal church in the area. He was somewhat younger than would have been expected of one holding such a responsible position. Theo was representative of the new youth wave in the church. He was an effective, relating minister. He rapped with the young; communicated with the middle aged, and empathized with the elderly. But the young, and the young middle aged were his devoted followers, and the source of his strength. In keeping with this important fact, Theo identified with the more mod set. He wore a mustache, and a goatee. His hair was collar length. The overall effect of his appearance was unintentionally, and unwittingly paradoxical. Theo's young followers saw in him a certain Christlike resemblance, while some of the more staid, traditional element occasionally perceived a disturbing Mephistophelean impression, perhaps enhanced by the long, dark eyebrows turned up at the ends. And then, there was a perceptive portion of his followers who loved him for his humanistic qualities, and took delight at the communion rail when occasionally protruding from beneath his vestal raiment could be seen a pair of dirty, comfortable, totally incongruous pair of sneakers. One delighted communicant was known to have nearly strangled on the consecrated bread after reverently lowering his eyes to receive, and spotting those irreverent sneakers peering up at him, allowed the bread into his gaping, surprised mouth, and was immediately seized with an almost uncontrollable spasm of laughter and coughing. Fortunately, Theo and the co-communicants took this as a demonstrative outlet of religious fervor.

Seeking the solution to his pressing parish problems, Theo's mind turned to Gilbert Erectus. Theo had the intuitive feeling that Gilbert was the key, and properly persuaded, could unlock the coffers. Gilbert Erectus was the most successful contractor and builder in the area. The city abounded with towering testimony to Gilbert's construction genius; bridges, commercial buildings, schools, and factories, all brilliant monuments to his driving passion to erect edifices for man's use. In Gilbert's engineering mind, filled with stresses and trusses, squares and angles, girders and glass, the world was one gigantic erector set. He could build the new wing for the church school, and not even disturb his busy schedule. The monetary aspect however, might not be so trivial to him. Gaining Gilbert's support would be very decisive in persuading some of the more affluent church members to underwrite the robes, hymnals, and classroom materials. Mentally settling his sights upon Gilbert, Theo's thoughts were brashly broken by a familiar voice from the intercom speaker on his desk.

"Your favorite propagator of the faith is here to see you," said his secretary, an unmistakable tone of amusement in her voice.

"Who?" Theo asked, trying to wrestle his mind away from Gilbert, and onto the statement from the speaker box.

"Gladayss Louisbottome," answered his secretary. Continuing, she added, "And you'd better get some more holy water. She's that way again."

Gladayss Louisbottome was a recurring thorn in Theo's toe. She was a religious zealot, and a convert from Roman Catholicism. During her conversion, Gladayss enthusiastically embraced the Episcopal faith. She did however, fail to divest herself of one catholic philosophic flaw. Gladayss was unalterably opposed to birth control. As living proof of her catholic carryover, Gladayss was the mother of eleven boys. She gave the impression she felt it was her divinely ordained calling to over run the world with little Episcopalians. Additionally, Gladayss suffered, among other shortcomings, from a limited capacity to orally express her religious fervor. Her inability to verbally articulate was more than compensated for by her willing facility to ovulate, copulate, and populate.

Knocking, then without waiting for an invitation, Gladayss peremptorily opened the door, and strode forcefully into Theo's office. As she advanced toward his desk, Theo had the foreboding impression of being trampled under by brute bulk. He had a fleeting mental picture of an old World War Two newsreel clip of an American battleship, all guns blazing, belching smoke from its stacks, steaming invincibly and inexorably toward victory over a demoralized Japanese fleet. Theo felt demoralized.

Gladayss was normally a large woman, but in her present condition, she was massive. Theo almost cringed, and very nearly took refuge in 23rd Psalm. ". . . . the valley of the shadow of death," he momentarily thought, and then, jumping hastily to his feet, indicated a comfortable chair for Gladayss. He did so as much in deference to her displaced center of gravity as to his desire to keep her from towering over him.

"Theo," Gladayss said, using the familiar first name, informal address now popular in the progressive, youth oriented church. "I have a problem."

Theo looked at Gladayss for a long, intense moment. While doing so, the thought passed through his mind, "Problem? Maybe she's trying to duplicate the twelve apostles, or recreate the twelve tribes of Israel."

"What is it, Gladayss?" Theo asked, a wary edge to his voice.

"We have to work in a baptism date, Theo. I know you have a busy schedule, but I'm sure you can squeeze it in."

"Truly my font runneth over," Theo thought. He then leaned over, and began to leaf through the pages of his desk calendar. Apparently engrossed in seeking a satisfactory date for the baptismal service, he thought, "Perhaps I should get a recirculating pump hooked up to the font. With Gladayss' prodigious production potential, I really need a Niagara Falls to keep up with her." This thought was followed by rolling his eyes upward slightly, silently seeking forgiveness for his irreverent treatment of the holy rite of baptism. Selecting a date, Theo extended the calendar for Gladayss to see, and asked, "How about this Sunday?"

Studying the calendar, Gladayss replied. "Yes, that will be fine." Theo made a notation on the calendar, then extending a helping hand, anxiously assisted Gladayss on her way. "See you in church this Sunday," Theo said in farewell.

"Yes, Theo. Thank you."

Theo breathed a sigh of relief as Gladayss departed.

Deciding to take the bull by the horns, and at the same time get out of the office for a while, Theo punched the intercom button on his desk speaker, and asked his secretary to get him an appointment with Gilbert Erectus as soon as Gilbert could see him. Momentarily she called back, saying, "I have Gilbert on the phone now. He says he will see you right away, if you wish."

"Fine. Tell him I'm on my way," Theo replied, grabbing his coat, and heading for the exit from his office.

Parking his car in front of Gilbert's office building, Theo was impressed by the modernistic, sleek, and simultaneous aura of permanence emanating from the structure. Theo had visions of just such an addition to the church school, and was more than ever convinced that Gilbert was the key to his problems. All he had to do was exert the right pressure on Gilbert to bring him around.

As Theo entered the building, Gilbert's receptionist caught sight of him, and stood respectfully. Motioning to an inner office door, she said, "Go on in, Father. He's waiting for you."

"Thank you," Theo said, knocking, and then entering Gilbert's office.

Inside the office, Theo was instantly impressed with the tasteful and expensive decor. The walls were paneled in mahogany; the floor covered with deep piled carpet, and floor-to-ceiling bookcases stood adjacent to a large picture window behind Gilbert's desk. Expensive, comfortable seating furniture was located around the room, arranged in such a manner as to focus attention on Gilbert behind his desk. Gilbert's desk itself looked to be the size of a railroad car, dwarfing Gilbert seated behind it. Observing Theo enter, Gilbert stood, and walked around the end of his desk, welcoming hand extended; face wreathed in a warm smile.

Gilbert was not a large man; standing a diminutive five feet, seven. He was given to a tendency to portliness, very cleverly concealed by the skill of an expert tailor. His smooth shaven face was topped with a pair of rimless glasses, giving his eyes an innocent, round, Orphan Annie like appearance, leading Theo to expect, "Leaping Lizzards, Sandy!" Gilbert's gleaming, pink pate was fringed with a thick, graying halo of hair, circumscribing the rear of his head from one ear to the other.

"Good morning, Theo," Gilbert said, in his best basso profundo voice, at the same time, gripping Theo's hand in a firm, masculine handshake.

Theo returned the greeting, allowing himself to be guided to one of the lush chairs facing Gilbert's desk.

"Good to see you, Theo. May I offer you a drink? What can I do for you?" Gilbert said in rapid fire order, as he returned to his chair behind his desk. Shaking his head in a negative nod to the drink, Theo thought, "This desk is an impregnable fortress. I hope I can bridge the chasm."

Then, Theo opened with, "Gilbert, the church has a problem. We are sorely in need of a new wing to the parish school. As the leading builder in the area, and a member of our church, you're the best qualified to help."

"How can I help, Theo?" Gilbert asked, pleased that his professional advice was being sought for such a noble endeavor.

"The church would like you to build the new wing, Gilbert." Gilbert received this statement with slightly mixed emotions. He was at once flattered the church would turn to him in time of need, but at the same time, he had an uneasy feeling it was going to cost him some money. Gilbert didn't become successful and wealthy by giving money away. "Probably want me to build the wing at a cut rate price," he thought, his facial expression losing some of its benevolence.

"Were you looking for a bargain price, Theo?"

Taking a firm grip on the bull's horns, coughing, and clearing his throat, Theo then replied, "No, Gilbert. I was in hopes you would build the wing as a consecrated donation to the church in support of Episcopal, Christian, educational goals."

"Donate?" Gilbert echoed, his tone of voice incredulous with disbelief, as the last shred of benevolence disappeared from his face.

"Do you know what you're asking, Theo?" Gilbert asked, his voice now bereft of its basso profundo, having elevated at least an octave. He continued, "You're talking about thousands of dollars!"

"Yes. Two hundred and fifty thousand," Theo concurred.

"A quarter of a million!" Gilbert spluttered, and then continued, "You want me to donate a quarter of a million dollars?" Gilbert's voice had now ascended to the tender tonal range of a eunuch.

Wishing to retain the initiative, and momentum of attack, and to exploit the advantage of shock, Theo issued an impressively pontifical reminder.

"Remember the words of our Lord Jesus, how he said it is more blessed to give than to receive." And in a further effort to secure his beachhead before Gilbert could recover, he again quoted, "Let your light so shine before men that they may see your good works, and glorify your Father which is in heaven."

"Give and receive. Light and good works," muttered Gilbert, obviously reeling from Theo's onslaught.

Perceiving a crack in Gilbert's weakening defense, Theo aggressively followed up his advantage by switching to a persuasive approach. "Gilbert, think of the nearly incalculable benefits. A gigantic tax deduction right off the top; invaluable free advertising; appropriate homage to you, inscribed on the school wing, for people to read years and years in the future, honoring your noble gesture, and best of all, you would be laying the foundation for your eternal castle in heaven."

Gilbert lapsed into sullen silence. His normally pink face was now flushed a deep red. He realized he was at a distinct disadvantage. Gilbert was totally at ease with a slide rule, or when pondering a scale of logarithms. He was fully capable of coping with stress from an engineering point of view, but in the face of stress such as Theo was exerting, Gilbert could not draw upon the irrefutable maxims of physical law that normally stood him in such good stead. Gilbert was very limited in his biblical knowledge. The only thing he knew about the bible was that it was holy, made a good paperweight, and could almost always be found in a motel room. Gilbert didn't like being outmaneuvered, especially here in his own office; his own battleground, cunningly calculated to place his adversaries at a psychological disadvantage. At the same time, Gilbert had to admit to himself that there were a few kernels of truth in what Theo said about the advantages accruing from his donating and building the new school wing, although he knew more profitable ways to avoid paying taxes.

"Let me think about it, Theo," Gilbert grudgingly conceded. Sniffing the smell of victory, Theo thought it prudent not to humiliate Gilbert to the point of stubborn counterproductive resistance. Instead, rising from his chair, Theo said, "I knew you would agree with me, Gilbert. God bless you! I'll be back in touch with you." Giving Gilbert no chance for rebuttal, Theo turned and walked to the door. Pausing in the doorway, Theo turned again, and said, "Gilbert, why don't you have that drink you offered me a few minutes ago?" With that, Theo stepped through the doorway, leaned over, and kissed Gilbert's surprised secretary on the forehead, and left the magnificent building, merrily whistling a nondescript tune to himself.

Theo's next encounter with Gilbert came during Sunday services several weeks later. It was a blustery, rainy, fall morning when the second services were held that memorable day. The turnout, for some inexplicable reason, was unusually large, particularly when considering the unpleasant weather conditions. Before services were over, Theo was to wish that it had been raining for forty days and forty nights. At any rate, the wet weather accounted for many umbrellas and raincoats in evidence. Gilbert entered the church with his coat buttoned to the chin. Even so, he was very distinguished looking, wearing an obviously expensive coat, shined patent leather shoes, and an impressive homburg hat covering his pink pate.

The services were routine, without the climactic sharing of the bread and wine. Theo's sermon was neither inspirational, nor hypnotic. His theme was about money, and the necessity for church support by the parishioners, a topic guaranteed to turn off the wealthy, and turn on the poor. The sermon, for better or worse, was over; the collection plate passed, and now, the final hymn was in the midst of the second stanza, when the atonal, desultory singing was overridden by a blood curdling scream. The congregation halted its devotional voice in mid-phrase. The choir singing dwindled off into a trailing silence like the echo of a train disappearing in the distance. Theo, standing in the pulpit, hymnal in hand, looked out over the congregation, a quizzical expression on his face. The organist stopped in mid-chord. The look on the parish faces was that of one gigantic, collective congregational question mark. And then, as silence settled slowly over the sanctuary, the air was again rent with a reverberating scream.

"Oh my God! Gladayss is berthing!" thought Theo, catching sight of her, mouth wide open, quivering in full bay. And then, also sighting Gladayss' pew neighbor, Gilbert Erectus, Theo's mouth dropped agape.

Gilbert was a flasher! He was stark naked! Theo was astonished. Gilbert stood there, hymnal in hand, a serene, beatific look upon his face, the very picture of innocence. Gilbert's pink, portly, pneumatic body perfectly matched the pink of his bald dome. Gilbert was definitely not a eunuch. His expensive raincoat, mingled with his trousers, lay rumpled about his feet. The overall effect was like a stop action shot on TV; a frozen tableau in time. There was a momentary period when everyone seemed riveted in place by the enormity of Gilbert's nude notion of devotion.

The organist, a young fortyish divorcee, leaned forward over the face of the organ in order to gain a better view of the cause of the commotion. Spotting Gilbert, in all his male glory, she sat back on the organ seat, and with a gleam in her eye, and an appreciative look upon her face, began a lusty rendition of, "I Need Thee Every Hour." Gilbert smiled. Theo glared. Gladayss fainted, dropping into her pew like a headshot moose.

The familiar tune from the organ galvanized the church goers. Those immediately adjacent to Gilbert began a simultaneous outward movement very much like a tidal wave of ripples in a placid pond, expanding from the splash of a large stone. The effect was that of a viper dropped in their midst. Gilbert was the snake. Three of the more clearly thinking, male church goers, grabbed Gilbert's coat, draped it around his shoulders, and hustled him, entangled feet and all, out the rear of the sanctuary. The organist sounded a terminal "Amen!" Theo spoke a brief, unheard benediction, and beat a hasty retreat out the side exit of the nave. And now, pandemonium prevailed.

Released from Theo's stabilizing influence, the congregational members gave vent to their varied emotions. "Have you ever . . . . !" "Oh my, I've never been so shocked!" "Did you see that?" "What a nasty little man!" were some of the more audible comments, as the babble of voices continued. One sleepy eyed celebrant, disgruntled over the disturbance, asked, "What the hell's going on?" Two elderly spinsters attended Gladayss, fanning her face with their church bulletins. Gradually shock subsided, and order returned as the celebrants, realizing the activities were ended, departed the church.

That evening, the vestry was called into emergency session. For once, all elected members were present. Their mood was vengeful and vindictive. There were demands for Gilbert's arrest and jailing; for his excommunication; and even expulsion from the church. Theo finally established some semblance of order, and got the meeting under way.

Theo opened with, "Now, we're all aware of the immodest display with which Gilbert endowed us this morning during services; a display demanding disciplinary decision on our part."

"A heavenly endowed display, and unmarried, too," murmured the organist, who was also a vestry member.

"What was that?" snapped Theo, resentful of her suspected levity.

"Endowed with money," replied the organist, lowering her eyes demurely.

"Oh yes, money," repeated Theo, moderately mollified, but still slightly suspicious.

The mention of money however, did bolster Theo's intent to present a well thought out solution to several problems. During the interval between morning services, and the vestry meeting, Theo seized upon what he saw as a divinely offered opportunity to obtain funds for the new church school wing. Theo was pragmatic enough not to be above a little clerical extortion, expertly expended. Now, he had to sell it to the vestry.

"As I was saying," Theo began again, casting a caustic glance at the organist, "We know what Gilbert did, and we know we have to take appropriate action. Before we fly off in all directions, allow me to remind you of some relevant facts, and how Gilbert's indiscretion may have been a blessing in disguise."

"Not much of a disguise," muttered one of the vestry members.

"Definitely not," concurred the organist, a lecherous look on her face.

Ignoring the comments, Theo continued, "It occurs to me that we need a new wing on our parish school. Gilbert is the most successful builder in the area, and could, if so persuaded, build us a beautiful new addition to our school. Would it not be most magnanimous of the church to accept Gilbert's humble apology, provided, of course, it was accompanied with an appropriate, and utilitarian symbol of his contrition. I admonish you not to act in haste, and repent at leisure. We have a golden opportunity to help accomplish God's work." Theo's presentation was both eloquent and persuasive. He could have been a successful used car salesman.

The vestry members reacted with an immediate explosion into discussion. Everyone talked at once. Pairs of vestry members argued heatedly among themselves. As the discussion became louder, the organist quietly, and without concern, buffed her nails. She had reached her decision, and, her mind being thus unfettered, roamed over more pleasant thoughts, mostly of Gilbert. She smiled at no one in particular. Finally, out of the chaos, a pattern of opinion began to emerge.

It appeared the more avant-garde element of the vestry was having its sway over the conservative constituents. Gradually the youthful, vigorous and progressive members successfully imposed their will. The loud talk and hubbub subsided. As order and dignity returned to this august body, one voice could be clearly heard.

"The church has adopted a liberal view toward homosexuality. Women can now be ordained. Why, even one publicly confessed and acknowledged lesbian was recently ordained to administer the holy sacraments. So what's wrong with this congregation having one little exhibitionist among its membership?"

"Little?" wondered the organist, as she finished buffing her nails, and smiled once again to herself.

Theo, realizing decision time was at hand, stood, and called the meeting back to order. "Ladies and Gentlemen, have you decided upon a course of action?"

One young vestry member, a self-appointed leader, said, "Yes, Theo, we have decided to accept Gilbert's apology, and his donation of the new church school wing."

"Well, then," Theo responded, in deference to Roberts' parliamentary procedures, "Let's put it to a vote. All those in favor, raise your hands." All but one member raised a hand, signifying approval.

"All opposed?"

No hands. One abstention from an older, anachronistic member.

"The ayes have it," said Theo. "Any further business? The meeting is adjourned."

The next morning, upon entering his office, Theo said to his secretary, "Get Gilbert on the phone for me, please." When she called on the intercom, and said Gilbert was waiting, Theo thanked her, and picked up his phone. "Good morning, Gilbert." Then, with a stern tone of voice, Theo continued, "I think we had better have a talk. Could you meet me here in the office at five this afternoon?" Theo wanted to make sure there were no eavesdropping ears around, and he also wanted to make sure he nailed Gilbert before he had a chance to leave town on a sudden business trip.

"Strike while the iron is hot," Theo thought.

"I'll be there at five," Gilbert replied.

"Good. See you at five."

Theo dismissed his secretary shortly after four that afternoon, telling her he would lock up when he left. He then made a quick swing through the church, making sure no one else was on the premises. Theo wanted no witnesses to what was sure to be extortion of a magnitude to make the Mafia misty eyed with envy.

Gilbert arrived promptly at five, nervously scanning his watch as he knocked on Theo's office door.

"Come in!" came the less than friendly command from behind the door.

Feeling akin to the ancient Christians as they must have felt when walking hesitantly into the arena of a Roman coliseum, wondering from which quarter the slavering, growling beasts would attack, Gilbert opened the door. Then, squaring his shoulders, and setting his jaw, Gilbert walked onto Theo's battleground. No lush, expensively decorated office was this. The carpet showed the effects of many feet having passed over it. The furniture, what there was, had a well used look. The desk, behind which Theo sat, was a postage stamp compared to Gilbert's. The unimposing and lackluster effect gave the impression of a ragtag, disorganized army arrayed against the awesome might of Caesar's legions. This apparent inequity was somewhat offset by the pervasive aura of Divine Presence, and the visible, somewhat somber atmosphere of Theo's ministerial garb.

"Sit down, Gilbert," said Theo, indicating a less than comfortable, straight-backed chair facing his desk. Theo had placed a floor lamp behind his own chair, thus enhancing the intentional atmosphere of inquisitorial tension. Theo was not the least opposed to taking full advantage of his own psychological options.

Gilbert sat in the proffered chair. The two sat for a long, pregnant moment, eyeing one another like two gladiators catching first sight of the other on the field of combat. Each silently took the other's measure. The battle was joined!

Theo immediately took the initiative. He probed and parried, maneuvering with inspired brilliance, confident he had the might of the church behind him. He was to discover however, that Gilbert was a cunning, skillful, and difficult adversary. Gilbert met the thrusts with deft, and determined, deflective dexterity, equally as confident he had the support of a strong base of wealth. His reserve was the knowledge that Theo wanted the new church school wing, and only he, Gilbert, would possibly provide this, free of any encumbrance to the church.

The conflict raged long, and with vigorous, vitriolic exchange. Finally, as the hour grew late, and the antagonists grew weary, a mutually acceptable agreement was reached. Then, with unspoken assent, they simultaneously stood. Each looked at the other with an expression of grudging respect. Each had given as good as he had gotten.

Theo then spoke. "You'll have the documents to me by this coming Saturday?"

Gilbert responded, "And you agree to my terms?"

Theo affirmed his agreement, wincing inwardly as he did.

"You'll have the papers by Saturday," Gilbert said. With that, he turned and left Theo's office. Departing, Gilbert thought to himself, "It's going to cost me, but it's worth it. Theo is a smart cooky. Wish I had him on my sales staff." Watching Gilbert depart, Theo thought, "He's a fighter. He sure knew how to get to me. Well, it's for a good cause."

The following Sunday, turnout for services was even greater than the previous week. Perhaps the activities of last Sunday had been taken as a preview. Whatever, there was a feeling of almost tangible tension in the air. Everyone was talking excitedly while entering church. No doubt, they all felt something very memorable was about to happen; an event, at least in their eyes, equivalent to that never to be forgotten occurrence at Golgotha many centuries ago.

Theo delivered an inspired sermon, the topic being, "To Forgive Is Divine." All the church members present hung on his every word. No drowsy, heavy lidded, head nodding today. The tension mounted. No one noticed Gilbert unobtrusively enter the church a few minutes after services began, and take a seat in the last pew at the rear of the sanctuary.

Finally, at that moment during the services when Theo normally read the announcements from the bulletin, a point somewhat like the seventh inning stretch, Theo tucked his prayer book under his arm, and strode purposefully to the center of the steps leading up to the altar. The congregation leaned forward in unison, almost as if preparing to kneel. There was an audible intake of breath. This was it! Had someone yelled "Fire!" total congregational cardiac collapse would have resulted.

Theo began, "I would like to remind you, one and all, God works in mysterious ways His wonders to accomplish." Then, extracting a letter from his prayer book, he continued, "I have a letter from Gilbert, addressed to the church. In this letter, Gilbert makes a full, beseeching apology for his momentary and inexplicable aberration of last Sunday. Also in the letter," Theo went on, "Gilbert has volunteered to totally underwrite, and build the new wing to the church school." Before there could be any recovery, or reaction, Theo then pulled another document from his prayer book. "I also have a check from Gilbert covering the costs of new hymnals, new choir robes, and complete replenishment of school supplies."

Pausing momentarily to allow the impact of his announcement to sink in, Theo then continued, "This whole matter has been brought before the vestry; the vestry you elected, and acceptance of Gilbert's apology and donation put to a vote. The vote for acceptance was nearly unanimous, with one abstention." Theo then paused again, allowing his intense gaze to shift to first one member, and then another. Momentarily, there was a simultaneous release of breath, and a break in the tension. The congregation leaned back to a normal sitting posture.

Theo then said, "Let him who is without sin cast the first stone." With that, he turned abruptly, and resumed conduct of the services.

When the congregation began the final stanza of the last hymn, Theo, as was his custom, walked down the aisle to the rear of the sanctuary. Arriving at that position, he turned, and finished the hymn along with the celebrants. When the last Amen was sung, and all heads were collectively bowed, Theo administered the benediction. Blessing all those present, Theo raised his outstretched arms heavenward. As he did so, his clerical robes slipped to the floor. Theo was totally nude!

Gilbert, looking on intently, displayed an expression of triumphant satisfaction. The organist, with a clear view of the rear of the sanctuary, gave vent to a sigh of admiration. Gladayss felt the internal beginnings of labor. Zebulon Black, the church sexton, looking on from the opened door at the rear of the sanctuary, his mouth open wide in disbelief, red eyes bulging like two over ripe plums, muttered, "Oh, Lawd!"

Theo, having met the terms of the hard fought negotiations, and unseen by the others present, quickly snatched his garments from the floor, and draping them protectively about himself, hastened from the church. Zebulon, still in shock, pulled a flask from his pocket, and downed its contents in one long, gurgling gulp.

The following afternoon, amid pomp and publicity, and with the Bishop present, ground was broken for the new school wing. The Bishop, a shrewd and ambitious old curmudgeon, with his most photogenic cheek turned to the TV cameras, gave a rousing talk about the nobility of Christian education, and building castles in heaven. Then, with TV cameras grinding, and reporters writing, Theo and Gilbert, each wielding a chrome plated spade, turned the first symbolic sod. Gilbert then presented his spade to the Bishop in appreciation for his stalwart leadership. The Bishop, again acknowledging the cameras, consecrated the ground for the new church school wing.

Also that afternoon, Gladayss whelped her twelfth boy. The attending physician, in response to a request from her harried, harassed husband, performed a tube tying operation, thus averting the need for a recirculating pump at the font.

That evening, the organist, in eager anticipation, laid a beautiful table for her guest; Gilbert.

Also that evening, Theo hung his chrome plated spade on the wall behind the desk in his office. He then pulled a small silver rectangle from his pocket, and affixed it to the wall beneath the spade. Stepping back, Theo repeated the appropriately engraved inscription on the silver plaque. It read, "Naked we come; Naked we go." The letters of the inscription were engraved in the precise, block style favored by engineers. On each end of the plate was engraved a pair of miniature trowels, symbolic of the builder.

THE END

# A LITTLE BOY'S LETTER TO SANTA

## BY: DANA T. MOORE, II

A Military Post
Anywhere, USA
Several Weeks Before Christmas
Santa Claus
North Pole

Dear Santa Claus,

I hope this letter doesn't bother you. I only wanted to ask you for a few gifts for Christmas. I know you're busy, but I thought perhaps you might find time to look at my letter.

As you know, Santa, my father is a professional soldier. He isn't always home for Christmas. When he does come home, he brings so many gifts that there is very little left for you to bring. But, Santa, some gifts he can't bring. Sometimes he can't bring himself.

I know it's a lot to ask, but I would like for you to bring my father home for Christmas. I'm sure you're busy with all the toys you have to make and deliver, but I thought, if you had only a minute, you might find my Dad, and bring him home. Christmas without my Dad will be pretty sad.

One Christmas my Dad brought the most wonderful electric train, and I would have enjoyed it, if he had let me play with it. Another

Christmas, he brought me a set to build toys with; called an erector set. But, you know what? He wanted to play with that, too. That was okay. My Dad was home for Christmas.

I can remember some of the Christmas seasons, Santa, when my Dad wasn't too happy. Once I asked him why, and he said he kept thinking of the children of the parents against whom he had fought in war. I don't think I know what war is, Santa. I asked my Dad, and he said he hoped I never found out. Dad told me that one time he had seen some of the little children whose mothers, and fathers had been killed in the war, and he said he felt like crying. He said he saw one little boy who reminded him exactly of me. The little boy was asking for food for himself and his little brother and sister for Christmas.

Anyway, Santa, I hope you can bring my Dad home for me on Christmas, and bring food to that little boy and his family.

One time, Santa, my Dad came home just a day or two before Christmas, and I swear, he had a bag so loaded with gifts, he couldn't unload all of them at home. Do you know what he asked me to do with him? He said he had a friend killed overseas, whose children wouldn't have any toys for Christmas. He said he would like for us to share some of our toys with them, and he wanted me to go with him to take some of the toys to their house. I knew you would bring them toys, but I thought we could help you by taking them some of the toys my Dad brought home. We did, and I think the kids really liked them. I know their mother told my Dad, "God bless you," which I couldn't quite understand. But then, there's lots about grownups I don't understand.

But, Santa, there have been Christmas times when I wasn't sure I wanted my Dad home. I don't know why, but when he was home, he and Mommy argued about him being away so much. They would get pretty loud when they fussed. I remember one Christmas, real early in the morning on Christmas day, I heard them arguing, and I got up to see who was making all the noise. I came out of my bedroom, and found them in the kitchen. Mommy was crying. She had a big, blue spot under one eye. When I asked her what caused it, she said she had fallen, and hit her face. They both looked awfully funny to me. And they were drinking that old smelly stuff they called whiskey. I can't understand why grownups drink that stuff. I tasted it once, and it almost made me sick. After I asked Mommy what had happened to her eye, my Dad mumbled something about being sleepy, and went to bed. He slept most of Christmas day that year. It wasn't much fun having him home just to sleep all day Christmas.

That wasn't a very happy Christmas.

I remember one Christmas when my Dad came home several weeks before Christmas. When the holiday season started, Dad and Mommy went to a lot of parties. They were drinking a lot of that stinky, old whiskey that year, too.

On Christmas morning, my sisters Beth and Bonny, and I came out of our bedrooms to see what you had brought. Santa, the floor was piled high with toys. Mommy and Dad were sleeping on the floor in front of the Christmas tree, and they had spilled a bottle of that nasty whiskey on the floor. It really smelled bad. Santa, you brought a lot of toys for us that year, but I guess you were in a hurry. Maybe you were behind schedule. All the toys were in a heap, waiting for us, but none of them were wrapped like you usually leave them, and they weren't under the tree. I understand, though. I know you have a lot of places to go on that one night of the year, and a lot of children's homes to visit in a short time. Another reason I know you were in a hurry is that you didn't take time to eat your cookies, nor drink the milk we left out for you. They were still under the tree.

This year, Santa, we're all looking forward to a nice Christmas, if you can only bring my Dad home. I am going to write down my Christmas list for you. I hope it isn't too much to ask for.

1. My Dad home.
2. A new coat for Mommy.
3. A new doll called Emma Em for my older sister, Beth.
4. A toy building set called Leggo for my younger sister, Bonny.
5. Some food for that little boy I was telling you about; the one that my Dad said reminded him of me.

Santa, I hope this letter reaches you in time, and you're not too busy to read it. Thank you.

Merry Christmas,
Bill

P. S.

Dear Santa,

This letter must have gotten lost. I found it the day after Christmas. I don't know what happened to it. Maybe Mommy forgot to mail it. I'm going to send it to you anyway. Maybe you've already seen this letter, but I want to make sure. I want to thank you for this Christmas.

Santa, this was the best Christmas of all!

I awakened early on Christmas morning. I thought I would slip out to the Christmas tree early, and see what you had brought, then go wake my sisters to come out and open their gifts. Santa, the Christmas tree was so pretty! It was almost coverd with presents. I didn't touch anything; just looked. I started to get my sisters, and then I heard someone talking. I thought perhaps you were still here. The sound of voices was coming from the kitchen.

I knew I shouldn't do it, but I wanted to look and see if you were still here. I slipped over to the kitchen door, and peeked around the corner. Santa, my Dad was home! Thank you! My Dad and Mommy were sitting at the kitchen table. They were acting like a couple of kids themselves. They were holding hands across the table. And best of all, Santa, they weren't drinking whiskey. They were drinking coffee.

My Mommy was acting funny. She was crying and laughing at the same time. I never will understand grownups. When I saw she was crying, I couldn't stand still. I went into the kitchen, and asked her what was wrong. She told me nothing was wrong, but this was the best Christmas we would ever have.

My Dad pulled me up on his lap, and gave me a big hug and a kiss. He said the reason Mommy was crying was because she was so happy. I still couldn't understand it. Why do grownups cry when they're happy? My Dad then told me there would be no more war for him. I still didn't understand, and told him so. He told me he wouldn't be going away any more. He said he had stacked arms. I didn't know what that meant. He said when soldiers were through fighting, they stacked their guns in neat little rows, which meant there would be no more fighting for them. He said he had done his part, and didn't want to see any more little boys like me whose mothers and fathers had been killed, and maybe he was responsible. I know my Dad wouldn't hurt anyone on purpose, especially if they had children like me.

And then Dad told me the best news of all. He said that right after

New Years, we were going to move back to his home in the mountains, and we would never have to be apart again. He said we would spend all our Christmases together from now on, and that he and Mommy would do all their celebrating with coffee.

Santa, it must make you feel good to bring such nice gifts and happiness to people on Christmas. This year you brought the best gift of all; the one my Dad was never able to bring before. Knowing Dad and Mommy will be together with us for all our Christmases made this the best Christmas ever.

Thank you, Santa.
Bill

# STARK TERROR!

By: Dana T. Moore, II

I was extremely fortunate to spend the happiest, and most productive years of my adult life as a fighter pilot in the USAF. During that period, I frequently heard flying defined as, "Hours and hours of sheer boredom, interspersed with occasional moments of stark terror." The following is an account of one of those moments of stark terror.

When I was still a gold-bar, Second Lieutenant in the USAF, the most knowledgeable pilot in the world, and a recent assignee as an advanced flight instructor in the Fighter School at Williams AFB, Chandler, Arizona, I had occasion to take a weekend, proficiency cross-country training flight. A friend, and flight school classmate of mine, also an instructor, and I, took two F-80 jet fighters on a weekend training flight. Contrary to popular opinion, the purpose of the weekend flying was not for fun and games, but actually for training, and experience. This type of flying exposed us to navigational practice, weather flying, strange field approaches and landings, and occasionally, as I was to learn this particular weekend, in-flight problems of potentially terminal magnitude.

As was customary, we took off after work on a Friday afternoon. Following several refueling stops, we ended up at Biggs AFB, at El Paso, Texas, where we spent the night. The next day, we put in a full schedule flying around the southwestern United States, finally calling it a night at Bergstrom AFB, Austin, Texas.

A brief author intrusion here might be in order. The F-80 was designed with one fuselage tank, a pair of internal main wing tanks, a pair of leading edge tanks, also in the wings, and a pair of external wing-tip drop tanks. All the fuel tanks fed into the fuselage tank, and thence to the engine for consumption. The pilot managed the fuel by selectively transferring fuel from the drops, main wing, and/or the leading edge tanks. Fuel transfer was done by electrically driven fuel pumps within the wing tanks, and air pressure from the drops. The normal order of transfer was from the drops first, main wings second, and leading edge tanks last. When the fuel aboard was down to the fuselage tank only, there were 207 gallons remaining, and thus, approximately 40 minutes flight before landing.

And now, on to the thrill of this weekend odyssey. On Sunday we filed out of Bergstrom AFB for Kirtland AFB in Albuquerque, New Mexico. The weather for our flight was predicted to be clear to partially scattered, with no significant wind or weather problems en route. We estimated the flight to take approximately an hour and a half. This leg was my turn to plan, file, and lead, with my friend flying my wing.

After departure, we switched our radios to our pre-briefed en route frequency. I could not contact my wingman, so by hand signal, instructed him to return to our last radio channel. Still no contact. The only channel we could talk to one another on was a squadron common, which we then resorted to. My youth and inexperience didn't allow for concern over this minor communications glitch.

The next occurrence, which should have alerted me to the fact that all was not as it should be, was a complete fizzle on the en route weather forecast. We had to climb over a cloud layer, and could no longer navigate by visual reference to the ground. No problem for a couple of intrepid aviators such as we.

Now, as we drew closer to our destination than to our departure point, just past the point of no return, I noted my main wing tanks were dry, and turned that switch off, then the leading edge tanks on. As usual, I watched the fuselage tank gauge to ensure that it remained full, indicating the fuel was transferring normally. The fuselage gauge began a disconcerting drop from the full mark. No transfer of leading edge fuel! As the needle on the gauge continued its inexorable decrease, I called my wingman, and told him of my predicament. After roughly pumping the stick sideways, and back and forth, to hopefully jar the internal fuel pumps into operation, and watching the fuselage tank continue to empty, being the fast thinker I am, I came to the conclusion I had a real problem. Some quick mental math told me that I would arrive at Kirtland just as the last of my fuselage fuel was used up. Not too good, since Kirtland was located in mountains reaching up to 12,000 feet. The unpredicted cloud coverage beneath us was growing thicker by the mile.

I asked my wingman to call Kirtland DF (Direction Finder) for a steer into Kirtland. I didn't want to waste time wandering around on top of the clouds hoping for a hole to peer down through, and find the field. By this time, my only radio navigation aid, a radio compass, was wandering aimlessly around. I felt I was doing likewise. The fuselage gauge continued to drop, along with my self assurance. And to make matters worse, the only channel I could talk to anyone on was our squadron common.

Observing the fuel gauge hovering almost on the "E," I began to think about bailing out. I had no desire to tangle with one of those high mountains. I was mentally reviewing the bailout procedure when my wingman called me, and said we had just passed over Kirtland AFB. Looking down, I saw nothing but solid clouds.

Mindful of the rocks in those clouds, I throttled back, and began a circling descent. Entering the clouds at 20,000 feet, I decided that if I were not in the clear, with the field in sight at 14,000 feet altitude, I was going to roll over, and take to my chute. We didn't have ejection seats in those days. At that precise moment, my engine flamed out! No more fuel.

Tensing myself for what I was certain was going to be a nylon letdown, I saw the clouds rise above me, and I could see the ground. Directly below me was beautiful Kirtland AFB!

Continuing in a descending 360 degree turn, I arrived over the runway with about 1,500 feet altitude. I continued in a descending turn. Lowering the landing gear and flaps, I rolled out on final, and glided to a perfect dead-stick landing. The engine had windmilled enough to provide the hydraulic pressure for the wheels to lower and lock.

In the early days of jet flying, there weren't any such maneuvers as simulated flame-out patterns and landings. Those evolved later as the training program for student pilots expanded. I did what I knew best, and that was to make a normal overhead traffic pattern. We were still in the old days of striving for power off, glide and land patterns.

After rolling to a stop, I turned on the leading edge fuel transfer pumps, and wonder of wonders! The pumps functioned normally, rapidly transferring fuel into my fuselage tank. Cause of the malfunction? Gasoline, or jet fuel, has a slight percentage of water in it. This water is normally precipitated out when the aircraft is on the ground, and separates from the fuel, settling to the bottom of the fuel tank. Part of the normal daily pre-flight inspection is to drain the water from all the tanks via a petcock drain on each tank, under the wing. Had I done this?

This best aviator in the world had neglected to drain the water from the fuel; a very basic precaution taught to the most inexperienced student pilots. Age and accurate hindsight allow me to admit to this error of omission. I also allow that it taught the best pilot in the world something he needed; just a little less cocksure attitude, and a little more adherence to established procedures designed to prolong life in the air. No more kick the tire, and light the fire!

# TOKE 'N ROACH

## BY: DANA T. MOORE, II

"I'd never believe it!" the petite little nun said, her tone of voice, and facial expression lending credence to the exclamation of disbelief.

"Me neither," replied her equally disbelieving companion, also dressed in the habit of a Roman Catholic Nun.

The two middle aged women, sworn advocates in the service of God, and wed to Jesus through their vows, sat and stared at the cache of funny money, and equally funny tobacco. The two had stumbled upon a hidden trove of counterfeit money, and perhaps an even more valuable treasure of marijuana. The site of this find was almost as unbelievable as the find itself; in the sacristy of the church; the place where the ladies of the altar guild normally prepared the elements of bread, wine, and water for administration of holy communion.

And to make the find even more troubling than violation of the law was the fact the site was in the local Episcopal Church of The Eternally Devoted. The pot was in a large cardboard box marked "Altar candles." Inside the box were several layers of neatly laid rows of compressed, brown-paper wrapped, one pound rectangles of marijuana, commonly referred to as "Bricks;" two and a half bricks totaling one kilo. The counterfeit money was in an equally symbolic box labeled "Unconsecrated bread." The funny money was new, and banded together in small stacks of $20 dollar bills. Taken at face value, the money must have been worth several hundred thousand dollars, or perhaps even more.

"Wonder what kind of sermons this pot produced?" mused the first to discover the contraband. Her name was Sister Lisa, originally christened Lisa Thomas, but for years known to her intimate friends as "Toke," the nickname deriving from her nearly ethereal size and translucent skin. Her former habit of using marijuana, before entering the nunnery, may have been a factor in settling the nom-de-plume upon her by some long forgotten, casually met, sharing user of the weed.

Toke's companion chuckled in a raspy voice, then said, "And I wonder how much of the fine trappings of this wealthy den of protestant infidels was bought with funny money like this?" The acidly sarcastic remark came from Sister Marie, once legally known as Janelle Marie Rollins, also bearing a nickname, "Roach," derived from her prenunnery past; the name perhaps evolving from her diminutive stature.

The two nuns, both former successful ladies of the night, and denizens of the street, had seen the wasteful, destructive destiny in their lifestyle, and with neither knowing either, converted to the Roman Catholic faith, and together entered the nunnery as novitiates. Completing training, and taking their vows, they were wed to Christ, and began a life of servitude in an attempt to help man, rather than skin him. Before conversion, they had both been frequent partakers of marijuana, among other drugs, and though never becoming dependent upon the substance, did become intimately familiar with the use of narcotics, and its attendant evils.

Lately, Toke and Roach had become involved in a community wide crusade to gather a large sum of money to help in the foundation of a new nursing home for the elderly of all faiths. This crusade was to peak out during the current Christmas season, terminating with a bazaar held at the Episcopal Church of The Eternally Devoted several days before Christmas. The bazaar was on the near immediate horizon, three days hence. Toke and Roach, possibly as a result of their tendency to over compensate when dealing with the human derelicts of the street, had been "volunteered" to the fund drive chairman as representatives from the local Catholic church by the Mother Superior. Their caste standing was probably reflected in Mother Superior's nominating statement to the two nuns, "Perhaps this will use up some of your inexhaustible energy, and simultaneously keep you out of my hair."

"Wonder where this stuff came from?" Roach mused, the incredulity now gone from her voice. "Wonder also how it got here, and who it belongs to," she continued in the manner of thinking aloud.

"The pot looks like good stuff," Toke observed.

"Yes, good Colombian," Roach concurred, crumpling a pinch, then sniffing it. "And that funny money looks authentic to me." Toke went on.

"Don't suppose the funny money was to pay for the pot, do you?" Roach asked, still clenching the pinch of pot in her right hand.

"Could be," Toke replied. Then, "You know, Roach, I think it's our duty to find out if this stuff is what we think it is."

"Think we oughta?" Roach asked, a crafty expression sliding over her face, while her hand extended a package of rolling papers.

"Our bounden duty," Toke replied, taking a slip of paper, and in the flash of an eye, quickly, and single handedly rolling a joint, demonstrating amazing retention of a habit long since discarded. "Pretty good, huh," she said, a smile of self-satisfaction on her face.

"Well," Roach observed, "You always were a slight-of-hand artist." This comment evolved from their novitiate years together.

Placing a lighted match to the joint dangling from a corner of her mouth, Toke took a long pull, and inhaled deeply. "Aaahh," she exhaled, a look of pleasant reaction on her face. "The best! High grade Colombian!" she said, the expression on her face corroborating the verbal ecstasy.

Lighting her own cigarette, Roach confirmed Toke's finding. "Yeah, this is high grade stuff. Wonder whose it is?"

"Don't know, but we oughta find out, and decide what to do with it," Toke replied, still thinking aloud.

"Do with it?" Roach echoed. "Whattaya mean do with it?"

"Well," Toke again replied, "We sure can't leave this stuff here, even if it is in a protestant church. We gotta get it outta here, and take it some place where it'll be safe while we figure out what to do with it."

"Looks like we're already doing with it," Roach replied, a languorous look lowering upon her face, while she took another long pull on the joint.

"Maybe," Toke countered, but remember, we have a big need for a big pile of money right away for the new nursing home. This stash of funny money and pot might just be the answer to our prayers. Maybe we can convert this lucky find to a bankroll for the nursing home."

"You're right, Toke," Roach agreed, bowing to the wisdom of her pragmatic, prelatic partner. "But just what do you have in mind for it? How do we go about getting it out of here?"

"Tell you what, Roach. With the labels on those boxes, who's gonna look inside them? We can call a cab, and get the driver to carry them out for us. He'll not likely be inquisitive about the contents with us being nuns. We can take the stuff to our room in the sister's home. Once inside the home, I feel sure no one will be the wiser. Then we can take our time, and figure out what to do with it. I still think we can convert it to a big bundle of cash."

Sometime later, between labored grunts, and spasmodic intakes of breath, the cabbie, straining under the liturgical load, managed a pathetic admonition. "Sister, I sure hope you don't have to move any more of these boxes of bread and candles." "If we do, we'll get one of the Fathers to move it. And we're sure beholden to you for your help," Toke answered, a benign expression on her face. Roach's face had the same look. An observer, experienced with the dream weed, might have perceived their expressions as being more exotic than divine in origin.

The next day, following morning Mass, and a Spartan breakfast, as was their custom, Toke and Roach retired to their quarters, telling Mother Superior they had to develop a recap on the fund drive activity for the man in charge, Theo Elysium, Rector of The Church of The Eternally Devoted.

"Well, what now?" Roach asked, not really expecting an answer.

"Maybe we should call on some of our former connections to find out where this stuff came from, Roach. Think you still have any contacts who might give us a straight answer?"

"I think I might come up with a name or two."

"Well then, let's get on with it," Toke replied. "This stuff is too hot to let any grass grow under our feet, no nun pun intended."

Some time later, the two nuns arrived at a back-alley pool hall, beer parlor, and numbers betting shop where they had done business before. Taking an unobtrusive seat in the dimly lighted area adjacent to the end of the bar, Toke called to the bartender.

"How about some service over here, Fred?"

"Well, I'll be damned! Toke! Ain't seen you in years! What's with the costume? Don't tell me you've gone straight. Who's that with you? Is that Roach Rollins, former well-known lady of the evening?" This last was followed with a deep chuckle.

"Okay, Fred, knock off the jokes," Roach replied. "Toke and I need some info, and we think you're the man to talk to."

"Whattaya need, Ladies?" Fred responded, the corners of his mouth still quivering upward in the traces of a smile. "Howzabout a beer?"

"No," Toke answered. "But we could use some coffee."

"Here's the coffee. Now, what kinda info you after?" Fred asked, placing the coffee before them, then settling into the booth beside Roach.

"Hear anything about a load of funny money, and grass hitting town?" Toke asked, sipping her coffee.

"Don't know if I want to talk to you two or not," Fred said, rising from his sitting position.

"Come on, Roach, let's go see the D. A. and talk to him about some numbers. Numbers, and betting."

"Awright, awright!" Fred countered, sinking back into his seat. "I heard something about some funny money being brought into town to be unloaded at the Christmas Bazaar. Also heard a bundle of grass was parked here for the same reason. Apparently there's going to be a lot of loose money in town during the bazaar."

"Who brought the stuff in?" Roach asked.

"Joe Gutenberger brought the funny money in from Chicago. Max Overgross, pilot for Great Smokey Air Line out of Fort Liquordale brought the grass in," Fred answered.

"Great Smokey Air Line? When'd Max get into the air line business?" Toke asked.

"Oh, 'bout seven or eight years back," Fred replied. "Seems he helped start the air line with money going south for laundering, and grass coming north for distribution. Shoulda been called the Green Dream Line."

"How do they plan to unload it, Fred?" Toke asked, afraid of the answer.

"Street talk has it they're going to set up a booth at the bazaar, and peddle the stuff there." Pausing for a moment, Fred continued, his brows lowering in a scowl. "How'd you two get wind of this? It's got high powered connections here in town. You could be asking for big trouble."

"The Lord looks after those who look after themselves," Roach replied.

"Well, if you two do what I'm thinking you're thinking of doing, you're gonna need the Lord," Fred warned.

"Thanks, Fred, for the coffee, the info, and the warning," Toke said, rising from the booth, followed by Roach.

"Girls, I'd be careful, if I was you," Fred said in farewell.

Once more in the privacy of a taxi, Toke acknowledged the folly of bringing in the authorities, who might already be involved as moneyed investors. "They'd just confiscate the stuff, and before we knew it, they'd have the pot back on the market," Toke lamented.

"You're right, Toke," Roach concurred. "Whattaya think we oughta do with this boodle bundle?"

"Let's do some dealing, Roach. Who's gonna think to look in the Catholic Sister's home for a load of pot and funny money? We're in the Catbird Seat. Let's see if we can make a deal, turn the real money over to the chairman of the drive, and then worry about getting rid of the bad booty."

"That's the best shot, Toke. Who do you think we should work with?" "Probably our best bet would be to get in touch with Max Overgross. Maybe we can talk to him, if he isn't completely zonked on coke," Toke replied.

Leaning forward, Toke spoke to the cabbie, "Take us out to the county airport, Driver."

As the taxi pulled into the airport operations area, Toke again leaned forward, and spoke, "Drop us at the Great Smokey Air Line's office, please."

"You ain't figuring to fly with that bunch, are you, Sister?" the cabbie asked, a look of apprehension on his face. "If you are, you're gonna need an extra set of rosary beads."

"No," Roach replied, "We just have some business with one of their officials. How much we owe you?"

"Ten even, Sister."

"Here," Roach said, extending the fare to the cabbie, "And Merry Christmas," she added.

Boldly entering the door marked, "Operations, Great Smokey Air Line," Toke and Roach were greeted with a somnambulistic air line pilot, sleeping at a desk behind the ticket counter. The middle-aged man was dressed in a well-worn, World War II leather flight jacket, dark sun glasses, western style cowboy hat with a long, incongruous feather arcing back over his shoulder, and a pair of gray, alligator-skin cowboy boots covering his feet reposing on the desk before him. He was laid well back in the swivel desk chair, mouth agape, snoring like a chain saw working through a chord of lumber. His face sported a well grayed beard, and mustache, somewhat in need of trimming.

"That's Max. Hope he isn't too far gone," Toke said. Then, pounding on the counter top, she yelled, "Wake up, Max!"

Reflexively slamming his feet to the floor, Max snapped abruptly upright. "Check our six o'clock position! What's up? What the hell's goin' on?" he muttered, feather quivering back and forth behind his head. Blinking his unseeing, sleep and drug dazed eyes, he tried to focus on the two nuns standing before him.

"What's the matter, Max. Still airborne? Maybe a little case of the strings?" Roach asked, a grin on her face.

Huh?" Max muttered, mind trying to penetrate drug fogged sleep, and bridge the gap between the present, and the dim past embodied in the vocal familiarity of the two Nuns.

"Don't know your old friends any more, Max? Toke asked.

Max stared, brow knit in toiling thought, trying to make the connection. No use. All the mental circuits were overloaded.

"Come on, Max. It's Toke and Roach," Roach volunteered.

Recognition! Max stared in disbelief, then asked, "What the hell you two doin' dressed like that? You gone straight? Too much!"

"Yeah, Max, we've turned over a new leaf. And speaking of the leaf, we're here to talk to you about some leaves; a lot of them," Roach continued.

"Leaves?" What kinda leaves?" Max asked, suspicion strong in his tone of voice.

"Well, Max, Man of The Wild Blue Yonder, seems there's a fresh load of pot and funny money in town. Plans are to move the stuff at the bazaar being held to raise funds for the nursing home," Toke answered.

Mention of pot and funny money sent Max's eyebrows arcing almost to the same height his nose candy usually sent his mind. Up and out!

"Now, Max," Toke continued, "We know where this stuff came from, and we also know the plans for moving it. We want in for some of the real money!"

"Sure!" Max retorted derisively, "What makes you think anyone's gonna deal you in?" Think those religious robes will cut anything? No way!"

"The robes, maybe not," Roach replied, "But you will. You have a problem, and don't even know it yet."

"Like what?" Max asked sarcastically.

"Like where's your pot and funny money? It's no longer blessed with the church's unwitting sanctuary."

"Huh?" Max replied, his face a dull mask of incomprehension.

"Yeah, Max, your investment is gone. We've got it. It's no longer stashed away in the church. Feel like dealing a little now?" Roach continued her relentless probing of a not too well organized defense.

"I'm listening," Max grunted grudgingly.

"Why not give Toke and me half the face value of the funny money, and half the street value of the pot. Then, once we have the money, we'll put you onto the lost cache of dream and green."

"What's to guarantee me you won't try working both ends against the middle, and deal with someone else at the same time?" Max growled, his face taking on the cunning expression of a survivor.

"Max, if you can't trust two nuns, who's left in the world to trust?" Toke asked, her face benign, and free of guile.

"Hmm," Max responded, weighing the offer. "What if I refuse?" He asked, face showing a combination of distrust, and disgust.

"Well, Max, ole flyboy buddy, we can always dump this stuff on the Feds. They'll be tickled to get their hands on it, and the only rebate you'll get is loss of your investment. We might even get a finder's fee, which is a lot better than nothing, and more than you'll have," Toke warned.

Max glowered.

Roach followed up. "And think, Max, it's Christmas; the time for giving. Wouldn't you like to make some people happy with a big contribution; a big gift to the fund for the nursing home? Think of all the people who will be infinitely happier because of your generosity." Roach smiled, tongue in cheek.

Max glowered even more intensely. Then, "I make lots of people happy with my imports. And I also make myself happy. Howzabout you give me back the load, and I give you a donation?"

"C'mon, Max. Think we were born yesterday?" Toke asked disgustedly. "Once you get your hands on that pile again, it's s'long to ole Max." Then, turning, Toke continued, "Let's go, Roach. Max would rather we give the stuff to the Feds, anyway." The two nuns turned to leave the operations building.

"Awright! Awright! Just how much you figure the total take to be?" Max asked, caving in to the two nuns, and his strung out condition.

177

"Well, Max," Roach replied, grinning victoriously, "A conservative guess would be $500 thousand in real money for us." "Half a million!" Max exploded. "Where'm I gonna get that kinda green?"

"Your business associates could underwrite it as 'Import Tarrif,' and not even miss it. The option is much more expensive," Toke answered. "Probably more expensive to you than anyone else, all things considered."

The implication was'nt wasted on Max.

"How we gonna set it up?" he asked.

"Tell you what, Max. "You're the big time operator from dreamland. You set it up, and get in touch with us. You have two days until the bazaar. You can reach us at either the Catholic Sister's home, or through Theo Elysium, Rector of The Episcopal Church of The Eternally Devoted. And Max," Toke went on, "Don't try anything funny. Your business associates would take a dim view of your rousting a couple of poor, defenseless nuns trying to help the elderly."

"Especially at Christmas," Roach added.

With that, the two nuns turned to leave. "We'll be waiting to hear from you, Max. Merry Christmas!" Toke tossed over her shoulder.

"Bah! Humbug!" was the only seasonal reply Max could call to mind.

Later that afternoon, Toke took a call from Theo Elysium. "Sister Lisa, do you know a man named Overgross, President of Great Smokey Air Line?"

"Yes, Father, I know the man," Toke answered in a neutral tone of voice, not sure just what Max may have said to the good Rector.

"Well, Sister," Theo went on, Mr. Overgross was by to see me in the rectory a few minutes ago. He left something for you. Said you would be most anxious to see it."

"What is it, Father?" Toke asked.

"It's a large manila envelope, addressed to you and Sister Marie. I thought you would want to come on down and pick it up. Might be important." "Be right there, Father," Toke answered.

Shortly thereafter, Toke and Roach disembarked from a taxi, and hurried into the Episcopal rectory, where Theo still labored at his rectorial duties. Accepting the envelope from Theo, Toke glanced worriedly at Roach, then quickly ripped it open.

"Wow!" Toke exhaled in astonishment. The envelope contained a thick wad of greenbacks. Toke checked them for authenticity, recalling the presence of Joe Gutenberger in the area. All old, all good.

"You got yours. I want mine," read the accompanying note. Toke saw the money was in large bills, totaling $500 thousand, as specified. Pocketing the message, Toke soundlessly handed the money over to Theo, whose eyes were by now bulging in disbelief.

"A donation from a former acquaintance," Toke explained.

"His name sure wasn't 'Scrooge,'" Theo allowed.

Roach nodded wordlessly, wondering now what they were going to do with the pot and funny money.

"That oughta help with the nursing home, Father," Toke offered, diverting Theo from the source of cash to the pressing problem of the new home. "Help? It should see us over the top!" Theo replied excitedly.

"Merry Christmas, Father," Toke said, the two nuns turning to leave.

"And the same to you," Theo replied tonelessly, his mind still on the cash clutched in his hand.

Once again in the privacy of their room, the two nuns confronted the thorny question of what to do with the counterfeit money and marijuana. "We can't just give it back to Max," Roach lamented.

"No, we have to dispose of it permanently, but how?" Toke asked.

"If we don't produce this stuff for Max and Joe to set up in their booth at the bazaar, things are going to get nasty," Roach reminded Toke.

"Don't you know it!" Toke agreed. Then, thinking through the problem, she came to a conclusion. "Roach, we can't let this pot get loose at the bazaar. The funny money doesn't make any difference, since the Feds will get their hands on it pretty quickly. The money may upset the local economy for a few days, but no permanent damage is likely to occur. The pot, however, is a horse of another garage. If that stuff is pushed at the bazaar, a lot of people are going to be hurt, and once sold, there's very little chance of getting it back, and out of circulation." Toke paused.

Roach nodded in agreement. "Well, whattaya think we oughta do?"

"Let's give the funny money back to them. As for the dream weed, I think we need to be a little more crooked than they are," Toke replied, a determined look on her face.

"Don't quite understand," Roach replied.

"Come on, Sister Marie. You remember what used to happen when the Narcs put the squeeze on people like Max, and the weed was cut off.

The street vendors had to come up with something to keep their regular customers happy."

"You wouldn't!" Roach responded, recalling the situation Toke referenced. "That could be dangerous; very dangerous!"

"It's a risk we gotta take," Toke answered. Then, "Let's get on downtown, and do some shopping."

That evening, in the security of their room, equipped with the necessary tools and ingredients to implement their deception, the two nuns set to work. "It's gonna be a long night," Toke commented.

"Just as well," Roach replied. "We'll have to be down in the basement at the furnace. Sure hope the heating system is good and tight. Hate to have everyone in this convent stoned."

"That'd be great!" Toke concurred. "The whole church staff stoned! Best we keep an eye out for that. Even so, as late as we'll be working, most all the folks will sleep it off before morning."

During Mass the next morning, The Mother Superior seemed to be watching the two naughty nuns very closely. After service, she approached them, a worried look in her eye.

"How's the fund drive going, Sisters?" Mother Superior solicitously asked.

"Very well, Mother," Toke answered.

"You two look as if you've been putting in some long, hard hours. Your eyes are pretty red. Sleeping well at night?"

Toke and Roach fidgeted before the interrogation. "Yes, Mother, well enough," Roach replied.

"Me, too," Mother Superior acknowledged. "Funny thing, though. I had the most weird dreams last night. Can't understand it. Almost like that time I was under anesthesia in the hospital for surgery. Sure was peculiar." She shook her head wonderingly.

"Perhaps you're just overworked, Mother," Toke volunteered.

"Maybe," Mother Superior acknowledged in farewell, a suspicious look on her face as she walked down the hall to her office.

"Suppose she knows anything?" Roach asked.

"Doubt it. She's a smart cooky, though. Don't sell her short," Toke answered. "Well, let's get on with the delivery to the Episcopal Church. The bazaar is tomorrow. We'll just put things back where we found them, and let Joe and Max see to their own booth arrangements."

"Hope Max doesn't get too curious about the grass," Roach commented.

"I doubt that he will, Roach. I'm willing to bet he'll be so spaced out on his nose candy, he won't know what's going on. By the time any customers decide to complain, the bazaar will be over, and Max most likely will be on his way back to Fort Liquordale. Be quite a while before he realizes he's become the Christmas Bazaar Salad King."

The bazaar was a smashing success. Theo took in almost twice the total money set as the target for the nursing home, thanks to the contribution Max made to Toke and Roach. Joe Gutenberger unloaded his funny money. Max passed his grass, and personally loaded with coke and cash, and with visions of sugar plums nestled in his head, made a wobbly, unsteady takeoff from the county airport, his feather quivering in perfect synchronization with the quavering roar of the straining old engines on his World War II, B-25.

A few weeks later, Toke and Roach feigned ignorance when Mother Superior asked them what was meant by the expression "The Bizarre Bazaar," a title given by local wags to the fund raising exercise in the Church of The Eternally Devoted.

"Perhaps some irreverent reference to the salad sold at the bazaar, Mother," Toke answered, eyes cast downward innocently.

"Salad?" Mother Superior echoed without understanding.

"Yes, Mother Superior. One of the booths at the bazaar featured the most delicious salad. It was loaded with Oregano and Parsley. I think it was one of the more popular booths there. The salad was sold out early in the day," Roach commented.

"Maybe they should have brought in more," Mother Superior said.

"No, Mother, I think they sold all the market would bear," Toke answered, glancing nervously at Roach.

Roach coughed, and shuffled her feet.

"Well, as long as the bazaar made money, and the nursing home will become a reality, we should be happy," Mother Superior said. With a resigned shrug of her shoulders, she turned, and walked off.

"All's well that ends well," Toke said in a low voice.

"Amen! Roach concurred.

## THE END

# WHOSE TRAIN IS IT?

BY: DANA T. MOORE, II

As it came out of the turn and began to pick up speed on the straightaway, the cars could be seen to sway back and forth in a sideways motion on their trucks, no doubt from the lateral forces induced in the just completed turn. It was a real beauty. The Santa Fe Special! It was of brilliant red and silver colors, with the red drawing the eye. There were two huge, powerful, streamlined diesels, followed by a long line of passenger cars. The entire effect was that of a very long, flexible arrow, moving rapidly along the track. Coming closer, it seemed to project an aura of immense, sleek power; a real tribute to man's mechanical ingenuity and his ability to combine artistic beauty and the strength of forceful efficiency.

Two pairs of watchful eyes stared intently at the train as it approached. One pair of eyes, brown, slightly tired, and wrinkled at the corners from too much looking into the sun, belonged to the older of the two observers. The other pair, young, bright blue, and eager, looked as if their owner would literally explode from the intensity and sheer happiness of the moment.

The train drew close. The long wail of its whistle could be heard as it approached the crossing not far from where the two were watching. Now they could see the small details of the train. It rumbled past them. It was a true marvel of color, sound, and motion. The flanged wheels tightly gripped the track and went "Clickety Clack," as they sped over the rail joints. The passenger cars, brightly lit from within, still swayed slightly, even though effectively checked by the strong coupling between the cars.

Watching the last car round a turn in the distance to their left, the one with the tired, brown eyes turned to his companion, and said, "Dana, I think we had better shut it down now. Mummy has the Christmas dinner almost ready.

"Okay, Dad," Dana reluctantly agreed, his blue eyes following the still moving train, his face a study in fascinated rapture.

Observing the train enter a turn in the track at the far end of the living room, I reduced the power, and let it come to rest beneath the overhanging boughs of the decorated Christmas tree, an appropriate setting for a boy's first electric train.

While Dana scampered off to look at the steaming brown turkey his mother, Joanne, was placing on the dinner table, I looked at the train under the tree, and paused for a moment in reflective thought. I had heard it said that boys don't grow up; they only get bigger toys. Perhaps. Although my toys were now supersonic jet fighters, and the games played with them considerably more serious, I still felt a flush of pride as I thought of the excitement and happiness that shone from my son's face that Christmas morning when he first spotted the electric train sitting under the tree. His face was still wrinkled from sleep, the blond ringlets tumbling down over his forehead, and a big yawn on his face as he rubbed his eyes, and looked around to see what Santa had brought. His first reaction was one of wide eyed, incredulous disbelief, replaced almost instantly with an expression of ecstasy.

"An electric train!" his voice pealed out, as he dashed over, and scooped up as much of the train as his young arms could embrace, almost knocking the Christmas tree over in the process. Although I wasn't sure it was pride in me, my son, the electric train, or all three, I had a good feeling about it all.

The decision to get the electric train for Dana came a week or so before Christmas. I had been pondering what to get for Joanne, when, with no apparent reason, the thought flashed through my mind, "I'm going to get Dana an electric train for Christmas." It was just one of those unexplainable, random thoughts that sometimes occur.

When I broached the idea to Joanne, she replied, "Isn't Dana a little young for an electric train?"

"No!" I countered with feeling. "No boy should grow up without an electric train," I continued to explain. Nor should a father be prohibited from his rightful opportunity to run such a train, I did not explain. Not that I needed any justification, but I remembered as a boy that I had an electric train predating my first memories of Christmas. Obtaining Joanne's approval of the train, I decided to go shopping the next day.

Walking along with the happy, jostling crowd of Christmas shoppers, I recalled Joanne's final admonition to me as I left the house that morning. "Dana is only three and a half, so you don't have to spend a fortune on his train." Thus reinforced, I strolled into the toy store, little knowing I was the toy merchant's dream come true; a father looking for an electric train for his son. I bought every piece of electric train equipment I could lay my hands on. I felt like a 19th Century Vanderbilt establishing a new railroad dynasty. Lionel stock really went up that day.

Returning home, and parking in front of the house, I was met by a rather stern-faced wife. "Let's see the train," Joanne demanded. I reluctantly opened the car trunk. Joanne stared at the trunk full of boxes, all bearing the Lionel label. "Oh well," she said in mock defeat, "I've always known that I had two little boys." I looked apprehensively at her, and saw that she was smiling.

That night, while the children slept, Joanne and I stealthily slipped stack after stack of boxes into the house. It took some doing, but with Joanne's resourcefulness, and some shuffling of the closet contents, we finally managed to hide the train away from curious, prying little eyes.

Late Christmas eve, after the children were asleep, and as Joanne and I were busy placing presents under the tree, Gus, a friend from next door, came over. He volunteered to help me set up the train. After an hour or so of working on our hands and knees, Gus and I had the train layout assembled, and in place. What a beauty it was! It had remote control switches, and uncouplers, crossings, and two engines for a train complete with whistles, plus a track pattern that covered most of the living room floor, much to Joanne's chagrin. After making sure that everything functioned properly, Gus started to leave. Pausing at the door, he turned to me, and said, "I'll be over tomorrow and help you check Dana out on running a railroad. Gus had two daughters, and no electric train.

Now, after having eaten much too much of a delicious Christmas dinner, followed by a needed post Christmas morning cleanup project,

Joanne and I were sitting on the couch, each of us trying to throw off the drowsy stupor of over eating. The children were dressed for bed. It had been a nice Christmas day. Dana walked over, and stood in front of me, looking very serious. The snap on the front of his pajamas, one that held the top and bottom together, was popped open. His pink, turkey filled tummy stuck out of the open gap in his pajamas. "Dad, can we run the train a little more before bed?" he asked.

"Sure, Son. Let's go."

Bending over to plug the transformer into the wall socket, I heard a knock on the front door. Before I could get to my feet, the door opened, and in stepped Gus. He was wearing a black and white striped engineer's cap. A red bandanna handkerchief trailed from his hip pocket. Taking in the situation at a glance, he said, "I see we're all ready for a demonstration in railroad operation."

"Sure, Gus. You can be the engineer, and the rest of us will be the conductors." Gus leaped eagerly to the task.

After several minutes of standing by the edge of the track, watching the train in total absorption, Dana did what any normal boy his age would do. As the train approached him, he leaned down, and with both hands, picked the engines off the track. The rest of the train tumbled onto the carpet in distorted disarray. Gus, his face slightly flushed, carefully replaced the train on the track, and slowly explained to Dana that this was not the way to run a train. Dana listened intently.

Several minutes later, the same thing happened again. Gus's face took on a deeper flushed appearance. Joanne and I exchanged glances of amusement. Once again Gus carefully replaced the train, and at the same time, administered the slow explanation to Dana. As before, Dana listened intently. Almost before we realized it, Dana once more grabbed the engines, with the same resulting pileup. Gus reached the end of his patience.

"How in the hell can I run this train with King Kong knocking it off the track!" he exploded.

Joanne stepped smoothly into the breach. "It's time for the kids to be in bed, anyway," she said. Turning to Dana, with a wink, she added, "Come on, Son. Tomorrow the boys have to go back to work, and then you can play with YOUR train all you want to." Joanne effectively gave a verbal underline to the pronoun 'Your.' As Joanne led the children off to bed, I thought I detected a look of sly determination on Dana's face.

"Come on, Gus, let's go out in the kitchen for a drink while Joanne puts the kids to bed." Gus accompanied me to the kitchen, still looking somewhat distraught. Joanne rejoined us in a few minutes, and helped herself to a drink.

Following some rambling conversation, a couple more drinks, and some foot shuffling, Gus finally blurted out, "Let's get back to the train." As we walked into the living room, there was no mistaking the look of anticipation on Joanne's face.

Stepping over to the train, Gus stopped abruptly, a look of horror on his face. "The engines! Where are the engines? They're gone!" he yelled out. I looked, and sure enough, the train engines were nowhere in sight.

Turning, I saw Joanne motion us to follow her. Signaling for silence, she quietly opened the door to Dana's room. As the hall light fell on that peaceful, blond-headed face, sheathed in the sheer tranquility of innocent childhood slumber, I looked at Dana, and almost burst out laughing. Clutched tightly, one under each arm, were the shiny engines to the Santa Fe Special.

Quietly retracing our steps, I was the last out the door. I turned for one more glance at Dana. As I did so, I saw him cautiously open one eye. Seeing that I was now alone in the doorway, he whispered to me, "Whose train is it now, Dad?" King Kong had the last word.

# THE CHRISTMAS CAKE

By: Dana T. Moore, II

Watching the snow steadily falling, he shivered in his foxhole.
"Damn!" He thought. "Christmas Eve, and here I sit, freezing my backside off!" He was convinced there could be no more intense cold than the cold in a foxhole on Christmas Eve, at midnight, in a hostile, foreign land, with snow pelting down. He pulled his heavy G.I. topcoat tighter around his neck. He already had his M-1 Garand rifle warming inside his topcoat. Rifles weren't much good when they froze. Neither were soldiers.

Christmas Eve, 1944. Outpost duty in a foxhole in Belgium. He was part of a thinly spread picket line on guard against attacking German troops. The Americans had been fighting a retreating, delaying action since December 16, the opening day of the German offensive. This soldier's unit was on the very front edge of the rear guard effort, almost in constant contact with the Germans. The fighting had been both bitter and bloody.

This particular American soldier didn't know what was going on. All he knew for sure was that it was cold enough to freeze the oil on his rifle, and the apparently unstoppable Germans were only a short distance east, probably not more than a few yards. He, along with a great many American troops, had thought he would be home by now, enjoying Christmas with his family. Somehow, the beaten German Wehrmacht did not agree, and the war roared bitterly on. The Americans were in the midst of the Battle of The Bulge, the last major German counteroffensive of the war. "Surely it won't last much longer!" he thought hopefully.

"Hey, Amerikaner! Wie geht es ihnen?" The voice came from the darkness, beyond his visual range. He kept quiet.

"American G. I. how are you? Are you hungry?" This time the question was in English, but with a decided German inflection, and in a pleading tone of voice.

He knew American soldiers had fallen for this trap in the past, and ended up with a bullet between the eyes, or a slit throat. He kept quiet, but now his M-1 was no longer warming inside his coat. It was cocked, and ready, pointed toward the sound of the German speaker.

"Ich habe, I have bockwurst und schwarzbrot, black bread. Would you like to share? It is Weinachtsfest, or Christmas, as you call it. Could we not call a brief halt to making war, and share a common Christian belief in Jesus? I also have some very good beer we could share. Perhaps you have something good to eat from home."

"I have a chocolate cake. Arrived from home this morning. It's still fresh. Flown over by air mail," the American shouted into the darkness. "I haven't even opened it yet."

"Mein Gott!" the German replied. "A real chocolate cake! I have not tasted chocolate in over a year. Bitte! Bitte! Please! Please! Let us share on this most glorious of nights; remembrance of the birth of our Christ."

"Should I take a chance?" the American thought. "Christ never knew what an American or a German was. Would Christ condemn either of them for sharing a few moments of Christian togetherness? I don't think He would," he thought further. "How to go about doing it?" he wondered.

"Do you have a flashlight?" he shouted at the German.

"Yah, Ich habe ein flashlight. I will turn it on." the German replied.

"You turn on your light, and I will turn mine on," the American replied.

Momentarily, approximately 50 yards to his front, the American spotted a small pinpoint of light, shining on the face of the German soldier. He turned on his light, and focused it on his own face. No gunfire erupted.

"I will meet you halfway," the American shouted. He saw the German soldier stand, and carefully step from his own foxhole. The American saw the German holding a Schmeisser machine pistol in his hand, sling looped loosely around his neck. What appeared to be a full musette bag hung from his shoulder. The American climbed from his foxhole, grasping his rifle, finger on the trigger. He held his chocolate cake gingerly under his left arm. The two men warily walked toward one another.

As they closed to a face-to-face distance, the German slowly sat. The American did likewise. The American spoke, "Wie heissen Sie? Ihr vornahme!"

"Du sprichst Deutsche!" the German exclaimed. "Wo lernen Sie?"

"Ihr namen, bitte?" The American repeated.

"Mein vornahme ist Dieter. Mein namen ist Dieter Schnetz. Bitte, let us speak English," the German answered. "Und your name?"

"My name is Liam Kelly," the American answered in English. "My mother came from Germany right after the first world war. My father is a first generation Irish American. That's something! I speak German, Gaelic, and English. Here I am, an American, with an Irish father, a German mother, talking to a German soldier in the middle of combat, on Christmas eve in Belgium! Froehliche Weinachten!"

"And Merry Christmas to you, also," the German said. He then reached into his musette bag, and extracted two, one-liter bottles of beer, a loaf of black bread, and a huge, looping rope of bockwurst, very similar to large American hot dogs.

The American tenderly lay the chocolate cake on the ground between them, and carefully unwrapped it. He had not yet seen the cake himself. There, in all its splendor, reposed a beautiful, uncut chocolate cake, with deep, rich fudge icing all over it. His mother had baked it. Deeply imbedded in the top center of the cake were two figurines, on their sides, facing one another. Careful scrutiny revealed them to be small, exquisitely crafted wooden, miniature mirror image reproductions of Jesus as He would have appeared in the manger. Staring at the cake, both the American and the German soldiers crossed themselves reverently. Then, both their mouths watered at the sight, and smell of the chocolate.

The American unsheathed his razor-sharp bayonet, and cutting a thick slice of the cake, handed it carefully to the German.

"Danke Schoen," the German said, placing the cake in his lap, then with his own knife, cut off a section of the bockwurst, and a chunk of the black bread. Extending the meat and bread to the American, he then grasped a liter bottle of beer, and likewise handed it to the American.

"Thank you," the American said.

The two men fell to their Christmas dinner with gusto, the German eating his slice of cake first.

Shortly, as their appeased appetites took hold, the two men relaxed, and began a conversation. Following the initial amenities, the conversation gradually lapsed into German.

"Where in Germany was your mother from?" Dieter asked.

"She came from a small town outside Munich," Liam replied. "Do you recall where?" Dieter asked, this time showing more than curious interest.

"Oberammergau."

"What was her maiden name?" Dieter continued.

"Shoffner, why?" Liam replied, also with a question.

"My mother," Dieter replied, "is also from Oberammergau, and her maiden name was Shoffner. She often spoke to me of her sister who had gone to America following the first world war. Is your mother a wood carver?"

"Yes," Liam replied. "I'm sure she carved the figurines in the cake."

Nodding his head in acknowledgement, Dieter replied, "My mother is also a wood carver. Oberammergau is the center of wood carving in Germany."

The two men sat in total silence, the enormity of the revelation settling in upon them.

"We are cousins!" Liam said abruptly.

"Yes, I think so," Dieter agreed.

Liam followed up with comments that his mother had also often spoken of her sister still living in Germany. Then, "I think it's nothing short of a miracle that you and I have met this way, and in this time. Of all the times and places each of us could have been in, we are here, now, on this Christmas night, in the middle of a war!" Liam shook his head in amazement.

The two then followed up with more confirming data such as their mothers' birthdates; their first names, hair and eye color. There was no doubt the two men were first cousins. A warm family feeling settled over the two men, perhaps engendered by their full stomachs.

Liam cut, and offered more cake. When he ran his bayonet through the cake, he was careful to leave the section with the two Christ figurines untouched. Shortly, a square column of cake stood, the two figurines still untouched.

Staring at the cake, their thoughts were abruptly interrupted by the loud sound of mechanical scraping, and clanking. Appearing from the dark behind the German, the fearsome figure of a German Tiger tank approached. The American and the German soldiers rolled sideways out of the path of the oncoming juggernaut. The Tiger's tank treads rolled straddled over the remains of the two soldier's Christmas dinner.

Watching the tank move ponderously toward the American lines, Dieter ran up to the still intact cake remainder, and snatched the two Christ figurines from the icing. Turning, he saw that Liam was unhurt. "Here, Liam!" Dieter shouted, and tossed one of the twin figurines to him. "See you after the war! I also live in Oberammergau." The two men hastily gathered their personal belongings, and dashed back to their foxholes.

Not long after, in the spring of 1945, following the collapse of the German Wehrmacht, the Americans went on to cross the Rhein River at Remagen, and very shortly, Germany capitulated. Liam's infantry unit ended up in Bavaria, in the area around Munich. He had no idea where Dieter was, nor even if he had survived the bitter ending of the war. He was determined, however, to locate Dieter, alive or dead, Dieter's mother, and the rest of his relatives.

With the loosely controlled Allied military conditions in the midst of the euphoric relief at the end of the killing, Liam had no trouble obtaining a pass, a jeep, and access to unlimited fuel. He quickly loaded the jeep with coffee, C rations, blankets, clothing, a portable cooking stove, and the prize of all prizes, a case of American cigarettes. Placing his ever present Garand into the jeep, and with a portable generator hooked to the tow hitch on the rear, Liam climbed in, departed his bivouac area, and headed for Oberammergau, the jeep almost a clone of a Santa Christmas sleigh.

Little over an hour later, Liam arrived in Oberammergau. He found his way to the German equivalent of town hall, parked his jeep, and went inside. Speaking fluent German, Liam soon located Dieter Schnetz' address. He was unable to obtain any information on whether or not Dieter had survived the war, and if he were now in Oberammergau. In response to his request, the town official gave Liam directions to Dieter's home.

During the drive to Dieter's home, Liam was very surprised to observe that Oberammergau appeared to have been exempt from the Allied obliteration bombing. Most of the residential area was untouched by the destruction of war. Locating Dieter's house, Liam parked the jeep at the side of the street in front of the house. Almost from reflex, Liam grasped his rifle in one hand, and extracted the Christ figurine from the breast pocket of his Olive Drab uniform jacket.

In response to his knock on the front door, Liam saw a middle age woman fearfully peer from the partially opened door.

"Yah?" she said in a subdued voice.

Liam immediately recognized his mother's sister. The family lines were unmistakable.

Extending the wooden Christ figurine so that it was in plain sight, Liam spoke tentatively, "Tantchen Greta? Ich bin euer neffe, Liam, auf Amerika."

The expression on the woman's face went from fear, to surprise, then to incredulity. Abruptly, as realization dawned, and she accepted that this American meant her no harm, she threw open the door, and grasped Liam in a loving, emotional embrace. "Oh, Danke, Gott," she repeated over and over.

And then, before Liam could free himself from the embrace, his aunt shouted, "Dieter! Dieter! Kommen Sie hier! Euer vetter, Liam, ist hier!"

Looking over his aunt's shoulder, Liam spotted Dieter emerging from a door in the rear of the room.

The three then broke into a cacophony of mixed English and German, all spoken in a breathless outpouring of emotional release.

And then, as a modicum of emotional stability returned, Liam asked, "Dieter, please help me bring in some supplies from the jeep. I would like to get them inside before someone is tempted to take them."

"Yes, of course," Dieter acknowledged in English. The two then went outside, and unloaded the jeep, bringing the packages into the house. They unhitched and rolled the generator to the rear of Dieter's house. Dieter and his mother were amazed at the gifts Liam had brought. Dieter then called his wife, who momentarily appeared from the back of the house, followed by two children; a boy about seven years of age, and a younger, wide-eyed sister, grasping her older brother's hand.

"My wife, Traute; my son Thomas, and my daughter Petra," Dieter announced by way of introduction. Continuing, he said to his family, "My cousin from America, Liam Kelly." Dieter's wife looked at Liam with an expression of curiosity. The two children stared at him as if he were a monster from an alien world.

Liam then suggested it might be a good idea to sample some of the American coffee he had brought. The adults agreed. The children were each given candy bars, and chewing gum; all they wanted. Dieter's wife, and mother retired to the kitchen to prepare the coffee.

While the women were busy in the kitchen, and the children enjoyed the candy and gum, Liam and Dieter brought each other up to date on their activities since their meeting in Belgium. Dieter was glad the war was over. He told Liam he had known from the outset that Germany could not win such a war on such a large scale. He then asked Liam what the future held for him.

"I think I will be returned to The States in a month or so, and be discharged from the army. Now that the war is over, we all want to return to as normal a life as we can. I have a wife and children waiting at home. I think we should make some tentative plans on getting together in the not too distant future. Perhaps I can bring my mother, wife, and children to Germany to spend time with all of you, and then perhaps you can do likewise with your family by bringing them to America. In the meantime, I want to help in any way I can in getting you and your family back on a normal footing. What does the future hold for you, Dieter?"

"Before the war, I had just started a small wood carving business. It failed during my extended absence, but I want to try and get it going again. My wife is also a wood carver. I hope my wife, my mother, and I can make a go of it." With that, Dieter withdrew the twin wood carving of Christ from his pocket. "Remember this?" he asked Liam.

"Sure. It was the mirror of this," Liam answered, also withdrawing his wood carving of Christ. "I think the cake, and the carvings are what brought us together, Dieter."

"Yes, I am sure you are right," Dieter concurred. "Christ did it, but the tool was the chocolate cake.

Liam answered, "From now on, whenever I eat chocolate cake, it will forever be *The Christmas cake!*

# WHY CHRISTMAS?

## BY: DANA T. MOORE, II

The old man knew something was wrong when he sat up, and tried to stand by the side of his bed. His gyros were completely tumbled. He collapsed in a dizzy fall, and lay on the floor, his thoughts, as well as his balance, in disarray. Momentarily, he screwed up his courage, and attempted to stand. At first, when he moved to a sitting position, he toppled over on his side again. Gyros still tumbled.

Chuckling to himself, he thought, "I must look like one of those kid's toys that, when knocked over, roll automatically to an upright position. The difference is I roll to a prone position. At least there's no pain."

Trying again, he found the annoying dizzy feeling abating to a tolerable level. "Let's get up," he said to himself. Struggling to a standing position, he braced himself against the bed, then gradually, his sense of balance returned to normal, and he was able to stand with no further difficulty.

"What in the heck happened?" he wondered. "Maybe I better get on down to see our family doctor," he thought further. "And I'm not going to tell Oma about it," he firmly resolved. "Just scare her unnecessarily."

The next day, he told his wife, Oma, that he wanted to go to the book store, and look at some Christmas books for their grandchildren. She nodded absent mindedly, knowing his penchant for browsing at the book store, and also remembering that Christmas was just a few weeks away.

Some time later, he walked into the doctor's office, and told the receptionist he had to see the doctor.

"Is it an emergency?" she asked, facial expression skeptical of the serious nature of the old man's demand to see the doctor.

"No," he replied, "but there'll be an emergency if I don't see him."

Looking at the old man, and knowing him from years of contentious contact as a patient, she said, with a resigned tone of voice, "I'll speak to the doctor. I think he'll work you in. Just have a seat, and I'll call you."

Following an extensive interview, and numerous thumps on the chest, the doctor told him, "I think you should see a specialist, and I also think you should see him today."

"What's wrong?" the old man asked.

"Until you see the specialist, I'd rather not say," the doctor replied.

"Harrumph! Wouldn't be hedging your bet, would you?"

"No, just want to be on solid ground," the doctor replied.

And so, later that day, following several hours of X-Rays, MRI exams, and numerous blood and urine specimens, the old man was allowed to go home. He was told that his family doctor would be in contact with him.

The next mornng, when the old man attempted to get out of bed, he had another episode of falling. Only this time, two things were worse about it. First, the fall was harder, and he struck his head on the bedside table. Secondly, Oma was still in bed, and was awakened by the sound of his fall.

"No keeping it from her now," he thought. He looked up, and saw Oma staring intently down at him, her facial expression one of extreme concern.

"What's the matter, Papa?" she asked.

"Don't know," he replied. "It's the second time. I fell yesterday morning, when I got up."

"Better go see the doctor," she said.

"Already have," he replied. He then told her about the visit to the doctor, and the further detailed specialist's examination yesterday afternoon. "I'll probably hear something in a day or two."

About noon that day, the doctor called, and said he would like to talk to Papa, and he suggested Oma come along.

For the second time, Papa was in the doctor's office, but now, with Oma at his side. The doctor stared ominously at a stack of papers on his desk. Finally, clearing his throat, he spoke. "It appears you have developed a brain tumor; a malignant brain tumor."

"Well, what do we do about it?" Papa asked.

This time, the doctor's expression was one of extreme sadness. "I'm afraid there's nothing we can do. The tumor has progressed beyond operable stage."

"I'm going to die!" Papa said quietly. "How long will it take?"

"A month. Perhaps six weeks," the doctor replied, eyes downcast, not wanting to confront the expressions on their old faces.

"Well, Oma," Papa said, "it looks like we must make sure this is a Christmas to be remembered."

"We will, Papa," Oma replied, her eyes brimming, an emotional lump growing in her old throat.

Saying their final goodbyes, the old couple left the doctor's office, and drove home.

Reflecting her strength of character, Oma, as soon as she could, began contacting their children. Without revealing the extent of Papa's illness, although allowing that he was ill, she prevailed upon them to bring their families home this Christmas. It had been several years since all the family was together, so she didn't have too much difficulty persuading them to bring everyone home for the holidays.

During Christmas week, Papa, and Oma, noted the dizzy spells erupting more frequently. It was no longer safe for Papa to walk around the house unescorted. Finally, as Christmas loomed close, only a few days away, Papa was forced to remain in bed.

The family, complete with grandchildren, had now assembled at home. The house was decorated to the point of living personification of Santa Claus, and his mythical North Pole. Christmas ornaments, several Christmas trees, holly and mistletoe all abounded everywhere one looked. Christmas music could be heard throughout the house. The grandchildren, the second youngest, being five, alternately ran happily around the house, then rested thoughtfully before the big tree in the living room, staring intently at the gaily wrapped gifts piling up at the base of the Christmas tree. Occasionally, one would carefully pick up a gift, and clutching it tightly, shake it slightly, while held next to the ear. Speculation ran wild about the contents of the gifts, and what Santa would leave on his Christmas eve visit. It was truly a most wonderful time of the year; an enchanted atmosphere prevailing constantly.

Following the evening meal on Christmas eve, most of the family gathered in the living room, and watched the Christmas programs on television. A few of the family had some last minute shopping to do, and were out. Papa was alone in bed.

Glancing up, Papa saw one of the youngest of his grandchildren, Katie, standing in the doorway. "Papa, may I come in and sit with you?" she asked.

"Certainly, Katie, come in and sit beside me here on the bed," Papa answered, patting a spot beside him. Katie scampered across the room, and clambered up on the bed beside Papa.

"Well, Katie, is Santa going to be nice to you tonight?"

"I hope so, Papa."

Then, with a very serious expression on her pretty, young face, Katie asked. "Papa, why do we have Christmas? What is Christmas?"

"Katie, we celebrate Christmas because it is the birthday of the little baby Jesus," Papa answered. Continuing, he said, "The name 'Christmas' comes from Jesus' last name, 'Christ.' Christ is the first half of the word 'Christmas.'"

Katie thought this over for a moment or two, then asked, "Papa, would you tell me the story of Jesus, and Christmas?"

An expression of concentration on his old face, Papa gathered his thoughts, then began speaking. "A long time ago, about 2000 years ago, in the land of Israel, a young woman, Mary, engaged to marry a man named Joseph, was visited by an Angel of the Lord. The Angel told Mary that she was to have a baby, and the baby was to be named 'Jesus.' But Mary was troubled. She could not understand how she could have a baby when she was not yet married.

"The Angel of the Lord told her not to worry, that she was sharing with the Lord God in the magic of this divine birth. Jesus would be the son of God."

At this moment, Oma looked into the bedroom, and then went quietly into the living room. She motioned for the rest of the family to be quiet, and follow her into the bedroom. They did, and seated themselves around Papa's bed. Papa continued to tell Katie the story of Jesus.

"Later that year, in December, all the citizens of Israel were directed to go back to the town of their birth, and pay their annual taxes. Mary and Joseph had to travel to the little village of Bethlehem.

"As was the custom in that time, a traveler either walked, rode a wagon, or rode atop a donkey or horse. Since Mary and Joseph were not wealthy enough to afford a horse, nor a wagon, Joseph, on foot, led their donkey, with Mary riding. The journey was difficult for Mary as she was uncomfortably large with the baby Jesus in her tummy. It was almost time for Jesus' birth, and both Mary and Joseph were worried about finding a place to stay when they arrived in Bethlehem.

"It was well after dark when Joseph led the donkey, and Mary into Bethlehem. It was also a cold night, with bright stars shining in a clear sky. Joseph led them from one inn to another, but was unable to find a place to stay for the night. The town was full of travelers in Bethlehem to pay their taxes. Joseph finally asked one innkeeper, his tone of voice pleading, "Is there no room at this inn? My wife is heavy with child, and due to deliver. We need a place to stay."

"The innkeeper, busy with other guests, thought for a moment, then said, "I have room in my manger. I will let you stay there for half price.

"Joseph gratefully accepted.

"In the meantime, there were three wise men traveling to Bethlehem. They had heard of the impending birth of Jesus, and knew that he was to be "The Prince of Peace." They were hurrying to arrive in time for the birth. They were carrying many gifts for the baby Jesus. The wise men were following the Star of Bethlehem as it moved across the clear sky, showing the way to go to be at Jesus' birthplace.

"Also, at this time, there were shepherds outside Bethlehem tending their flocks of sheep. They also saw the bright star, and, being ignorant, were afraid something bad was going to happen.

"And then, the shepherds heard trumpets sounding in the sky. They cringed, and looked up in fear. There, in the sky was a heavenly angel. The angel spoke. "Don't be afraid. Tonight a king is born. He is the son of God. He brings news of blessed good tidings, and peace to all men of good will." The shepherds followed the bright star into Bethlehem, and found the manger where Jesus was born. They saw the three wise men with their gifts for Baby Jesus. They saw Jesus, wrapped in baby clothes, laying in a small crib in the manger. It was from the wise men giving gifts to Jesus that we got our tradition of giving gifts at Christmas."

"This, Katie, is why we celebrate Christmas," Papa said.

"But, Papa, I still don't understand why it's such an important day for us to celebrate," Katie said. "What did Jesus do that made him so important to us?"

"Katie, Jesus was sent to earth to save all mankind."

"What do you mean, 'Save,' Papa?"

"Most people living then, as now, Katie, were living a sinful life."

"What's a sinful life, Papa?"

"Katie, they were people who did bad things to one another, and didn't seem to even care. God sent his son, Jesus, to earth to beg God's forgiveness for the people. Jesus also tried to teach the people how they should live; to love their neighbors as themselves.

"When Jesus was about 35 years old, he gave up his trade of being a carpenter, and became a full-time preacher. In doing this, he caused a lot of people to hate him. He tried even harder to teach people the right way to live, but it seemed the more he tried, the more the people hated him.

"And so, he was turned over to the Romans and tried in court as an imposter who claimed he was the son of God. When he was found guilty, he was sentenced to die on the cross; "to be crucified."

"What does that mean, Papa?" Katie asked.

"It meant He was nailed to the cross, His legs broken, and allowed to hang there until He died. The nails were driven through his wrists, and ankles. It was a very cruel death in which the victim suffered terribly. Just as He was on the verge of death, Jesus asked God, "Forgive them, Father, for they know not what they do."

"When Jesus was dead, the Roman soldiers who crucified Him, gambled for the only possession Jesus had; His robe. They then took Him down, and buried Him in a borrowed tomb. Jesus was too poor to have a burial plot. He had no money; did not own a house, had never been in business, and had no wife nor children.

"Three days later, Jesus arose from the dead, and went to heaven. He came back, and spent time with his followers, proving to them that He had truly arisen, and would sit at the right hand of His Father, God. Then He went to heaven to stay."

"It was from this selfless act that a mighty, worldwide religion was founded; Christianity. Jesus had more impact upon the world than anyone else who ever lived."

"Papa, why did He die?"

"It was Jesus way of obtaining forgiveness for all mankind. And besides, Katie, I think God wanted His son back with Him, just as Oma and I want you with us. God loved His son, just as Oma and I love you."

Katie nodded her head in apparent understanding.

And then, "Will you die, Papa?"

"Yes, Katie. We all have to die."

"When will you die, Papa?"

"I think, Katie, it will be pretty soon now."

"Papa," Katie began to sniffle, "I don't want you to die." Big tears welled up, and ran down her cheeks.

"Katie, we all have to die some time. I'm old, and my time is near. And besides," he said, squeezing her hand tightly, "It will seem like no time at all until you are with me in heaven. You, Oma, your mom and dad; we'll all be together in heaven. We will be with the one whom we really celebrate Christmas for, Katie."

"Papa, do you really believe that?" Katie asked, turning her face to look him directly in the eyes.

"Yes, Katie, I really do believe that."

Papa's grip on Katie's hand relaxed. He said in a soft voice, "Merry Christmas, Katie." His old eyes closed, and, hearing heavenly angels singing, accompanied by legions of trumpets, he descended into total relaxation as he embarked on his last journey.

Katie, still holding Papa's now limp hand, heard the distant trumpets and voices of angels.

"Merry Christmas, Papa."

# THE TUNNEL

BY: DANA T. MOORE, II

Ahah! The tunnel at the end of the light! It draws ominously close. As a reminder of the close proximity of this terminal tunnel, I am painfully aware that I have become the object of an ever increasing volume of subtle signals telling me that I ought to get on with those things I have put off until "some other time." These undeniable signals are falling hair; trifocal lenses; muscular coordination shot all to hell; a prostate the size of a grapefruit, leading to unreliable bladder control; liver spots on my hands and face; a red, bulbous, blue veined nose; diabetes; a survived coronary occlusion, complete with angioplasty, and the most difficult to ignore, the endless lament of a wife who is now plagued with a retired husband on her hands 24 hours a day.

As life benevolently moves on, allowing my years to pile up like a stale stack of pancakes in a greasy spoon restaurant, I am slowly, but surely evolving some theories that, if put into use, might make the world a better place to live. A few to consider. We see throughout the world, even in our modern, advanced civilization, the ravages of disease that seem immune to prevention or cure; hereditary afflictions such as insanity, diabetes, coronary disease, multiple sclerosis, cystic fibrosis, asthma, and on and on ad nauseum. What would be the ill effects of sterilization of newborn babes whose parents had passed on these illnesses? Now, I don't propose castration in this case; just sterilization. If such a practice were implemented worldwide, it would be only a matter of two, or maybe three generations, and those hereditary diseases would be eradicated from the world's worry menu. Think of the horribly crippled child suffering from one of the above diseases.

Another of my observations from the lofty pinnacle of age; the appropriate response to the incurable child molester. Perhaps, if the child molester, following appropriate court conviction, were castrated, he would no longer be a threat to anyone. No second offense allowed! How about the rapist? Why not treat him to the same reward for his deviations? In both cases, the bleeding heart, liberal do-gooders would have to be ignored. They are the ones who always want to turn the other cheek; someone else's cheek.

While I'm at it, why not a few amendments to our democratic representation in Washington? Why not term limits of a realistic nature? Why not limit our elected public officials to an eight year, four term stay in the house of representatives? Certainly, they should be able to line their pockets thoroughly in eight years! How about two terms in the Senate? And one term as President? Granted, to make the President's term effective, it should be extended to six years, but one six year term only! And in all cases, the elected public official should be required to complete his term in office no later than the age of 65. If age 65 looms too close, the aspiring lawmaker should be disqualified from even standing for election.

There are a number of recommendations that I think would make our representative form of government better. The period of public competition for elective office should be limited to four months, including the primaries. The maximum money that any individual could spend should be limited to a fixed amount. Limiting cash expenditure should level the playing field, and prevent the process of running for election becoming a function of blatant purchase by the wealthy.

Another requirement that might limit the swollen payroll in Washington; have the elected public official pay his staff out of his own pocket, and no allowances provided for this overhead. I suspect we would see, should this be imposed, a panic evacuation from the Washington area. We might even see some of the politicians become involved in meaningful work for the tax payer.

Another theory of mine is about the public education system. We should get the politicians out of it completely. That would be difficult, since there is big money involved in public education, and politicians swarm to big money like sharks to a wounded, bleeding whale in the ocean.

If the politician were excised, or perhaps I should say "exorcised," from the public education system, then some objective, non-vote getting decisions could be made. If the decision making people had the courage, and would stand up to the various organizations, such as the NAACP, ACLU, and other militants, then the most important decision in the public school system could be made; establish meaningful, and inflexible academic standards. Enforce these standards across the board, regardless of race or ethnic origin. Don't pass incorrigible, trouble making students just to get rid of them. No pass, no diploma!

How about this recommendation for the public education system? Let's allow prayer in the public schools. Why not? The coin of the realm has the motto, "In God We Trust" stamped upon it. A little respect for the Almighty would help a lot. Our youngsters need to know that they have to respect something, or someone.

Another decision that should be faced is to put aside the political pap of teaching students in their original native tongue. We are Americans, product of the melting pot. We should teach American English in the public schools, and those who have come here from another land, as part of their Americanization, should learn our language.

When choosing a personal physician, stay away from the new doctor just out of medical school. He has a new education, a new house, a new car, a new office with new equipment, and a new, young family to pay for, and he always wants to do it in his first year of practice. Also, this is not compatible with medicare. The young physician wants to charge the maximum fee the market will bear, and has no time for regulated fees, assignment, nor patients who are economically forced to rely on medicare. Stay away from physicians who own stock in pharmacies, or health maintenance organizations. They have a vested, self-serving interest in discovering new health problems; in you. Avoid physicians in their early sixties. They are in the burned out stage, and listen to you with one ear only, while they think longingly of retirement, the old fishing hole, and the golf course. They find your litany of health problems a genuine bore. You'll become dependent upon him, and he'll quit on you.

And now, the most critical problem of all. This is the problem the politician is terrified to confront. We must face up to, and address the problem of cultural/moral decay in our society. We have to acknowledge that the problem truly exists, and then forcefully correct it. We must stop the wildly out-of-control act of children bearing babies, and then laughing at the drive by shooting of these children; shooting in many cases spawned by the rampant drug problem in our country.

The family is the core of our society. We have seen, in the last 50 years, the destruction of family values. This has spread, as it inevitably would, to our society. Because the family is at the core of our problem, it is also at the core of the solution to social and moral decay. Parents, *not government*, must shoulder the responsibility of straightening out the mess our society has sunk into. Gun control laws won't do it. Federal legislation won't do it. People, and families must do it. We have to get a firm grasp on the problem of young people who have absolutely no loyalty to anyone, or anything, but themselves. The young have ascended the heights of hedonistic philosophy, and most of them aren't sufficiently educated to define hedonism. We must also deal with the adults, beyond recovery, who are a central part of our runaway criminal element. These adults are thoroughly intermingled with the young people growing into the same adult criminal element.

The foregoing is a short summary of my conclusions gleaned from acquired years. Most of the young would find this a bitter pill. They are naive, and in good health, and so, don't worry. When their children get into middle, and high school, the reluctance of people to make the hard, but necessary decisions about the public school will drive them to consider private schools. This is an affluent technique of turning their backs on the problem.

There are a few other problems crying for corrective attention. The deadbeat father who abandons his family, and leaves them in the financial lurch. There are very effective means available right now to track them down, and bring them to heel. The IRS should be turned loose on them. They would wrap this problem up in very short order. The drug problem is a national shame, as well as a disaster. We should deal with it the same as we would an invading army from Colombia or Turkey menacing our national safety.

Having written this, I conclude by saying, "Good Luck!"

# WHY CHRISTMAS SAD?

BY: DANA T. MOORE, II

Joy To The World! Jingle Bells, Jingle Bells! Oh, Holy Night! Oh, Come All Ye Faithful! "More Booze, Bartender!" "Bah! Humbug!" "To hell with getting up early to set out those toys! You do it!"

Why, on this most joyous occasion of the year; this time celebrated by Christians as the birthday of Christ; this time of gift giving in remembrance of the tradition established by the Three Wise Men that long ago day in Bethlehem, do we find such widespread sadness? Why, in the most opulent land in the free world do we find people in the depths of despair at this most happy time of the year? Why is it we can look around at the joyful throngs of Christmas shoppers, walking brisk and red cheeked in the winter cold, chattering happily with one another, tossing coins in the pots of the bell ringing Salvation Army collectors, carrying stuffed shopping bags with gaily wrapped gifts peeping out, and still see sadness abound? What is it that causes people with every apparent reason to be joyful instead to be plagued with soul wrenching sadness at Christmas? Why does the sound of Christmas carols bring on tears? What makes these people seek refuge in a frenzy of partying and drinking at the onset of the Christmas season?

Some of the answer is obvious. Some, even in this land of plenty, are on the bottom of the socio-economic order, and though even they have much for which to be thankful and happy, relatively speaking, can find cause for despondency this time of the year. Others lament the loss of a loved one, or grieve over the absence of loved ones far away, and in the case of some, are just lonely, having no one to love and cheer them. Loneliness is a severe burden to bear at Christmas time; especially the loneliness of old age, and poor health.

What about the others suffering sadness at Christmas? The others who have everything money can buy? The ones whose families are near? Why is it we see such a widespread case of "Christmas Blues" among those who have every reason to be happy. Whence come the rivers of alcohol at Christmas; the volume far in excess of that considered socially acceptable for Christmas cheer? What is the source of this near disabling despondency?

The psychiatrists have numerous reasons to cite for "Christmas Blues." They would have us believe that the world's population suffers from extensive psychotic disorders; manifesting themselves at Christmas. A small portion of the head shrink's conjecture may be based on fact. Most, however, I think, is just that; conjecture. After all, if we didn't have the psychiatric conjecture to dwell on, why then have the shrinks?

Being no psychiatrist, I will accept the risk of putting forth a homespun analysis, and an even more basic remedial recommendation. I think the Rector at my church unknowingly hit on the root cause of this end-of-the-year, seasonal malady, accurately summing it up in one simple sentence. I was the December usher for early church services that year, and as such, had to clean up the pews after services; collecting the bulletins, hymnals, gloves, glasses and other items left behind by the bolting worshipers. The church was still adorned in its Christmas decorations, although the holiday had passed. I knew the decorations would be gone before services next Sunday. As I completed my chores, the Rector paused in the aisle next to me. I looked up and commented on the decorations, observing that it would be nice to have them all year round. The Rector concurred, adding the wish for also having the Christmas spirit all year round. Therein, I concluded several years later, lay the answer.

Simple, huh? Don't bet on it! Let's examine. The Rector's wish for year-round Christmas spirit was the expression of an idealistic desire. I am confident he would agree, and would agree also this condition is not readily attainable.

What then? Could we perhaps reduce, just a little, the near manic level of sales hucksterism so prevalent at Christmas? Could we possibly eliminate the idea that one must receive a gift to balance the one given? What has happened to the old fashioned Christmas spirit of, "It is better to give than to receive."? Where did the idea come from that we must drink ourselves into sotted oblivion repeatedly during the Christmas season? Why must we spend money as if it were going out of style, particularly when we don't have it to spend? Who originated the idea that women must be smothered in jewels and furs at Christmas? That men receive cases of expensive whiskey and an irresistible urge to consume it? Why must the credit card receipts exceed by the cube the dwindling number of Christmas cards we receive each holiday season? I think our Christmas celebration has grown into a compulsive condition much akin to that of a bobsled on its icy downhill plunge; locked into the accelerating track of dizzying descent while seemingly out of control; the eventual ending-up place not at all certain. And perhaps even worse, with no one caring.

What ever happened to the real idea of Christmas; love? Not the current, widely accepted four letter version of love, but that old fashioned love one feels when his eyes brim as he watches his child behold the wonder of a brightly lit Christmas tree for the first time. What about that look on the child's face when he first confronts Santa Claus on a cold, snowy day during his earliest remembering Christmas season; that look of reverent wonder that only an innocent child can display? What about that look of wondrous love seen only in a mother's eyes when she first views her newborn child? Who could doubt for a second the love expressed in the eyes of a proud parent watching his child graduate from school. Love often masquerades as pride.

I wonder if it is possible that we have forgotten how to love. I wonder if the true meaning of love has become lost in the tinsel and surface finery we now accept as the meaning of Christmas. How many really believe that the original, and true meaning of love was demonstrated for all time almost 2000 years ago when an unworldly, part time carpenter and itinerant minister, was nailed ignominiously to a cross of wood; the cross he was forced to carry to a cloudy hilltop? Who believes the love embodied in his plea, "Forgive them, Father, for they know not what they do."?

The bottom line of love is commitment and sacrifice. Gifts given without commitment, and with no sacrifice do not commemorate the original cause for the celebration and gift giving. Could this hollow, shallow, commitment-free practice perhaps subconsciously subject us to feelings of guilt? In our fear of personal commitment, do we withhold the ultimate gift of love to those who cry out for it? Do we, as a result of this ever increasing burden of guilt try to expunge it annually with an outflow of meaningless gifts? Do we unwittingly attempt to drown this guilt in a flood of alcohol?

I think yes.

What then? How do we get the custom back on track? How do we slow this runaway bobsled, and replace it with the real sleigh; pulled by the reindeer, not propelled by guilt! Somehow we must get to a generation not yet contaminated with a consuming desire to corner all the money in the world. Somehow we have to convince this new, untainted generation that many of the best things in life are indeed free. We need to so thoroughly ground this group with the basic tenets of honesty, moral strength, and commitment to ideals that a few of them might even grow up to be honorable politicians. And that's asking a lot!

This most likely isn't the complete answer. Maybe some of it lies in the motto found on our money; "In God We Trust." Perhaps if we taught this new, as yet untried generation of youngsters to rely a little more on the Almighty, and a little less on self, we might retard the downhill velocity of the Xmas Bobsled, and convert it to a Christmas Sleigh. Maybe then, if we're extremely fortunate, we might find in this sleigh the real meaning of Christmas; Peace On Earth, and Good Will to All.

MAYBE THEN, INSTEAD OF CHRISTMAS SAD,
IT WILL BE TRULY A

# MERRY CHRISTMAS!

# WHY FLY?

## BY: DANA T. MOORE, II

What would make a normal, sane person want to fly? Better leave that function to the birds! The birds notwithstanding, since the days of Greek mythology, man has wanted to fly. Perhaps not all men, but some desperately wanted to fly. Icarus, son of Daedalus, is a good example. In accordance with Greek legend, he wanted to fly so badly, his father fashioned wings of feathers for him. Icarus, ignoring his father's advice, flew too close to the sun, the wax holding the feathers melted, and Icarus fell to his death. Probably the first instance of a young, headstrong pilot who brought on his own death by ignoring competent advice, thus creating the need for our first flying safety program.

This desire to fly, however, was denied fulfillment until early in the 20th century. True, there were some who managed a partial satisfaction of this desire by using balloons. As any pilot knows, balloons and airplanes are worlds apart. The pilot of a plane is free to go faster, slow down, climb, dive, turn, loop and roll to his heart's desire, providing his plane is built for such acrobatics. He can direct his plane on a designated course that will place him at a preplanned destination. The balloon is constrained to rise, or descend by use of greater or less volumes of hot air, and to change it's direction by descending or rising to a level of different wind direction. Winds aloft may adversely effect an airplane's speed over the ground, but will not interfere uncorrectibly with it's direction.

Why, then, fly? The non-flier sees an airplane as merely a way to travel from one point to another, so, to him, the question is meaningless. The flier, however, sees an airplane as the successful melding of wire, metal, delicate instruments, glass, and a powerful engine that will take one or more people aloft for enough time to accomplish one or more important goals. To the flier, the question is very meaningful. Having spent most of my productive adult years in the cockpit of a military fighter plane, I have had ample opportunity to develop and retain a deep feeling of permanent affection for flying, and for airplanes.

I well remember my first ride in an airplane. It was in an old Waco, with a bench seat for two in the front, open cockpit. I was just barely tall enough to see over the side. As the plane lifted from the ground, amid the roar of the radial engine, and the blast of wind in my face, I felt my first sensation of flight, watching the ground fall away below. The feeling was an almost indescribable thrill to this now permanent aviation devotee.

While preferring the more nimble fighter aircraft, I am fond of all airplanes. I took my first dual instruction in a Cub Coupe in the early years of World War II, and was ready to solo long before my 16th birthday. Gasoline and money shortage dictated an interruption to my flying activity until after the war when I was able to resume flying on the GI Bill of Rights. This led to a 21 year tour in the USAF as first an aviation cadet, then a rated pilot. I even managed to squeeze in a two year exchange tour with the US Navy, flying jets off the carrier USS Intrepid, CVA-11.

Well, then, what prompts me to sit here at my word processor, trying to cobble together a collection of words expressing my heart felt feelings of love and affection for flying and airplanes? They are indeed heart felt feelings, and I feel compelled to pass them on to others while I can still assemble them into an intelligent, if nostalgic expression of love for flight.

I clearly remember when I first soloed in a venerable surplus Piper J-3. It was winter of 1947, and I took off and landed on a runway covered with snow, and thought nothing about it. My pre-solo dual instruction was administered off snow convered runways, so flying off snow was perfectly natural to this fledgling aviator.

Later, in 1948, in what was then still the Army Air Corps, I soloed the mighty T-6, and felt as if I had truly "slipped the surly bonds of earth!" This was a feeling I was to experience repeatedly during my flying years; first flight in an F-51; first flight in an F-80; first takeoff in an F-86F; first penetration of Mach 1, also in an F-86F, straight down, under full power; first takeoff in an F-100C, and experiencing the Super Sabre's almost effortless passage through Mach 1 in level flight, followed by an impressive final approach speed of 180 knots. And then on to my first arrested landing on the USS Independence in a Grumman F11-F, followed by the near indescribable sensation of my first catapult launch. Probably the most memorable feeling was my first night catapult shot, followed by my first night arrested landing, both emotional conditions I likened to flying in a bottle of ink! My first flight in the Navy's F8U Crusader also left an indelible print on my flying memory. My introductory flight in an F-104D was an impressive feat, especially the 4 G 180 degree turn with no loss of speed. There were many other highlights; first non-stop deployment across the Atlantic; first flight I took my children on in a civil light plane, and others too numerous to list here.

One nostalgic comment I feel appropriate here. It's an observation that will make sense to other pilots, especially those who have experienced the F-51 of World War Two fame. When I was first introduced to the Mighty Mustang, one of the requirements was for we pre-checkout students to go to mobile control at the approach end of the runway, and observe takeoffs of the F-51, and their landings. When the Rolls Royce Merlin cranked up to full power on takeoff, it gave me goose bumps. It still does, but unfortunately, I never hear it any more. The sound of that 12 cylinder, inline engine turning up to 3000 rpm is one that I will never forget.

At an age now where I would be considered a risky candidate for a trip as a passenger in a commercial airliner, I look back on the above mentioned highlights of my flying career with extreme affection, and sadness; affection that I was fortunate enough to experience them, and sadness that I will never again be able to enjoy those thrills.

My mind jumps to a career point when I was a very junior first Lieutenant, advanced flight instructor, and was orbiting one of the turning points of a cadet night cross country out of Williams AFB, Arizona. The cadets were flying F-80's. My job was to check off each cadet as he passed the check point I was orbiting, and called in his position to me as he turned on the next leg. I was at an altitude of 30,000 feet, well above the cadet traffic, and happened to be in and out of a layer of cirrus clouds. The cirrus, ice crystal clouds, caused my plane, an F-80, to be wreathed in St. Elmo's fire. The electrical phenomena caused a series of blue bundles of static electricity to dance slowly in and out along the leading edges of the wings; and simultaneously to ride up and down the metal structure of my cockpit, instrument panel, and canopy bow. I reached up, and placed my hand in one of the blue bundles of energy, and was surprised there was no sensation. The visual electrical energy danced around a ring I wore, but was harmless. Just one of those interesting occurrences that has remained in my memory for over 40 years.

In the spring of 1957, my fighter squadron, I was operations officer, was getting ready for an overseas deployment. One of our most intense training requirements was learning to mid-air refuel. We were using the F-100D Super Sabre equipped with probe for refueling. The idea was to approach the tanker, usually a KB-50, all that TAC fighters could scrounge for refueling, and insert the probe into a basket approximately three feet in diameter. Once hooked up, the boom operator in the tanker turned on the fuel, if it was to be a "Wet Hookup," and transferred fuel. Most of our hookups then were dry, no fuel transfer, just for the practice of making the hookup.

Tactical Air Command Headquarters had sent a detachment of KB-50's to George AFB, where we were stationed, and directed that we learn to refuel. The tankers had to fly a certain minimum number of sorties, and we as trainees had to fly a certain number of refueling sorties. If we fell short of the number of prescribed training sorties, we were in trouble. If the tankers fell short of their prescribed number of sorties they were in trouble. Falls under the heading of "Utilization." The result was a heavy training schedule, day and night, and on weekends. Once our squadron attained refueling proficiency, we then had to continue refueling training to conform to programmed utilization. Many of the young pilots were unhappy with the weekend schedule. They wanted to be with their families, especially since they knew we were on the eve of a six month overseas deployment. In order to free a maximum of the young pilots to stay home on the weekends, I scheduled myself for as many of the weekend sorties as I could handle. They were all local flights. I clearly recall one Saturday when the refueling area was in the vicinity of Bakersfield, California. To get back and forth to the tankers, the fighters flew from our desert base at Victorville, and met the tankers.

Completing the refueling portion of the sortie, we went home, landed, turned the planes around, then flew back to the refueling area. The tankers all this time were orbiting in a race track pattern working with the receivers. After my time on the tanker, I would descend to about 1000 feet over the desert, and head for home. The weather was clear. I remember looking down on the desert floor, and seeing a mass of bright desert flowers in bloom. I also clearly remember thinking at the time that I was extremely fortunate to be flying the best aircraft the world had to offer, and being paid for doing it. I also recall that I was aware at the time that it was a pleasure I could only enjoy during the beautiful youth of my life. Military flying, like professional sports, is an activity restricted to the young. You get into it, and before you know it, it's gone.

I've heard flying described, perhaps not originally, but certainly appropriately, as "Hours and hours of total boredom, interspersed with occasional moments of stark terror." I think to that should be added, "and rare moments of amusement." I recall a training flight out of George AFB in the F-86H. I had three young pilots flying with me, and a fifth plane scheduled to fly as aerial target. We were to set up a fighter gunnery pattern using the 5th fighter. Naturally it was a dry, no-fire, camera gunnery mission. The briefing included, among other things, a pre-determined fuel minimum at which point that pilot would call me with a "Bingo."

We had been in the practice pattern for some time, still well above bingo fuel, when one of the junior birdmen called me with a "Bingo," well below the fuel of the rest of the flight members. In fact, he was critically low, and we had a good distance to go to get home. I instructed him to head straight for home, remaining at altitude, and I would fly his wing. The rest of the flight was sent off to fly an alternate mission, with directions to return home as fuel dictated.

My junior birdman with the low fuel headed off to Lake Arrowhead, rather than directly home. I called him, and corrected his course, but in a few minutes, he was again headed off to Lake Arrowhead, a course about 45 degrees away from home base. I became puzzled, and asked him what he was doing. He replied that he had practiced simulated flame out patterns a number of times from Lake Arrowhead, and he figured by starting his emergency pattern from there, he would have it made. I ordered him to go directly home, set up a flameout pattern, and land. His decision to go to Lake Arrowhead originally would have taken him an additional 15 minutes, and most likely another 500 pounds of fuel. The end of the flight was uneventful, but the illogic of the inexperienced junior birdman remained in my mind for years as an amusing display of faulty headwork.

And, while on the topic of amusement, I recall two vivid experiences I had, both during initial checkout in a plane new to me. The first, in an F-80, involved a little pain. I had cranked up, taxied to the end of the runway, and in accordance with established checkout procedure, ran the engine up to 100% power, and then, while holding my position with brakes, read off over the radio to mobile control the critical engine gauge readings. At that moment, I decided, no doubt in error, that my seat needed lowering. I reached down with my left hand, and moved the seat locking lever. Unknown to me, the bungee cords that allowed the seat to lower and rise easily had been removed. The seat fell, with my weight on it, and caught my left middle finger. The crunch tore the fingernail off. I jerked my hand up, and saw the bloody glove, at the same time, inadvertently releasing the brakes. Looking up, I saw that I was well down the runway. Nothing to do but continue the takeoff. The remainder of the flight was uneventful. Made a forceful impact upon my memory, though.

Another, more pleasantly amusing occurrence was my initial checkout in the F-86. After I had taken off, and gone through the required training maneuvers, I returned to base for landing. Pattern and landing were normal. Upon touchdown, I held the nose off for deceleration, and when it started to fall, me not being used to the attitude on the ground, I was convinced I had landed with the nose wheel retracted. I turned off the end of the runway before my breathing and pulse returned to normal.

There are other occasions I recall that draw forth feelings of affection. I well recall a time when I was returning to Victorville in an F-100D, having launched from Homestead AFB, Florida. I was flying at 35,000 feet over west Texas, without a cloud in the sky, and for some reason, not a bit of haze. The sky was crystal clear. I felt I could see half way around the world. Although under positive radar control from the ground, I could very readily navigate by reference to my map, and the surface terrain. It gave me a feeling of being able to see the earth much as The Almighty must from his omniscient vantage point.

I was fortunate to spend the productive years of my life doing something I loved to do, and doing it very well. Not many people can lay claim to that. I think also, that a non-flier reading this treatise will miss the whole point of it. The experienced flier will absorb, and take pleasure from everything I have set down. I tried not to let this become a "There I was," narrative, but an outlet for my feelings about flying.

So, why fly? Only the truly dedicated pilot can answer that. I think, for one who really wants to fly, and who loves airplanes, not to fly would leave a void impossible to fill. The real pilot has a love for flight, regardless of the type of plane that endures for all his conscious life.

# PIXILATED PIXIE

By: Dana T. Moore, II

'T was two nights before Christmas, and all through the house, all that could be heard was Mrs. Claus' grouse, "Get off that jolly juice, you old gasbag! Tomorrow night you have to make your rounds, and right now, you couldn't find your way out of the barn if I led you with a bottle of bourbon in front of your nose!"

Santa belched, a deep, rumbling, roiling rumble. Shaking his head, he mumbled, "I gotta get outta here! Maybe some fresh air will clear my head." With that, he stumbled out of their North Pole home, and waded through knee high snow to the reindeer barn. The air on this December 23rd evening was crisp and cold, and indeed, it did clear a few of the cobwebs from his head.

Opening the door to the barn, Santa reached in, and turned on the lights. He saw the reindeer standing in their stalls, some pawing the floor fitfully as if anxious to be on their way to deliver the annual load of Christmas gifts. He glanced at the sleigh.

"Doesn't look like it's good for another round-the-world flight," he thought. Rusty runners, paint peeling, sides of the gift compartment cracked, and bulging from last year. Walking to the sleigh, Santa reached into the glove compartment, and extracted a well-worn flask. Shaking the container, he heard a welcome gurgle, and removing the cap, turned the flask up for a reinforcing draught of his favorite thirst slacker. "Ahhh," he sighed with satisfaction, and replaced the flask in the glove compartment. "Better fill that with Christmas Cheer before launch time tomorrow night," he thought.

Weaving slightly, hands stuffed deeply in his pockets, Santa stared morosely at the sleigh. I really should have given this Christmas chariot a complete overhaul after my trip last year. He noted one of the side doors hanging askew on a loose hinge, and a navigation light dangling from a long wire. "Never pass a safety inspection," he thought. Flipping on the power switch, he noted the battery was dead. "Good thing I have a spare in the house. Can't make the trip without power for lights and music. It's surprising how important the sounds of Christmas carols are when I get close enough to the ground for people to hear them."

Walking to the row of reindeer stalls, he reached in and affectionately scratched Donner behind the ear, and heard a groan of pleasure. "You guys have to be good this year," Santa said. "No snap rolls, nor loops. The old sleigh just might not take the extra G forces. For that matter, I'm not sure I could either." Stepping to the next stall, he began scratching Blitzen behind the ear, and received the same groan of pleasure from inside the stall. "And no lazy, half-hearted output on takeoff. We're gonna need all the thrust all of you can generate this year. We've never had such a long list of requests for computers. They're heavy. The old sleigh is really gonna be over grossed on launch this time. On the first few takeoffs, we'll need long takeoff runs until I can offload some of the heavy stuff at our first few stops. Hope the sleigh runners will take the longer run." Cupid pawed the floor of his stall, wanting his ear scratched. Dancer did the same. Before long, Comet, Dasher, Prancer and Vixen joined the stamping demand for affection, and the barn sounded like a chorus of tap-dancers. "I'll make sure you have plenty to eat tomorrow so that your energy level is at its peak," Santa said.

Santa decided to be up early tomorrow morning, and complete the repairs needed on the sleigh. In the meantime, his Brownie helpers would be busy organizing, and loading the precious gifts aboard. It was going to be a difficult task to get the cargo properly loaded. Even then, he knew he had to make several stops along the way at his isolated, prepositioned toy troves, and other Christmas gifts. No way he could get everything on the sleigh at one loading. "Oh well," he thought, "it only comes once a year."

"See you guys in the morning," Santa said in farewell, turning out the light and heading back to his house.

Shaking the snow from his boots, Santa began a mental review of his gift list. He smiled with affection at the recall of many of the good little children who had asked for Christmas gifts. Then he remembered those who hadn't been so good. "The ones whose behavior left a little to be desired would get toys marked, 'Some assembly required.' Those whose fathers perhaps lacked proper Christmas spirit would have to do the assembling. Make the slack fathers, and not so good little kids think before next year's Christmas list.

The next day, Christmas Eve, was spent in refurbishing the sleigh. The Brownies managed to pack an unbelievable volume of gifts into the creaking old vehicle. Finally, as launch time drew near, the sleigh was loaded, and so was Santa. Donning his cold weather, thick, heavy clothing, Santa climbed unsteadily into the cockpit of his sleigh. The reindeer were all in harness, and raring to go, stamping and snorting their anticipation. After all, it wasn't every night they took a round-the-world trip.

Mrs. Claus climbed upon the runner brace, and leaned in to give Santa a goodbye kiss. "Please, Santa," she intoned, "please drive carefully, and leave that flask alone. You have a lot of children around the world depending on you tonight."

"Burp!" Santa replied. Continuing, "Maw, I'll be good, and I'll be back by daylight tomorrow morning." With that, noting Mrs. Claus to be off the edge of the sleigh, Santa yelled, "All right, you guys! Let's be on our way! Merry Christmas, Maw!"

Following an unusually long run across the smooth snow, the eight reindeer staggered into the air, the sleigh hanging at a precariously high, near stall angle of attack as the deer power thrust slowly accelerated the whole creaking, wobbling, overloaded sleigh and driver to climb speed. The navigation lights flickered erratically in the night. Climbing over the horizon, and out of sight, Santa shouted, "Good takeoff, my trusty steeds! Settle down now, and I'll set her on automatic cruise climb. Merry Christmas!"

Approaching the first stop for the evening, a farm house, Santa noted a long, open field before the house. "We can get this load stopped in that field," he thought.

Calling out, he shouted to the reindeer, "Okay, be extra careful on this landing. We still have a full load. I'm gonna let you do it, and I'll monitor, just in case."

"Monitor?" Blitzen thought disdainfully. "The old guzzler, with his full load, doesn't even know which end of this rig we reindeer are hitched to. Good thing he's gonna let us make the landing. Otherwise, we might have Christmas gifts scattered all over the northern hemisphere." The landing was smooth. The reindeer pulled the sleigh up to the farmhouse.

Santa took his bag of gifts, and entered the house through an unlocked door. "Not even going to attempt the chimney routine," he thought. I can just see me half way down the chimney, stuck, with all these gifts jammed in with me. Don't know who ever thought up the silly idea of me entering a house that way!"

Inside, Santa hurried to his task of placing the gifts around the tree, and in the socks hanging from the mantle. "Pretty home," he thought. Then, spotting a plate of cookies, and a mug of milk on a table in the living room, he walked to the table. Picking up the cookies, he slid them into his coat pocket. "The reindeer will like these." Then, extracting his flask from a deep coat pocket, he laced the milk, and downed it in one swallow. "Need that antifreeze!" he thought.

Out to the sleigh with his empty gift bag, he paused by the deer long enough to hand out the cookies. Then hopping into the cockpit, he yelled, "Make as good a takeoff as your landing was, and you get all the cookies tonight!"

"Humph! he's been into the antifreeze again," Donner thought, eyeing Santa warily as he took up the reins.

This launch was both shorter, and smoother than the first. The lighter load in the sleigh, plus Santa's slightly reduced load of bottled frivolity made for improved operations.

The next stop was uneventful. When placing the gifts around the tree, Santa noted another glass of milk, and a huge pile of cookies. Again reinforcing the milk with his private stock, and quaffing it in a gulp, Santa took the cookies, and his empty gift bag, and returned to the sleigh. The reindeer were stamping their paws in anticipation of the cookies. Maybe they were cold. It was indeed a cold night. The reindeer were emitting huge clouds of steam as they exhaled in the cold air. Santa handed out the cookies. Burping a loud rumble, he once again mounted the sleigh.

"I'll hand fly this takeoff, boys!" Santa shouted to the deer.

"This will be good," Cupid whispered to Vixen, having observed Santa's less than steady gait on his return to the sleigh. "We better be ready to take over in case he lets it get away from him." Vixen nodded and whispered to the next reindeer, who then passed the word to the others. Nothing beat alert preparedness.

Rattling the reins, Santa shouted, "On Donner! On Blitzen! Let's get this show on the road!" The sleigh moved across the snow, and with Santa wobbling in the cockpit, lifted abruptly into the air. Donner and Blitzen set the new course as they climbed back up to cruise altitude. Santa hiccupped loudly, relaxing his grip on the reins as he slipped off into a snooze.

Sometime later, Santa became aware of the descending sleigh, and once again took the reins. Completing an uneventful landing, Santa again staggered into the house with the bag of gifts across his shoulder. Filling the stockings, and piling a stack of gifts under the tree, Santa retrieved the cookies for the deer, and returned to the sleigh. Handing out the cookies, Santa spoke, "You know the itinerary, Donner. Take us to the next stop. Then I think we have to replenish the supply of toys and gifts." Climbing into the sleigh, Santa settled gratefully into his seat, and drifted immediately into slumber.

As their itinerary took them ever deeper into populated areas of the United States, the sleigh load grew lighter, and Santa's heavier. Crossing Chicago, Santa noted a deep layer of new snow on the ground. He didn't like it when they had to land in areas where there was no snow, such as Miami, or Hollywood. On the next stop, their approach path took them in the vicinity of Ohare International airport, the civil air traffic grew progressively heavier. One commercial 747 had to take violent evasive action to avoid a collision. Santa was rubbernecking, and had just taken a reinforcing draught of his Christmas cheer.

"Damned crazy pilots," Santa thought. "Watch where you're going," he yelled explosively to the 747 disappearing in the distance to his rear.

The rest of the night's joyful journey was completed without mishap. A few near misses, perhaps, but nothing serious.

As night slipped away, and the sun began to slip above the horizon, Santa and his weary reindeer made a careful approach to their north pole landing strip. Santa was bleary eyed from the now empty flask in his glove compartment. The reindeer were just as bleary eyed from their night of exhausting work. The landing was uneventful. One side door fell off the sleigh on touchdown, and went slithering off through the snow.

"One of the brownies can come out and retrieve it," Santa thought. "I'm too tired and cold. What a long trip!"

Greeting a crew of his Brownies, Santa pointed to the barn, and said, "Merry Christmas! These fellows did a splendid job tonight. Give them a good rubdown, and an extra ration of food. I'm in for a few hours rest."

With that, Santa walked wearily into his home, calling out, "Hey, Maw! I'm back! Didn't miss a stop either. And now, I'm ready for a little eggnog, a hot shower, and a long winter's nap. Merry Christmas!"

Steaming in the relaxing shower, Santa thought, "I've gotta get me a permanent assistant. I'm getting too old for this cold weather, open cockpit travel. Well, enough for now. A few hours rest, and I'll be as good as new."

MERRY CHRISTMAS!

www.ingramcontent.com/pod-product-compliance
Lightning Source LLC
Chambersburg PA
CBHW020317260626
47156CB00004B/1262